# BENELLI'S Elle

## DEBBIE MITCHELL
### &
## LESLIE STAFFEY

Benelli's Elle (Unfortunate Souls MC Book One)

By Debbie Mitchell & Leslie Staffey

Published by: Archer Quill Publishing

Cover Design: Debbie Mitchell w/Canva

Model: Alfie Gordillo

Photographer: RLS Model Images Photography

Editing: Book & Mark It Editing by Lexis Ann

Amazon ISBN: 9798582415190

# Dedications

*Oh, our dear sweet KC, we cannot thank you enough for all that you have done. You've taught us Scrivener, hours of video chats helping format and compile, how to do POV's, our cheerleader, we could go on and on. Without a canceled book signing, we may have never met. Who would have thought a trip to New Orleans would give us one of our dearest and best of friends, from Canada to boot.*

*Some of the authors we need to thank for all their help, advice, & support: Darlene Tallman, Liberty Parker, MariaLisa Demora, Dove Cavanaugh King, Christine Michelle, Jessica Coulter Smith, B.B. Blaque, Teagan Brooks and Avelyn Page. You amazing authors who took us newbies under your wing, for that, we thank you. We can't forget our Facebook friend Fabiola Cadet-Destil.*

*We would like to thank the Beta Readers that sent us feedback, Karen Laurent, Becky Jean, Brandy Goodman, Brea Cagle Trundle, Sha Dagley, Shannon Heighton Hicks, Mary Jo Porter, Melissa Burke, Melissa Kristy, and Trish Kranawetter.*

*(Debbie) I need to thank my kids, Randy, Jamie, and Lanie and my grandson. You believed in me and never questioned if your mom could write. Thank you, Jamie, for the photo shoots, twist your arm, right? Thank you, Lanie for letting mom spend countless hours writing without disturbance. Thank you to Brenda and Joe, my sister and brother for believing in me and Brenda, anytime I needed you, you were there. Now, get to writing that mystery, you've got this!!! Mom, thanks for being you. I love you all so much.*

*I want to thank Debbie and James Clover for their advice.*

3

*(Leslie) Thank you Sam, for always standing by my side, cheering me on and loving me. You will never know how much that means to me! Love you more, my Superman.*

*To Jaclyn and James, thank you for always being there for me, for encouraging me to write a book and for just loving your momma, you don't know how proud I am of you, love you always. To my Nolan and Nathan for giving me absolute joy of seeing your faces, and those faces you make, lol. Mimi loves you. I want to thank you Laura for being my person. You have always been in my corner. Love ya, L. Marty, our awesome Marty, thanks for always listening to me talk about the book and always being there to bounce ideas off of.*

*Thank you to each and every person that we haven't mentioned but asked how our book was going, it meant a lot.*

# *About the authors*

Debbie and Leslie grew up going to the same high school in Southern Illinois. Years later they began working together and that's when the real fun started. When Leslie transferred, the two lost touch but one day Leslie called Debbie up and invited her to an Indie Author Event in Indianapolis. She brought Debbie into a world she didn't know existed. The world of binge reading, MC romance, and fun. From there the two dove headfirst into this world and even took a road trip to New Orleans, that is where the two decided to start co-writing an MC series. Writing has become a new passion, and this is the first of the Unfortunate Soul series.

*For anyone out there that has a dream, no matter how crazy it may seem to you... go for it, you won't regret it.*

# CHAPTER ONE

## Elle

Staring at myself in the intricate oak mirror, curling my long, dark reddish-brown hair into spirals, I didn't know how dramatically my life was about to change. Looking at the vibrant teal-blue eyes in the mirror, then at the photograph of my father, they are the same. The dad I've never known. I look down at the old, worn picture of my mom and dad when they were young, and I smile. Mom was only eighteen then. She has come so far in life, and it fills me with pride, and she's made a glorious life for the two of us. She sent me to college to follow my dreams, where I studied business management and photography. The business classes were mom's idea, but she was definitely right because I learned so much about owning a business. I made a promise to her I wouldn't look for him until graduation and today is that day. I wanted to go when I graduated from high school, but life got in the way. Something horrible happened to my friend Zen, and there is no way I wouldn't drop everything to help her. This is the right time now, and I'm going to find my father. I came outside with two bags, set them down, and I popped the trunk up on my red VW Beetle convertible.

"Elle, I just don't understand why it has to be the second you graduate," mom pleaded, following me to my car. "Can't you spend a little of summer with your momma before you go out and search for your dad, move out, grow up?" my mom, Michelle, says as she is getting teary-eyed.

"Mom, you know I've been wanting to do this ever since you told me about him. It will be fine," I stated. "I just don't get why you never told him about us. Maybe things could have been different."

"Baby girl, we've had a glorious life, right? I mean, no, there wasn't a man in it, but we did okay. I was so young, and you know your grandparents would have never accepted me being with a biker. That's if Johnny would have even accepted me and being pregnant. I didn't find out I was pregnant until I was back home for a month. It was a fling, and that's all it was. A foolish fall romance that gave me the most beautiful, smart, mostly well-behaved girl I could have ever hoped for. I'll never regret having you," she gently spoke the last as she cupped my face in her hands and kissed my cheeks. "I love you, my baby girl."

"I love you too, mom, and you know I think you are amazing. It's just that you've never married and maybe he never found the one either," I say, hugging my mom back tightly. She really was the greatest mom, and to raise me on her own was something. Even picturing myself doing that now seemed crazy. Sure, she dated sometimes, and a couple even proposed, but she always turned them down. I honestly don't think anyone turned her into goo like my father. They took a lot of pictures that fall because sometimes when she thought I was in bed, I'd sneak out of my room and see her sipping a glass of wine and looking at an old photo album. She didn't hide it from me. When I was little and asked about having a dad, she pulled it out and showed me the pictures of my father, the club, the other club members and some of their kids and pictures of her friend Izzy who she went to visit back then. She even took one out of the album and gave it to me, and I've had it on my mirror ever since. They were sitting, him behind her and their legs stretched out and his arms wrapped around her. You can tell how in love they were.

7

We let go of each other and I gave her a kiss and went back inside and continued going back and forth to grab stuff loading my small trunk like never coming back was the goal. My plan was the couple of months like mom had and genuinely believing everything would go great.

# Michelle

Watching my daughter gather her things, I started drifting off into my own memories of my first trip alone. It was fall; the leaves were changing. I was going to visit my friend Izzy for a couple months after high school and summer vacation. Not seeing her in years, she suggested me being there in October because the nearby town went all out with festivals, haunted houses, and all things witchy near Halloween, so we decided all of September and October would be good. I had traveled the first year before starting college, and my plan was talking Izzy into going with me. My family sent me to Europe during the summer thinking if I traveled all summer studying art, I would not take the year off to "find myself." Well, that was my plan anyway.

Two weeks after being in New Freedom, IL, we ran into each other. The most handsome man I had ever seen. I was walking down the sidewalk with my friend, eating ice cream, and jabbering as young girls do, and ran smack dab into him. Smashing the cone right between my Prince T-shirt and his cut, I didn't know that's what they called it. Seeing his cut initially frightened me, but he just looked into my hazel eyes and stared. I was stammering around frantically, trying to wipe it off and apologize. He just chuckled and took my ice cream drenched fingers and licked them clean. That's all it took.

We were inseparable from that moment on. For the next six weeks, you wouldn't see one of us without the other. Him with his dreamy rocker look about him, except with

8

more muscles, of course. Damn those arms, those eyes. Yep, I was a goner. I still spent some time with Izzy, and she got to know some of the club members as well. Remembering she had a crush on one of them, but not remembering his name.

He had been out of the army a couple of years and started a motorcycle club with some of his army buddies, Ruger, Winchester, and several others. I really enjoyed my time with them, and they were nothing like what my parents had me believe bikers were like. There was Ruger and Malibu Barbie and their two young boys, Matteo and Dante, and there was his brother Winchester and his wife Tequila Sheila and their son Luca. Sheila was a hoot. She was about six years older than me, with wild blonde hair, big boobs, and an even bigger personality. They were all older than me, but they welcomed me with open arms even though I was just a teenager.

I remembered that last day before I left for home. The club had a Halloween party, and we ladies had talked the men into dressing up in costumes. I went as Diane Lane/Cherry in the Outsiders. It was easy because people always said I looked like her. The guys all dressed in hair band attire, Reaper as Jon Bon Jovi, Ruger as Eddie Van Halen, Tank was Sammy Hagar and Winchester as David Lee Roth. I laugh out loud, thinking about how Sheila talked him into bleaching his hair for the part. Of course, they dyed it back to brownish black the next morning when I said my goodbyes. After the party he took me to the banks of the Mississippi River where he laid down a big blanket and we made sweet love in the light of the full moon but that thought quickly subsides when I remember Cuda being dressed like Angus Young from AC/DC. I am outside in my driveway laughing like a lunatic when my daughter slams the trunk and jolts me out of my thoughts.

"What on Earth are you laughing at?" Elle asks, looking all around.

"I was just thinking of the Halloween party at the clubhouse the night before I left. One guy dressed like Angus Young," and I bust out laughing again.

"Who?" she asks, and I shake my head.

"Please tell me I raised you right, Angus Young. You know, the guy in AC/DC in the schoolboy shorts and tie?" I plead she knows this, or I've seriously lacked in parenting all these years.

"You Shook Me All Night Long?" she asks with her head cocked like a little cocker spaniel pup.

"YES! I have NOT failed as a parent!" I say excitedly, bringing my elbow down as I raise my knee.

"Mom, you are cracking me up," Elle says, laughing with me and tossing her purse in the passenger seat.

## Elle

"I'm all locked and loaded," I say as I sway anxiously from foot to foot, dreading saying goodbye to my mom. I'm kind of nervous about leaving her, but excited. She had to be two parents, and she rocked at both. She taught me strength, courage, and gave me so much love. My mom is beautiful inside and out. I look at my mom with her curves and shiny, light brown hair glistening in the sun. She could have had the pick of any man around. Many men tried to date her, but she wouldn't give most the time of day. Now that I'm older, I know what she meant. Some men are only after one thing and aren't worth it. If you won't get to know me, I'm certainly not going to jump in bed with you.

I'm fairly certain with Mom's looks, she encountered the same problems.

"You be careful! Call me 3 times a day and let me know where you are," mom says.

"And don't pick up hitchhikers and don't take candy from strangers," I laugh and tell her, "I know mom, I'll be fine." I give mom one last hug before I hop in the car, start the GPS, crank up the radio and leave Cottonwood, Arizona to find my dad. It's a small little town about 30 minutes from Sedona. I've lived here all my life. Mom moved here shortly before I was born, and she started her art studio. She fell in love with Mingus Mountain, Slide Rock, and our favorite burger place in Jerome, Haunted Hamburger. Mom asked me to stop by her art shop in Sedona to drop off a couple of pieces for her. I love these red mountains and the vibe in Sedona. It's became a real art mecca over the years and mom got in on the ground floor.

I whip into the parking lot and Christopher, her assistant, comes out to meet me. "Your mom said you were on your way. Let me help you carry that in," he says about the heavy sculpture that rode shotgun with me from the house. I unbuckle the seat belt around it as he opens the passenger door. "Dang, this sucker is heavy! Be a love and grab the dolly for me."

I run inside and grab it and push it out of the car. "Mom said she's already got a buyer for this one," I say.

"Yes, it's commissioned by that fancy lawyer in Phoenix," he says.

"Oh God, please don't tell me it's the one she's about to dump!" I say.

"The same. You know your mom, no one will give her the butterflies like..." he says, but I finish him.

"Like my dad. I know. Really, I think she just needs to give up on trying to find someone that does that and just find a decent guy," I say. "I've never felt butterflies for anyone in my life, so I think she's just stuck in the past. I'm going to meet him, ya know?"

"Your mom told me. She's so nervous. Part of her wanted to go with you. Did you know that?" he asks as he gently lifts and sets the sculpture down with my help.

"No, I didn't. Maybe I should have asked her to go," I say hesitantly, feeling bad for not thinking of it myself.

"Do not do that! You need to have an adventure on your own. Your mom knows that and that's why she said nothing," he says, "besides, she's afraid if she sees him again, she really won't be able to move on."

I snort, "Yeah, like THAT'S ever going to happen!"

Christopher laughs with me, "I know right, I really liked that Bill guy from a few years ago. He proposed, and she broke it off."

"Yeah, he was pretty cool. We got along great, but she gets melancholy in October. All I can say is he must have been one hell of a man to be that hooked. That's another reason I want to meet him so bad. I mean, how could you love someone that much and not just try to be together? Did he search for us? I mean mom, since he doesn't know about me. Won't that just blow his mind?" I try to shake off how my introducing myself is going to go as we walk into the studio. I haven't quite figured out how I'm going to do it. All these years dreaming about meeting him and I haven't planned the perfect introduction.

"You are so like your mother!" he says.

"What? I'm not doing anything," I protest.

"You get that same faraway look as your momma when you overthink. Tell me I'm wrong?" he says, tapping his fingers on the counter.

"Your wrong," I say and try to make a joke of it, but he gives me a knowing look. "Okay, okay, I do, sometimes, take after my mom."

"Everything is going to work out just like it's supposed to," he says and kisses me on the cheek, "now get out of here and start your future!"

"Thanks, Christopher. Take care of mom, okay?" I ask.

"I always do," he says, and with that I get back in my car and head down the road.

I'm jamming to all kinds of music, from pop to heavy metal rap to oldies. I love pretty much all music. The wind blowing through my hair, shades on, damn, this is so exciting! I make a quick stop around lunchtime to fill up both my tank and my stomach and call mom.

"Hey baby girl! Where are you now?" mom asks.

"I just stopped in Albuquerque and I'm getting ready to go to a little Mexican place to eat," I tell her.

"Wow, you're making pretty good time. Call me when you stop for the night. Sorry, gotta run. I'm in the middle of something," mom tells me and hangs up. I'd bet money that she's giving the lawyer the sculpture, along with the boot. It's not like my mom is a serial dater by any means.

She may meet a guy once a year, if that even. Most of them I've never met because they never make it past the first date. Hell, I didn't even know she dated at all until I got older and kept pressuring her to meet someone.

I make a couple of stops here and there, not paying any attention, and miss my exit. I'm pretty far out of my way before I realize and stop and stretch in Shreveport, Louisiana. Of course, taking pics of Riverboat Casinos on the Red River. I check out the RW Norton Art Gallery. Raised in an artist's world, it's in my blood. This place is a whole different world from where I'm from. It's like everything got greener the further I got away from home. I pick up some food and I check in to the hotel and call mom.

"I was worrying about you. It's pretty late," mom tells me.

"I know, mom, but I just wanted to get as far as I could before I got a hotel. Then, I missed an exit and ended up in Shreveport." I tell her.

"Shreveport!" mom shrieks.

We have a longer conversation this time, mostly her wondering why I got so far off my route, but I told her that sometimes missing exits are the right way to travel. Afterward, I hop in the shower and settle into bed. Never having gone far alone, I feel like I'm officially adulting now. I am snuggled up in bed loading the pics from my camera I'd taken today on to my laptop while eating some amazing Jambalaya and Boudin Balls. Once I'm stuffed, I realize how beat I am and before I know it, I'm asleep.

I wake up and decide my route. With a quick stop to get Beignets at a place called Another Broken Egg Cafe because, well, you have to. No more out of the way adventures for me, I need to make a straight shot. But how could I not take the long way and try some Cajun food? Now I must stop in Memphis and take a tour, but that's on the way and Groupon had a hell of a deal. I load my things back up, call mom and tell her I'll probably not call her when I get to Memphis since it's not too far and that I'll just call her when I get to dad's place. Mom isn't too keen on the idea, but she tells me okay.

On the road, one of my mom's favorite songs comes on. I get lost in the music of Uncle Kracker singing "Drift Away." Cranking it up, I sing along with it. I think about mom holding me and dancing me around the kitchen as she sings. Did this song remind her of my dad? The lyrics hit me a little differently this time.

Memphis is really cool. I listened to Blues and Jazz. I saw Sun Studio and even watched them make guitars at the Gibson Beale Street Showcase. My mouth was watering, smelling the amazing barbecue. The smoky taste, the dry rub and tangy sauce was to die for. I spent way too much time taking snapshots, going on tours, and losing track of time.

I love taking pictures, though. It's my passion. From landscapes to interesting places, and the faces. That's what I love the most. Capturing a face in a moment of time, ahhhh bliss. I feel like I see into someone's soul and get a secret piece of them hidden from the world. Whether it be a smile and a twinkle in the eyes of an elderly couple still in love or the wrinkles and crow's feet that show how much a person smiled in their life, it's a story to me. I imagine their lives in the pictures I take.

I get back on the road a lot later than I had wanted. In fact, it had already gotten dark, which is late for summer. I only have a little over 3 hours to go, but that's going to put it at around midnight. I was stressing over pulling up to meet my father and introducing myself at that late of an hour, and completely forgot to call my mom after breakfast.

"Dammit, Elle, focus!" I think to myself. I have always got distracted. Kind of how I ventured off into Louisiana to start with. I took a wrong exit because I forgot to turn my GPS back on when I left Albuquerque and just went with it. When I saw I was heading toward Cajun food, it was get upset or go with it. My stomach said go with it because let's be honest, I can eat.

I love food, I can't help it. Mom and I would watch cooking shows or save pins on Pinterest of cool recipes, and on Sundays, we would spend the day together in the kitchen. We would whip up so much food we had leftovers for the rest of the week. When I got into high school and college, our house was the place to go for all my friends. They may eat Ramen all week in their dorm rooms in Phoenix, but on Sundays, they all knew they were going to eat well.

My best friend Harlow would even come over early that day to help. We all call her Zen because she is our group's Hippie Child. All peace and love. Long, blonde hair with carefree waves and curls. A boho style in her clothes. She has this inner light about her. When you are around her, you automatically feel a calmness come over you. That's not saying she hasn't had her share of tragedy. Believe me, she has. But she came out of it as a better, stronger person. Not me. I'm more the flame. The loud one that loves to laugh. If you need strength, you come to me. I'm the friend that makes you feel like a powerful woman when I'm done with my pep talks. Where Zen gives you peace and calm, I give you the roar. However, she has gotten better at it with her degree. Somehow, she just knows which you need and flat out gives it to you. Sometimes, it's a hug and to cry with you, sometimes it's a kick in the ass. She's the yin to my yang. Give me my black eye liner, my torn blue jean shorts, and my scrunchie, give her an

16

embroidered peasant blouse and her flip-flops. God, I miss that girl! If stressed about anything, she's your go to girl. Unfortunately, she's spending the summer in India getting more enlightened or she would be on this trip with me, no doubt.

I look down at the clock. No wonder I'm so exhausted, it's One AM and I've passed the bigger part of Devil's Backbone, but I can't go one more mile. Maybe I can find a place to stop and get a hotel and a bite to eat. I'll just get some rest and a fresh start and find my dad in the morning. That makes way more sense than walking to his door at this hour and saying, "Hi, you don't know me, but I'm Elle Burrow, you know, Michelle Burrow? Yep, I'm your daughter." Yeah, that would make a great first impression.

# CHAPTER TWO

## Elle

Several stops for gas, bathroom, food, and directions later from leaving home, I end up in Devil's Backbone, one state over but near New Freedom. Completely exhausted from driving and unable to go any further, there is only one place open... a little dive bar and grill on the outskirts of town called The Old Rusty Barn Bar and Grill. It looks a little shady but there is nothing else around. Hopefully they will let me in for a quick bite and directions to the nearest hotel.

Straightening my clothes, trying to calm my wild, windblown hair, I head in, trying to seem more confident than I really am. When I get in, I'm spotted by a dark complected, thick make-upped waitress with black hair and big blonde chunks and a stacked body for her age. "What brings a young girl like you in here?" the name tag of Lilith asks me.

"I realize I'm not too far from New Freedom, but I can't drive anymore. Can I have a Dr. Pepper? I think it's a bar and grill. Is your kitchen still open?" I meekly plead.

"Sure sweetie, it's okay, it's dead in here, anyway. Let me go back in the kitchen. I'll see what I can come up with." Lilith slides me the Dr. Pepper and heads into the kitchen.

In about five minutes, she brings back two plates of sandwiches and chips. "I hope you don't mind if I eat with you. I haven't had dinner yet, and I haven't met a stranger in forever. Besides, you look like you could use some company."

"Yeah, that would be great! Thanks for the food too. I really appreciate it," I reply.

"It's no trouble at all. So, what are you doing in these parts?" she asks.

"Well, it's a long story but my mom, Michelle, fell for this man... my father, twenty-two years ago and she got pregnant with me. He never learned about me. She was just here visiting a friend, you understand. She didn't find out she was pregnant with me until she was back home. Mom was too afraid to tell him. I'm hoping he accepts me and lets me get to know him before finding a new job in my field. I want to get to know him." Why did I just tell her all that?

"Well, if he's from New Freedom, it's a small town. Maybe I know him. What do you know about him? Do you have a picture, a name?" she inquires.

"Here's a picture of him and my mom. It's kind of worn. His name is Jonathan Samuel Holmes."

"I know EXACTLY who that is, sweetie. I should have seen it before. You have the same eyes. We all know him as Reaper," Lilith says, entirely too syrupy.

I look at her, alarmed. "My dad goes by Reaper?" What was I thinking looking for my biker dad? Why did I just expect him to be this awesome TV dad kind of guy? With a name like Reaper, he probably kills people for looking at him wrong. All these thoughts rushing through my over-active brain.

"He's a good man and a friend," Lilith quickly tells me when she notices the panic in my eyes. "Here's what I'm going to do. There aren't any hotels around here. I will take you back to the clubhouse. You can stay with me..."

But I stop her, "Oh that is so sweet, but I couldn't put you out like that, you just met me."

"Let me finish, girlie. As I've said, there aren't any hotels close and I'm friends with your dad. You come stay with me at the clubhouse. I will get you two all introduced first thing in the morning." She pours on the charm as much as she can without making herself sick. "We haven't had one person since you came in. Let me close up and we can head there in a few."

I throw my arms around Lilith because let's be real. Her idea is way better than anything I can think of. "Seriously? Oh my God, I can't thank you enough!"

"No need to thank me, dearie. Just seeing the look on his face will be thanks enough," she tells me.

We head out and lock up the bar just as the waitress says. "Why don't you grab what you will need for tonight and leave your car here and you can ride with me? You and your dad can come get it in the morning?"

I hesitate, but Lilith is being so nice, putting me up and introducing me to my dad. They are in the same club; it seems. Against my better judgment of following in my car, I grab a few things and climb into Lilith's truck.

We pull up to the clubhouse and Lilith tells me to sit in the truck for a second while she runs in. She informs me sometimes they can be pretty wild and doesn't want me to have to see anything I shouldn't.

## Lilith

I'm thinking this is just the opportunity to get back in good with my old man Chains. Chains has been in the trafficking business for a few years now. It's not as easy to come up with girls and people not noticing someone missing. I pour on the charm.

When she hands me the picture, I look at it and immediately notice the Unfortunate Souls cut. "Oh, this just gets better and better," my mind brewing up a plan. I had plans of drugging this girl and delivering her to Chains, the president of the Vengeful Demons, and my man. I have plotted up something even easier and more brilliant. I picture myself twisting an evil handlebar mustache and smile to myself. This girl is the president of the rival Unfortunate Souls daughter. Delivering her on a silver platter will have to make Chains take me back after our fight.

I con the girl into leaving her car here and we head to the Vengeful Demons clubhouse. When I go in first, I spot Chains leaned back in a recliner. A rough-looking guy at 6'3" and weighing in at 300lbs. A long scar twisted down the side of his face. That scar came from Ruger's old lady. I think her name was Barbie or something. He got even with that bitch, though. His long graying hair and beard looking rough and unkempt, but what do I care. You can still tell that he was probably handsome in his youth. He's dangerous with a dark arrogance about him and that's what I like. I strut over to him as suggestively as I can, "Hey Chains baby, you know why you should forgive me and take me back?" but when I enter the room fully and walk around the recliner to him, I see he's getting a blow job by a club girl and I am livid. I want to jerk her head up and drag her outside, but I've got to keep my eye on the prize here.

The brown-headed club girl was finishing taking in the explosion of Chains' cum as he pulls her back off of his cock. She is wiping her mouth and getting off her knees and walking away quickly when he answers me, "Jesus Lils, only you can ruin a blow job. It's not happening, but I'll bite. Why?"

"What would you say if I helped you not only get a pretty young thing to sell off, but you could get back at Unfortunate Souls at the same time?" I say, proud of my brilliant idea.

Chains jumps out of the recliner and grabs my arm, jerking me towards him. "What the fuck did you do now, woman? If you grabbed one of their girls, all hell's gonna break loose in here and it's going to be on you, you fucking cunt!" He is seething with anger. The spit hitting my face as he yells.

"Wait, wait, just listen," I plead as I am backed up against a wall. A hand around my throat now, "It's Reaper's long-

22

lost daughter. He doesn't even know about her yet. She thinks I'm going to introduce them in the morning."

"Reaper doesn't know about her? He doesn't know she exists? And you're telling me she came with you willingly and is sitting out in the truck?" he asks.

"Yeah, she even has a picture of her mom and Reaper she carries around," I say.

"Okay, get her in here. I'll play it up until we can lock her in a room and plan this shit out," Chains says.

I shuffle quickly outside to get Elle, "Ok, it's all clear. The only one in there right now is my old man Chains."

"Seriously, thank you again. I can't believe I get to see my dad!!" she tells me thankfully.

## Elle

As we walk in Chains is ending a conversation with someone on the phone. "There she is, Reaper's only child. Damn, he's going to be surprised. And look at you all sweet and pretty," he says as he takes my hand and spins me around.

Chains is making me nervous. Just the way he said that last part and he looks so rough and creepy. A scar goes down the side of his face, disappearing into his scruffy, long beard. The smell of strong liquor, pot and something that died on his breath. Lilith is noticing my nervousness and jumps in, "Well, come on, sweet girl. Let's show you to your room for the night."

She leads me down a long hall with Chains following. They open a door, and we head down a staircase.

"We have a room all set up downstairs for guests. It will be nice and quiet down there. The boys should be here soon, and they can get pretty rowdy."

They open another door at the bottom of the stairs. "There you go" and I step in and I'm looking around confused, "I can't seem to find the light switch." Just then Chains shoves me hard into the room and I hit the rough concrete floor and he slams the door. I can hear someone locking it.

I scream and bang on the door, "What's going on? Why are you doing this? Please, no!"

What have I gotten myself into? I'm smart enough to know that screaming and banging for long on that door is going to get me nowhere. Also, it will just make me weak. Think, Elle, think. They have all my belongings, and I don't have my phone. The last time I talked to my mom was around 7:30 am. I didn't call her this afternoon because I was so excited about seeing Memphis. Then was running behind after. Damn, wasn't that a joke now? I know my mom, after missing two of my check-in's, mom is already freaking out. Hopefully, she's so worried she calls the police, and they are looking for my car. Of course, the last time I spoke to mom I was in Shreveport, Louisiana checking out of a hotel.

I feel around this dark, dank room and touch a small table and lamp. Fumbling around, I turn on the switch and check out my surroundings. There's an old twin bed with messy, well-used sheets. I groan, just imaging what's all over them. A wooden chair at the table with the lamp. No food, no weapons, no bathroom. A dirty plastic trash can sits in the corner. My new toilet, gross. An acidic taste rises in my throat. I spot a broken ink pen with sharp, jagged edges on the floor under the table, so I crawl down and grab it. I've never been in the position where I had to defend myself. I doubt that would be enough to stop either of them, but maybe if I can get in an excellent shot, I can run. Assuming they won't be in until morning, I hold the pen for dear life, curl up into a ball on the filthy bed, and try to get some sleep.

The next morning, I wake to hear steps coming down the stairs and the key wiggling in the lock. I wake in a daze, not knowing where I am at first. It doesn't take me but a moment to remember what happened and my surroundings. "Holy crap, this is it! Just breathe Elle," I tell myself, trying to steady my racing heart. I continue to lie still and try to act like I am still asleep. I'm trying to slow my breathing and just take small breaths, as someone sleeping would be doing.

"Wake up, you lazy little bitch," Lilith slams some food down on the table and goes over to shake me. When she grabs my shoulder to roll me over, I jump up, jabbing Lilith in the side with the pen hard and deep. I take off running towards the door as Lilith is cussing and screaming and holding the pen sticking out of her bleeding flesh. I get out of the bedroom door and to the stairs, taking steps two at a time. It seems like forever but merely seconds. I make it up the stairs and into the upstairs area. I'm grabbed around the waist and spun around by another man I haven't seen before.

"Little spitfire, aren't ya?" he laughs as he's keeping a tight hold of me and I'm flailing uselessly. Chains walks over to me and though I'm fighting with all my might, it isn't enough. Chains sticks a needle in my arm while the other man holds it against my body and soon, I get really groggy. Calibar, the man that had grabbed me, starts walking me over to a chair, but before he lets me fall into it, Lilith comes up and punches me right in the face. I then fall into the recliner and am barely awake. My cheek is throbbing, and it's the only thing keeping me awake at this moment. I'm trying to hear and see what's going on, but it's getting harder and harder to keep my eyes open. When Lilith punched me, it hurt herself too from the stretching and she doubles over in pain herself from hitting me while wounded.

"Dammit Lils! I can't have her all beat the hell up when I meet with Reaper," Chains growls.

"Do you see what that cunt did to me?" she cries out in anger and pain. "I think she hit something important. I need a doc," she says weakly before falling to the floor. No one is paying any attention to me at that point, and I smile at that but I can no longer keep my eyes open. At that point, Lilith falls to the floor and passes out with a pool of blood gushing onto the floor from the stab wound I gave her.

"Now what?" Luther asks.

"Frodo, you take the girl. Put her in the car and take her to the back of the Old Rusty Barn. Park in the back, out of sight," orders Chains.

"What about Lils?" asks Luther.

"I'm done with that bitch and her causing me problems. Put her in the silo and meet me at O.R.B.," states their leader.

It's at that point I completely pass out and hear nothing else or know what is happening.

# CHAPTER THREE

## Benelli Vice President

It's a club party tonight for the guys to cut loose. We are celebrating the success of the weed dispensary contract we got with the state a few months ago when it became legal in Illinois. The club has been working our asses off to make this happen and our second quarterly report came in and it's been a very lucrative deal. We weren't hurting for money by any means with all the businesses the club owns, but this will set us up for life. This will allow us to get into the other avenues we want to take the club in. I want it to be more of a help to not only the community but to actually save people. I want us to make a difference in the world. We've had some smaller issues with the rival MC, the Vengeful Demons, for years. There was something involving my mom and dad, but we never got the story, just that there was bad blood between them. I know that club is into some shady shit. I can feel it. Maybe it's the soldier in me, but my gut says something major is coming our way and they are involved.

"Hey brother, why are you always so damn serious? Lighten up, it's a party," my brother Remington tells me, slapping a hand on my shoulder while reaching over the bar to grab a bottle of whiskey with the other.

"Who are you talking to? You get as serious as me. Remember that time someone was being mouthy to Lyric at the club? If I hadn't of stepped in before you, that man would be 6 feet under now," I remind him.

"Yeah, well, he deserved it for talking to her like that. If he talked to her like that, I guarantee you she's not the first. Besides, that's my job, right? The enforcer, the righter of wrongs?" he tries to laugh it off, but I know there's a special place in that icy heart of his for Lyric. He tries to deny it and does his best to not get involved with her since Cuda and Stilleto took her in and that makes her more like a sister. At least to me.

Remington pours the two of us a double shot and we down them with ease. "Seriously dude, look at all the ass in here tonight! I know you won't tap the club girls, but there are a shit ton of hang arounds here. Surely there has to be one or two here that will change that attitude. We are celebrating in case you forgot. Hell, I see twins over there that I think need some attention," he says, and I look over to where he motioned. I will not deny they aren't hot in a slutty kind-of way, but damn it, I want more than that.

I've gone through the wild stage, the party stage, the having any girl I wanted. We all go through that, but I'm over it now. I want what my Uncle Winchester and Aunt Sheila have. Those two have been in love since way before I was born, and they are still head over heels with each other. I want to find that, someone to laugh with and grow old with, someone that knows me even better than I know myself.

I look over and see my dad over by the pool table with Reaper. They've been best friends since they served together and then started this club. They are chugging beers, telling stories, laughing, and playing pool with Breezy and Goldie. The club girls being overly flirty and showing their cleavage and ass as they lean across the pool table to take their shots. Dad slaps Goldie's ass, and she giggles and shakes it more. I roll my eyes at them. I know dad didn't exactly have it easy with mom when she was alive and yeah; he has every right to do what he wants, but I really don't want to see it and turn around facing the bar again. I wish some damn woman would come along and knock the rug right out from under him. Truth be told, I wish that for me as well.

Phoenix and Lucky come over to the bar and ask the girl behind it for a couple of beers. Lucky tries to hand me a hit of his joint and I decline, so he takes in another hit. Phoenix lights a Marlboro and offers me one and that I accept. "Your dad and Reaper are drunk off their asses tonight," Lucky says.

"Yeah, they're gonna be feeling it in the morning," I say.

"I'm gonna go ride out to the river. You guys wanna go?" Phoenix asks.

Lucky is sitting and has his back to the bar, his arms propped against it. "Nah, I'm too lit to ride. I'm gonna hit it with Jinx." he nods his head towards where she is, and she bounces over. She immediately wraps her arms around him and starts kissing his neck.

"Yeah, let's get out of here," I tell Phoenix and put out my cigarette and take the last swig of my beer.

As we walk to the door, Justice walks in, all 6'6" of him. He scans the party and pulls his keys out of his pocket. "You ridin'?"

"Fuck yeah, we are," Phoenix says, "you in?"

"This ain't my scene, you feel me?" Justice says and we nod in agreement and head outside.

We climb on our bikes and hear the roar of them coming to life, and head off down the road. Phoenix cranks up the music on his bike and we look at him and smile. "Ah, hell nah!" Justice says and laughs. It was a song that Phoenix used to play in Bagram to get Justice riled because it was too country. Justice would try to change it to rap. Before we left Afghanistan, though, Phoenix had us all learning how to line dance to it. That was a good memory of our time there.

Phoenix wasn't much of a talker, but the guy loved his music, and could that boy sing! I swear he could have made it as a star, but he was happy coming back with me and joining the Unfortunate Souls and doing gigs locally. He said he was too big of a guy to be a heartthrob. Yeah, he's a bigger guy, but he's solid. He has medium length, dirty blonde hair that usually a mess between his overthinking things, running his hands through it and working in the garage.

Justice, on the other hand, is a really tall and, I'm secure enough in my manhood to say, good looking, black man. Women tend to drool when they see him and when they hear his deep voice, that's it. None of us stand a chance with the ladies if he's around.

Me, I have my black hair just like my dad and brother. Right now, it's at that needs to either grow out or be cut stage and drives me crazy. My beard and mustache I keep pretty trimmed. I'm not ripped but I keep in good shape. I have big brown eyes that give me an "I can kick your ass, don't try me," look about them. Mostly, though, I'm a laid-back kind of guy. I like to laugh and have fun, but I'll admit when dad stepped down, and I took his place as the VP, I may have taken things more seriously. I want this club to continue to succeed and I want so many things for it. The club is expanding with a charter in St. Louis and one in Indiana. They are rowdier than the original, but they are still willing to drop everything at a moment's notice and help us out when we need it. I was born and raised in the Unfortunate Souls MC. It's the only life other than the army that I've ever known.

We park our bikes on the Mississippi River and walk to the bank. A lonely barge slowly trudges by as Justice throws some wood in the fire pit we have at this spot, and Phoenix gets it started. We reminisce about our time at Bagram, Afghanistan and try to concentrate on the good things, but it's not all good times or we wouldn't have been needed there. We try to keep it as light as possible and enjoy our time at the river and our ride. Phoenix is going to help me put on the custom fenders I just got for my bike tomorrow. Justice has plans to go see his momma and auntie. After a couple hours, we put out the fire and they head back to their rooms at the clubhouse and I head for my house and my big, 'Ol dog Luna. That's the only woman I'll share my bed with right now. I have found no one yet that I'd want to take to my home.

# Reaper

## Club President

I wake up, pulling the naked girl off the top of me and head to the bathroom. "Get up, Breezy. It's morning and you need to get out of here," I tell her as I'm picking up all the clothes thrown around the room.

"Ah Reaper, come on, I was having the best dream," Breezy, the big busted, plump, curvy red head tells me. She looks at me with those big, hazel eyes and even bigger, full, pouty lips.

"Go on, Breezy, you know the rules. Out you go," I say, tossing Breezy her clothes that were scattered everywhere. Damn, we were pretty wild last night, I think to myself, remembering the drinking, dancing, and partying the club did. Hell, I don't even remember coming back to my room. Good times, I think as I head towards the bathroom. Breezy heads out as my phone goes off, alerting me of a text. I finish taking a piss and head back to the end table and grab it. "I need some damn coffee," I grumble while opening my cell. It says unknown.

I've got something of yours
Old Rusty Barn 60 minutes
Come alone

That's all it says, along with a picture. That picture knocked the breath out of me. I grab my gut then bend over, putting my hands on my knees. I take in a few deep breaths and look at the phone again. It's an old picture of me and the only woman I ever truly loved, Michelle. My mind isn't even fully awake yet, and it's racing. "FUUUUCK!" I yell loudly in a deep, scary tone.

"What is it? You ok?" Breezy asks frantically while running back towards the bedroom door. Lucky and Ruger that were in the main hall half asleep with Goldie and Jinx come rushing too. They all jumped at hearing my gruff shout and came running. Great, now I've got a crowd heading to my door. Ruger is my age and my right-hand man, even if he stepped down as VP a few years ago. Lucky is a huge guy with red hair and beard, extremely broad shoulders and covered in colorful tats. He's our treasurer and comic relief. Jinx is the newest and youngest of our girls at 21. She has long, thick, multi-colored hair with part of it pulled in pig tails. This month it's light pinks and blues, but you just never know with that girl. She's a little clumsy, hence her name, but she's fun to be around. Goldie. Well, she reminded us of Goldie Locks and the 3 bears the first time she showed up.

Lyric comes running too. She lives here, but she's not a club girl. She's Justice's cousin and Cuda's goddaughter. Lyric is in manager positions throughout the club. She moved in with Cuda and his woman after her parents died and then moved to the clubhouse when she turned eighteen. She oversees the club girls, and she doesn't take any shit from the girls, or us. Her black hair and beautiful hazel eyes can steal your soul. She's originally from New Orleans and you look at her and think all things creole, secrets, and magic. Lyric is in college and smart as fuck. She spends most of her time studying when she's not giving us hell.

"Get it together, man!" I tell myself. "It's cool guys, stubbed my fucking toe." I quickly yell back so they don't come in. Too late. I grab my foot, acting like I really did.

"Shit man, the way you yelled, I thought you got your dick stuck in something," Lucky chuckles.

"I'm fine, fucker. Why don't you go see if Goldie or Jinx needs your "Lucky Charms," I try to joke it off to get them out of my room at the clubhouse?

Jinx bops over to Lucky, wrapping around his body ready to get some "charms" for herself. Lyric just rolls her eyes and grabs my foot to check it out. She looks up at me, knowing there is nothing physically wrong with me, but keeps it to herself. Like I said, she's smart as fuck. "Alright everyone, let's give this man some peace and get out of here," Lyric tells them. They all file out and back into the main hall and kitchen. Thank God for that woman.

"You sure you're okay?" Breezy sympathetically asks as she's leaving.

"Yeah, Breezy, I'm good. I've gotta make a run to Devil's Backbone for some parts. Fix me a coffee, will ya?" I ask.

"Sure babe," Breezy says and bops along back to the kitchen.

Well, THAT took way more time that I don't have. I scramble around, throwing on my clothes and cut as quickly as I can. I carefully slide my knife down in my boot and my 9mm Beretta in the back of my jeans and head out of my bedroom at the clubhouse. Breezy runs up with my cup of coffee and I blow on it, then chug it down, needing the quick shot of caffeine. I hand the cup back to Breezy and light a smoke. She may be one of the club's community pussy, but she really was a sweet girl. I give a tug at her chin and give her a quick kiss. "Thanks, Breezy. If I'm not back in an hour, send the troops."

Lyric, hearing my comment about the troops, follows me outside, "anything we need to know?"

"I'll be okay, hon, you know me," I chuckle, trying to lighten the mood and fool her. I know it's useless, but I give it a shot.

"Yeah, I know you Reaper," she gives me a look, telling me she ain't dumb, and she knows something is up. I hop on my bike and start the engine, hearing it purr for me. It's not the classic I've been fixing up at the garage, but this is my baby, too. She leans over and kisses me on the cheek, "be careful old man."

"Old man? Hell Lyric, I'm only fifty. I'm in my prime. When I get back, I'll show you how prime," I tell her, laughing, knowing that would never happen.

Then it takes a more serious tone as I watch her lips and she softly whispers, "Just come back, okay." My head nods in a yes, but not sure if I will be able to keep that promise. Looking into my rearview mirror, she stands, almost hugging herself, watching me until she is no longer in sight.

I'm going down the road picking up speed and I'm wondering what the hell is going on. How the hell did they get Michelle? I haven't seen her in twenty-two years. How did they find her when I haven't been able to? My mind is going 90mph along with the Harley. I'm traveling from Illinois into Kentucky. Not a long drive, but long enough to fill my brain with ideas. It has to be the Vengeful Demons. They're the only bad news in Devil's Backbone where the Old Rusty Barn is. I mean, you have some meth heads and other drug addicts, but they wouldn't be able to find her and kidnap her. Vengeful Demons are the only explanation.

They're a dirty MC in Kentucky and we are in Illinois, but the only thing separating our clubs is that old Mississippi River bridge. Devil's Backbone is a way bigger city than our New Freedom, IL, but we like it like that. The slower pace, the less crime. Our club owns some businesses in New Freedom, Devil's Backbone and the neighboring towns including the weed dispensaries we have the contract for, a bar, strip joint, a mom-and-pop diner, a donut shop down the road from the dispensary and others. All up and up legal and that's the way it's going to stay. We're even considering purchasing a road construction company. I've spent many years building this club up since we all got out of the military. Ruger, my best friend, and I grew up and served together. When we got out, we started this club with his older brother Winchester and a few other retired soldiers.

I need to come up with a plan, but if truth be told, I am going in blind, and Chains is calling the shots. If he has hurt Michelle, he's a dead man. He's a dead man anyway for this. No one lays a hand on my Belle, and I look at the tat on my hand and remember her.

I can still remember the scent of her like it was yesterday, Love's Baby Soft. That perfume of soft, sweet innocence, of stolen kisses in the dark. Laying on a blanket out on the sandy dirt of the river as the moon shone down on our glistening bodies. Sweaty from the Indian summer and making out. Passion like I've never felt before or since, you know the one. When you're young and you're kissing and touching and feeling in a furious fever. Turning and tumbling with every sense heightened. Butterflies. Yeah, even I fucking felt them. Knowing though, I didn't have a curfew like she did while staying with her friend and her parents. Izzy was twenty, but they were strict with her. Though I knew who Izzy was with now and exactly how wild she was. I was going to get in every single taste and feel of Michelle I could get before she had to leave each night.

Before I knew it, I had already crossed the Mississippi River Bridge into Kentucky and was pulling up to the bar. Turning off my bike, I'm scoping out the area. I see a little red VW Beetle and 3 bikes. Chains', Calibar's and Luther's. I'd know those bikes anywhere. I covertly check the gun at my back and head in.

"Here, pull up a chair." Chains shoves one with his boot in my direction and I decline, taking one where my back is facing the wall. Never have your back open where someone can sneak up on you.

"What's the fucking deal, Chains? We don't mess with your club, and you don't mess with ours. Where the fuck did you get that picture?" I demand.

"Well, something jumped into our laps, so to speak, last night and you're going to want to help us out," Chains calmly states, also saying, "You see, old man, it turns out you have a daughter. Or should I say, we have your daughter, her name is Elle Burrow, ring any bells?"

What the fuck? A daughter? I have a daughter? With Michelle? My mind is spinning. "Prove it motherfucker," I state with detest.

Chains nods to Calibar, who heads back through the kitchen, and you can hear the back door open, feet shuffling, the door closing and some muffled cries. Luther is sitting at the bar across from Chains and Reaper. Luther is lanky and goofy. Brains were never his strong suit. Frodo forces her past the bar towards their table with one arm gripping hers and a gun to her head with the other. Calibar has her other arm gripped tightly as well, pushing her along. I jump out of my chair and pull out my gun. Luther and Calibar draw back on me as well. Four guys to one and a daughter to save. This will not work. Fuck, why didn't I just tell my club what was going on. I could have entered and seemed alone, but have my team ready.

Chains motions for all of them to put their guns away and states "listen, we have her and you're going to do us a favor you see. If you do for us, keep it on the D.L., you get her back. You don't cooperate, or your little soldiers get wind. She dies and I promise you it's going to be a cruel death. Fun for us at first," he chuckles, "but then slow and painful, and after that we come for you and your precious club." Shaking uncontrollably with tears streaming down her bruised face, Elle tries to plead.

"Looks like she has something to say," Chains strolls over and rips the duct tape off of her mouth.

"Please, I know you don't know me, daddy, but please don't let them hurt me! We have the same eyes. I'm your daughter. Please save me!" she begs.

We did, in fact, have the same eyes. I too, have this odd color of bright teal blue eyes. I've seen no one in my entire life with that color but me. I mean, maybe in a magazine or something, so I know she's mine. She looks like a perfect cross between me and Michelle. There is no denying that child. There is this immediate love for that girl, MY girl, and it blew me away. I've never been a father. Never known what it was like to love someone so strong and so immediately.

"Okay," I say, defeated, "what do you want from me?" knowing he's going to get it, no matter the cost. I'm not leaving my kid in the hands of that piece of shit.

Chains nods to Frodo and Calibar, who jerked Elle away and out the back. Luther stays behind with Chains. "We want some more businesses. Profitable businesses. Dispensaries and the contracts that go along with it." Chains states matter-of-factly.

"I can't just do that! It takes more than just my signature for something that huge." I try to explain. I don't give a shit about the money, but you can't just do big business dealings like this with the snap of a finger.

"Figure it out! And no letting your piss ant club know either, or daddy's little girl becomes our play toy. Then, when we are all done using her up, over and over, we lock her up and let her die a long... Slow... death. You feel me?"

I clench my fists in anger, but I answer. "I get it. Give me two days." I detested her being in their custody for that long and it made me sick to my stomach, but drawing up papers and getting contracts switched wasn't fast paperwork. Not to mention, how was I going to get the other signatures without my club getting involved and risking her death? They were soldiers, and I knew them as well as I knew myself... no man left behind. "No one touches her, no one hurts a hair on her head. Do you feel

ME?" I state with the forceful presence that a true club president demands.

Chain puts up his calloused hands. "You have till noon tomorrow. You honor your half of the deal, she won't be touched."

# CHAPTER FOUR

# **Elle**

Little did either of them know that Calibar and Frodo led me kicking and screaming outside to the hidden yellow Datsun out back. Frodo ripped the front of my dress, exposing my breasts. They were pawing and gripping at my exposed flesh. Calibar then grabbed me hard and spun me forcefully and bent me over the hood of the rusted car that the one they call Frodo had brought me in. With his one hand shoving my bruised cheek down to the hot steel of the car, I felt the tears stinging my eyes. His other hand lifted my dress up, exposing my panties. With his one forearm across my back, Frodo ripped off my panties with his loose hand. Calibar took his legs, forcing mine apart, and I heard his buckle being undone and a zipper being pulled down. The realization of what was about to happen to me made me try to fight. With two against one, one holding me down onto the car hood and the other pinning my legs, I didn't stand a chance, but I tried, oh how I struggled. I tried reaching my hands out and pushing them off of me, but Frodo bent them back and leaned on them too.

The more I struggled, the harder they pinned me. With my legs spread wide by his force, Calibar then, without mercy, shoved his dirty cock inside of me. Feeling every forceful violation as it slowly shattered me, piece by piece. My body

41

being tortured by the back-and-forth force of me pinned to the car hood that has sat in the scorching summer sun. I was being burned by the hot hood and violated over and over. It will forever etch the pale-yellow color with peeling paint in my nightmares as I felt him entering me. The smell of their disgusting scent of man sweat, cheap weed, booze and several day-old filth. One smell in particular. The potent smell of a cigarette that had been snuffed out and put back in a pack, then taken back out and relit.

When Calibar had gotten off inside me, he took his turn to the side of the car, holding me down as Frodo took his turn, forcing his body to slam into me hard, fast, and unforgiving. Calibar leaned down to the side of my bruised face, brushing the hair away. Hot, dank breath against my ear, "you know you loved my dick baby, show me how much you want this big, hard dick pounding your pussy again." It was at that moment I was officially broken. Just a shell, a body for them to use. No more tears. I wasn't even there. I couldn't think, I couldn't fight, I just lay there on that hood and left my body.

## Benelli

I pull up to the clubhouse and turn off my bike just as I'm getting a call from Lyric. "Something's up, I feel it," Lyric says to me before I can even say hello. Shit, when Lyric has a bad feeling, you take heed of whatever it is. She fills me in on what Reaper told Breezy as I'm walking through the door. As soon as I enter, I end the call.

"God Damn him, it's the mother fucking Vengeful Demons. Dammit Reaper, what did you do?" Ruger growls. "Get the guys here NOW!" everyone grabs their phones and starts gathering the troops. All the officers and Winchester are at the clubhouse and go straight to church, and Ruger tells them what little he knows.

"Maybe it's nothing. Maybe he IS getting parts in Devil's Backbone, but something ain't right. I can feel it! We're all heading there, ready for anything. If it turns out to be nothing, we went on a fucking joy ride, men. Saddle up," I call out and hit the gavel. As the VP, I'm in charge in Reaper's absence. Ruger, my dad, used to be the VP, but stepped down after my mom died and he thought us boys were mature enough to take over. We didn't want him to step down, but he took mom's death pretty hard, mostly I think he blamed himself because they fought before she left. He said he couldn't do it anymore and while he still would always be a member and mentor to us, he no longer wanted a title.

I asked Lyric to call the old ladies to get them and their kids to the clubhouse for lockdown just in case anything happens, and they don't have time after. Lyric was raised with all of us, though a little younger.

Ruger, Remington (my brother), Lucky, Justice, Phoenix, Colt, his dad Winchester (my uncle), and I all hop on our bikes and take off, locked, and loaded towards Kentucky. Virus stays behind to do any IT work we will need. We have GPS trackers on all the bikes, so we can find out the location of one of the members when needed. Sure enough, within moments, Virus has got the location of Reaper's bike at Old Rusty Barn and tells us throughout our earpieces. I motion to them to pull over at the gas station just over the bridge.

The Unfortunate Souls slow down and see Reaper's bike ahead at the Old Rusty Barn bar and grill, along with some bikes from the VD. The Old Rusty Barn is down a ways where it's all flat and open, surrounded by milo fields, so it's fairly easy to see around the building except for a big shed out back. We pull off when we are over the bridge at the gas station on the opposite side of the road behind a few semis.

"Okay, how do you wanna handle this, chief?" asks Justice.

"There's only three of their bikes and some little red car. That's a chick's car, so I'm not worried about whoever that is," I state.

"That's eight of us, nine counting Reaper, to their three. I say we fucking just bust in and take care of business!" says my brother, the enforcer, Remington, who is hungry for a slaughter.

"If it was a different scenario and we couldn't see what's around, we would handle this differently, but I'm gonna agree with ya, brother. Let's just storm up and blow in. Take them by surprise," I agree. "Pops, Unc, Rem, and me will go in the front. The rest of you take the back. We all good with that?" I ask, looking around at the rest of the club. Everyone nods in agreement, and we start our bikes back up and get back on the road.

## Elle

I didn't know it at the time but my mom, Michelle, hadn't heard from me most of the day yesterday and after having a horrible "mom" gut feeling, (you know the one) had gotten on a plane to Devil's Backbone, Ky where the closest airport is to the clubhouse earlier this morning.

Calibar and Frodo heard a bunch of motorcycles pulling up and turning off their engines, knowing a load of bikers were here. Not knowing if they were from the VD or not, something distracted them. When they pulled off of me, I snapped out of my comatose state and thought this was my only chance to get away. I slam my head back into Calibar, who grabs his broken nose and falls backwards. Frodo has stepped far enough back that I then donkey kick him in the balls. He grabs his crotch and staggers back. That's when I really gather myself and run. I run hard and fast towards the back door of the bar, thinking I had nowhere else to go and no one else to save me. I saw a gas station not far away but didn't think I'd make it and chose to run to my father. I don't even know if he is still there, but I am in fight-or-flight mode and I only see that door to the back of the bar as my safety. I didn't notice the two bikers coming around the side of the bar towards the back door or the other two bikers who were now with Calibar and Frodo fighting them.

Calibar broke free and took off, but Phoenix and Justice now overtook Frodo. As I run in the back door, I am followed by the two bikers that had come around from the side. I didn't know it wasn't those two that had violated me, so I ran even more desperately. I also didn't know that behind those two were the other two that had captured Frodo. All I knew was that I had to get away and get to my father.

When I burst through the back door and into the bar, four men had burst into the front door and guns were drawn by everyone, on everyone including me. Once the other men see that I'm a half-naked woman, they take their aim off of me and onto those dirty bikers that had taken me. A very tall, dark complected, black-haired, muscular biker heads my way and meets me as I enter the room by the bar. As he is coming, I notice he has the same patch that my father had and every bit of strength I had had from the endorphins, gone. I fall forward into his arms, wrapping mine around him as he catches me. Turning in his arms, frantically looking for my father, I see him across the room. I reach out an arm for him and he reaches one out for me and yells, "Elle!"

"You double crossing piece of shit!" Chains yells and pulls the trigger and shoots my dad in the center of his ribs. Reaper immediately falls to the ground, and I scream in the horror at watching my father I had finally just met get gunned down. I bury my face into the man whose patch says Benelli's chest. Everything moves at lightning speed. Ruger and Remington both pull the trigger on their guns, killing Chains. Luther is shooting at anything and everything, trying to back out of the bar. He hits Winchester with a bullet in the shoulder as Justice, Phoenix, Colt and Lucky come in from the back entrance with Frodo captured. Justice draws on Luther, hitting him in the back of his head. Then there was silence.

Three dead, one of them their own. It was a war zone with blood and bodies covering the floor. By now I'm hysterical and hyperventilating, still in Benelli's arms. Benelli walks me to the farthest seat, away from the bloodshed, turning my face away from it. He is now taking off his cut and T-shirt and putting the shirt on me to cover me. Then he puts his cut back on and sits me in a chair with him facing me. He is looking into my eyes, trying to get me to focus on him as he is facing all the bloodshed and I am facing a jukebox and wall. He is saying, "Sh, just breathe with me, sweetie. Look at me, just breathe," and I can't help but to get my breathing under control. I see or hear nothing in the bar anymore. Just his calming voice and kind face coaching me along.

# Michelle

I am driving from the airport heading to Illinois to the Unfortunate Souls clubhouse to find my daughter, Elle. Thank God I still had tracking on my daughter's phone from when she was younger. It narrowed the search down dramatically. I spot Elle's car and a bunch of bikes at this dive. I park hurriedly and head in. When I open the door, I become terrified as I see several guns drawn on me. When they see I am an unarmed woman, they stop immediately. Thank God! I look around the room with all the blood and there are three male bodies I can only assume dead on the floor in horror, but my baby girl is here somewhere. I am looking around the room like a madwoman and I'm seeing only cuts.

Silently, I look at the men on floor and I notice one with a bell and the word MY above it on his wrist. Reaper, oh my God, please don't let it be him. He always called me Michelle my Belle after a Beetles song. I clasp my hands over my mouth and gasp in sheer horror. I run over to the body and crouch down and roll his limp body over; I have to know. I brush the wild hair out of his face, and I know it's him. I grab him into my arms and just start rocking him back-and-forth, weeping for not just the man that fathered my daughter, our daughter, but for the man that was my past, my love. I was such a fool to not tell him about Elle. To not come back to him. I don't even know if he had a wife or other kids now or if he didn't want me, but I should have come back and tried to make it work. Why didn't I give us a chance? I had denied him of knowing his daughter and denied that I always longed for him.

I haven't even noticed my daughter yet. I'm just holding Reaper, rocking him and sobbing. I kiss his face, his forehead, his cheeks, his lips, and I see his bright eyes flutter open and look at me. Everyone around me is looking at me in confusion, not knowing who I am, but I don't even notice. I fixed my eyes on him.

Reaper, with his eyes now open, thinks he must be in heaven to see his beautiful angel holding him. "I didn't think I'd make it to heaven, but this has to be it, Michelle, my belle. Is it really you?" he manages to make out.

"Yes, babe, it's me. I'm right here. I'm not leaving you. I'm right here," I tell him with all the love in my heart.

I hadn't noticed that we are now surrounded by some of his other club members. Ruger, Reaper's best friend, leans down toward us with a confused look on his face. His chest tight from the moment they have all been witnessing.

"Mi... chelle? Is that you?" he recognizes the young girl from twenty-two years ago in the woman's face before him.

"Rug... er? Oh my God, Ruger, what happened?" She asks.

"Honestly, we don't really know. We had a feeling something wasn't right when he left the clubhouse this morning and ran into this mess, but we don't know why he was here," says Ruger, as he takes his friend's hand in his. "Reaper?" he says.

Reaper looks over at his friend and tries to grip his hand in firmness, but he is so weak. "Ruger...." He asks in barely a whisper and Ruger leans down closer to hear him, "She's yours now, take... care. Of... my... belle," and he his eyelids close and he fades away into death, his body goes limp.

"NOOOOOOOOO!!!!!" I scream and hold him tight to my body, droplet after droplet of tears falling from my face to his lifeless body.

Elle, hearing my scream, runs over to me, falling to her knees and wraps her arms around me and her father on the concrete floor of the Old Rusty Barn.

I look at my daughter. Disheveled and bruised, and release my arms from Reaper and grip her tightly, "Oh Elle! Baby girl, are you ok? What happened?"

"Mom, oh mom, I am so sorry. I'm just so sorry. It's all my fault. He's dead because of me, it's because of me my dad is dead," Elle is ranting hysterically.

"Ma'am, I don't mean to be rude, but can someone please tell me what the hell is going on?" Benelli asks.

I speak up knowing that my daughter doesn't have the ability right now, even though I don't know all the details myself. "Elle, Jesus, Elle left a couple of days ago to find Reaper.... her father. I never told him about her, you see. She wanted to know him. I haven't heard from her since yesterday morning, and I had a bad feeling and took the first flight out here late last night. Her car is out front. That's why I stopped," I tell him as calmly as I can, so I don't upset her more. "I don't know myself anything after that, but let's get her settled down. She's obviously been through more than what just happened here." I look at her torn dress hanging underneath the white T-shirt swallowing her.

"Yes, ma'am," the biker tells me with understanding eyes.

Benelli nods and walks over to Winchester and Colt. "He good?" he asks Colt.

"Yeah, he'll make it. We'll have to have the doc meet us at the clubhouse, but he's tough."

"Fucking A, I am," Winchester states back. Then he looks over to the girls, Reaper, and all the carnage. "We're going to have to get this all cleaned up," Winchester continues, but visibly upset.

"I've got it covered," Justice lets them know. "The cleaning crew will be here in thirty. We need to get out of here before anyone shows up. There's an old car out back. We'll put Reaper and Winchester in there. What are we gonna do with this guy?" as he nods his head towards Frodo.

"Take him with us. He's the only person who has a clue what the hell happened other than her," Benelli motions towards my daughter, "and I don't want to have her go through a bunch of questions right now. I have a feeling she's been through more than what just happened when we arrived."

I am listening to everything that's going on around me while still holding my daughter and looking at Reaper.

Ruger leans down and holds a hand out for me, "Michelle, sweetie, we've got to go. We need to get you two out of here." I don't take it yet. I can't leave Reaper. He looks back at the guys. "How are we going to get the bikes and two cars all back? There's no way they can drive," he motions towards Winchester and then back to me and my daughter.

"We can put Reaper and Winchester in the car that's out back. We'll destroy that car once we have everyone back at the club," offers Colt.

"That's covered too. We have Virus, MacGyver, Toxey, Fireball and some of the rest of the club coming in the SUV's, helping us get all these bikes and cars out of here. We'll chop their bikes for parts and burn the rest with the Vengeful Demons car," affirms Justice.

"Good thinking, thanks, man. Let's get everyone out of here," Benelli states when I hear the other members of the club pulling up out front.

Ruger reaches down for my hand again, and this time I take it in his. Benelli is reaching out for Elle's. That surprises me in the state that my daughter is in, but I don't question it. He's a handsome man with his dark, shorter, messy hair and his groomed mustache and beard. Much shorter than most of the bikers in this club. He has muscular arms and a powerful body, much like his father had at that age. It clicks in my head that the man holding her around the waist and walking her to the car is little Matteo that I had met so many years ago at a birthday party. I look around and spot his brother, the one they call Remington, but when I knew him, he was a wild little boy named Dante. He still looks wild with his long, dark hair and mysterious eyes, much more covered in tattoos than his older brother. He looks like he eats evil men for breakfast.

Before we head outside, I see them working on Winchester, Ruger's brother. He looks mostly the same, still long hair and a long beard, only grayer in it than last time. I wonder how he and Sheila are. I really adored that woman. Not so much of Ruger's wife, Barbie. There was something about that woman that didn't sit right with me, and I never understood why.

We walk out into the blindingly bright noon sun, shielding our eyes, and enter one of the black SUVs they have brought. I say nothing on the way back to the clubhouse, trying to process everything that just happened, and I just hold my daughter's hand that's in my lap with the two of mine and we look out the window in silence, knowing that whatever has happened in the last twenty-four hours has changed our futures forever.

# CHAPTER FIVE

## Benelli

We get back to the clubhouse and everyone is trying to pitch in and get everything done. We have Dexter, our club doc, stitching up Winchester, with Tequila Sheila, his wife, by his side. When I told Dex about the situation, he brought his daughter along to help with Elle. I don't have it confirmed yet, but I'm pretty sure those pieces of shit raped her. For some reason she is okay with me but won't let any other man near her, even to innocently help. Dex's daughter is a physician too and is as loyal to the club as her dad. You can never have enough people to mend us up if something happens.

The old ladies of the club have separated all the duties of getting the meal ready, caring for kids, and checking on Michelle and Elle. All very distraught their selves at the loss of their president but they are keeping things flowing. That's what a good woman does. When we are nothing but seas of rage, anger, and retribution, they are our captains steering us smoothly through the storm.

The entire club has such a somber vibe running through it. He was such a good man and had been our president since the inception of this club. What's going to happen now? There's nothing else to do, just carry on. I go into my office and get things lined out with Reaper's death. We know the coroner, so we have that covered. After he leaves, we have the funeral home to pick up Reaper's body. While they are here, dad is with me and tells them he wanted cremated and some other details that our president would have wanted. They have been best friends since the army over twenty-five years ago, he would know.

While dad is finishing up with them, I go check on the guys who have Frodo secluded and let them know church will start soon. The men have him hanging from chains in the warehouse/torture room. Our club location is a long-forgotten plot of land in New Freedom. There used to be an old shoe factory back in the 50s before the big tornado wiped out half the town. That end of town never recovered and got built back up. Reaper, dad, Nato, Cuda, Grinder, Tank, Rivet, Bricktop, Buddha and Rooster bought the factory, the abandoned schoolhouse next to it, along with some old homes and twenty acres of land, for a song. Some were army buddies, some went to school with Reaper, who was originally from New Freedom, just a bunch of guys wanting camaraderie and that feeling of home that a lot of them didn't have. They all had a passion for riding, so what better way to have that piece of freedom from being on a Harley and the family to belong to an aspect of the club? They made their own family.

My father, Ruger, had been stationed at Fort Benning, Georgia with Reaper, Nato, Grinder, and Rivet. They were in the Ranger program. Not everyone they met made it, but this group did, and they were in a brotherhood for life. In Saudi Arabia during The Gulf War to today. The size of the club has grown over the years, adding other retired military men. Bricktop, Tank and Buddha joined shortly after. They were all from the area and wanted all that this club was. Brotherhood and a place to belong. Buddha and his wife Calgon have been gone for a while. They went to the Smokies and got married and took Tank and Izzy with

54

them. Then they continued riding their Harley's all over the US. They always wanted to travel and since Tank and Izzy's son grew up and joined the Indiana Chapter, they figured, why not.

I enter the warehouse, looking at my men and then at Frodo. I stare at his dangling body hanging from chains. He is beaten, bloody, and missing a few fingers. Slices across his entire body with blood seeping out. He is currently passed out from the pain. "I told you he was mine!" I yell with authority. Fuming with anger not just because he was, in fact, mine to torture and end but that I made that abundantly clear and that how the fuck am I supposed to be president of this club if they, family included, were already not taking my orders seriously.

"We were just having some fun brother," Remington states, "just killing time till you got here." Just like my brother, the enforcer, to jump into this with both feet, eager to inflict pain on this worthless piece of shit. I love my brother and I let it slide. I know he wouldn't inflict enough to cause Frodo's death. He saved that for me.

"Church, five minutes," I tell them and walk away.

### ****Church***

The three prospects MacGyver, Toxey and Fireball will watch Frodo as the rest of us have church. "Men, I hate to do this, but we need to have an election. As the VP, I was acting Prez in Reaper's absence, but now we have to do this right. I'm going to have you all write down who you want to take over and I'll read the ballots," I say to the men.

"We don't need any damn ballots, Benelli. You've been a great VP, and you had shit handled as the Prez. I nominate Benelli to be President," states Phoenix, the club secretary.

"I second that," Virus, the IT officer, replies.

I look gratefully at Phoenix and Virus, "opposed?" no one raises a hand or makes a sound. "Okay men, I guess I'm your new President." A round of Hooah is spoken through the group. "Now, we need a new VP. I nominate Justice. You've always had our six, especially today."

Justice, the 6'6" muscular black biker with wicked good looks and the lightest green eyes, looks at me in shock and humbled by the nomination.

"I second that," says Lucky.

"All opposed?" I ask the members. Again, no one makes a sound or movement. "Justice is now the new Vice President." Another round of Hooah.

"Seriously, thank you guys. I won't let you down," Justice says with honor.

"Now, let's get down to business. We need to plan the funeral and what the fuck happened today. What do we know?" I ask.

The group goes around and adds suggestions to the funeral, and we decide on it. After that is complete, we all discuss what we know, and that is that Reaper left this morning to meet up with the Vengeful Demons. Obviously, it has to do with Reaper's daughter coming to meet him. We're betting the VD somehow got a hold of her first, and that's what all the mystery was about this morning.

"Apparently, when we pulled up and when we went around back, we distracted Calibar and Frodo enough that Elle was getting away from them. Calibar got away from us, but we grabbed Frodo. Man, they were raping her," said Phoenix. Anger rose around the room, but no one was more furious than me. "He's MINE!" I say forcefully and with a darkness none have them ever seen from me before. They all nodded in agreement. "Adjourned," and I slam down the gavel onto the wooden table that was engraved and burnished with the American flag in the background and several soldiers in different positions in the foreground. One soldier very similar to the famous kneeling one with the gun, cross and dog tags. The table matching their club patch.

Dad, Justice, and I stay behind in church to make all the appropriate calls and to the setup the funeral, as well as get a hold of the other two charters, one in St Louis, Missouri and the other in Indiana. Once done, we join the others in the main hall.

## Michelle

When we pull up to the club and exit the vehicle, several of the "old ladies" greeted us. A woman with big, "meet Jesus" hair loops arms with Elle and I and leads us toward a brick building that looks like a giant two-story school.

"Hello girls, I'm Aqua Net, but you can call me Nettie," she tells us, and I smile thinking her name suits her. "Elle, here is your room, we have a doctor there waiting for you, OK?' Elle takes in a breath and holds it but is relieved to see it's a female doctor.

"Hello, I'm Dr. Karen Lipe. Do you mind if I talk to you and check you out, just to make sure you're okay?" the doctor asks.

Elle agrees and Nettie leads me out of the room, not by my choice, but I'm assured that she is fantastic and will take good care of my girl. I follow Nettie around as she shows me my room and around the club, introducing me to people as we come across them. She shows me the kitchen where many of the woman are working together to prepare an enormous meal for the entire club. I meet several of the women, among them Lashes, Vamp, Kitty and Claws. I ask if I can help and reach my hand out to the knife Claws is cutting veggies with. She understands my need to keep busy and hands it over and getting another for herself. I feel at home in the kitchen and the girls keep my mind off things with their chatter.

I see Dr. Lipe enter the kitchen and she motions for me and pulls me to the side. "I gave her the morning-after pill. I didn't know if she was on any birth control. I gave her some antibiotics to be safe. Here is enough to last you till tomorrow and scripts for the rest. I also wrote for her to have Ambien for sleep if she needs it, but tonight, just give her this Ativan. She wanted to take a shower first before she rested, and it would be a good idea if you can get her to eat a little too before laying down. I also drew some blood just to rule out any STD's or diseases those P.O.S.'s might have had. I'm so sorry this happened," she said as she patted my hand.

I enter Elle's room and go to the bathroom where Elle was standing shaking in the shower. Holding the washcloth, I get it lathered up and start washing my daughter. I get her hair washed and rinsed and Elle tells me she's okay to finish up. I leave her to go get my clothes. Our rooms are adjoined sharing the bathroom. Elle scrubbed her body hard to get the grime of them off of her. She slid to the floor of the shower, curled up in a ball, still shaking. I come back in to see her and help her up and get her dried off, hair brushed, and she dressed and gave her the anxiety pill Dr. Lipe had handed me. I led her to the bed, had her lay down while I went and got myself cleaned and changed. Elle has dozed off, so I leave her sleeping and go out to the main hall where everyone is gathered together for the meal.

It was a solemn get together. Nothing like their normal big get-togethers. Children still ran around, but it was different. People chatted amongst those around them, and the other members came off and on to congratulate Benelli for becoming President and Justice getting the VP position. All agreeing it was a good call. After the meal, people left and headed home. The officers headed for the "factory," it's a concrete building across the lot. All but Benelli. Benelli rose and went over to me. "Is she ok?" he asks, sincerely concerned.

"No, but she will be," I tell him.

"We've set the funeral for next Tuesday. It's all taken care of," he softly lets me know.

"Thank you, we appreciate it. We'd like to stay until after the funeral if it's no problem," I thank him.

"Of course. Do you think I could speak with Elle, if you don't mind?" the handsome man around thirty asks me.

"She's sleeping now. I'm bringing her some food. Can we let her rest for a bit longer and let her eat? I will come get you before I give her another Ativan." I ask.

"I understand. That's fine. Let me know as soon as she wakes?" Benelli replies, and I only nod.

When I see my daughter stirring, I go to get Benelli. I don't want to, but I know they have one of the men and they need to know how to move forward.

"Elle, can I talk to you about what happened. If you're not ready, I understand, but we really need to get some clarity on the situation," Benelli asks.

"Can we talk with my mom here? I really can't bear to tell this more than once," Elle answers.

"Sure, anything you want," he replies.

Elle sits up on the bed hugging a pillow and I sit down on the bed next to her. Benelli pulls up a chair. "Let's start with how you ended up with the Vengeful Demons, OK?" Benelli asks gingerly.

She recounts the happenings of meeting Lilith and how she ended up at the club. She tells Benelli and her mom of how they locked her in a room. How she stabbed Lilith with a pen and tried to get away. She tells them how someone grabbed her before she could and then she went blank until she awoke in the car out back and they brought her in. Then she bursts out crying. "I can't, I just can't, I'm sorry, it's too horrible," she sobs.

"Oh baby girl, what did they do to you?" I ask while stroking Elle's long, dark wavy locks.

"Did any of them rape you?" Benelli asks.

"Yes, the two guys that had me out back. They both did." I wrap my arms around Elle and Benelli, clenches his fists and storms out and goes straight to the building and room they have Frodo chained in.

# CHAPTER SIX

# **Michelle**

I leave my room and go out to the main hall. One prospect asks if I am needing anything. "I need to talk to Ruger," I state with a demanding voice.

"Um, he's busy right now, ma'am. I can get you whatever you're needing," MacGyver, one prospect lets me know.

I reach up and grab the top of his shirt and twist, "Listen Bucko, I have a daughter in there and I need some vengeance. You can either get Ruger for me or I go psycho mom on this whole place."

MacGyver calls Ruger on the cell. "Kind of busy at the moment, prospect. This better be good," growls Ruger.

"Listen, I'm sorry. It's that mother," I caught myself grinning when he mentions Michelle and the prospect continues, "You know the one with the girl. She says she's going to go psycho mom if you don't talk to her," begs the prospect.

Ruger smirks. He always liked Michelle back in the day. She was smart, feisty and, let's be honest, hot as fuck even now. "Bring her to the outer building. I'll meet you two out there, and newbie..." Ruger says slowly.

"Yeah?" MacGyver asks.

"Pussy" Ruger gets off the phone with a laugh.

"Well?" I ask in a harsh tone.

"He's going to see you. I will take you too him," he states hesitantly.

I follow him out of the main hall and across the lot to a large brick building. Ruger is waiting outside the bunker as we walk up. Ruger nods for the prospect to leave and he does, gladly leaving just Ruger and I standing.

"Let me in there, Ruger. I know what you're doing, and I want my turn," I demand of him.

"Are you sure about this? It's pretty grizzly in there," he asks.

"It can't be anymore grizzly than what I saw this morning. Ruger, I NEED this. You know I do," I plead with him.

"Let me talk to Benelli. I can't guarantee you anything, but I'm telling you, if you go in there, you can't back out. What happens in there, stays in there," he tells me, making sure I whole heartedly understand. Trust me, I've got this, I think to myself.

## Ruger

"You really think she has it in her?" Benelli questions me after telling him what's going on.

"Yeah, I really do. She needs this. She needs this way more than you do," I state, quirking a grin at Benelli. My son gives me a look like he does not understand what I'm talking about. I know what's up. I saw how he was with

Elle, and I know he thinks he needs to deliver the punishment himself to right a wrong. He's not fooling me at all, and I just give him that look that tells him I know he's more interested in Elle than I think he even knows.

"Fine," Benelli gives in. "Dad, you better be right about this. If she can't handle it or this gets out, you know what this means for all of us."

"I know, son, but I'm telling you she's got this. If something ever happened to you..." I tell him, but he breaks in.

"I know, but there is a tremendous difference between you and that lady over there," he states and continues, "Oh, and dad?"

"Yeah?" I question.

"You may think I have the uncontrollable urge to take care of Elle and yeah, maybe I do... but I also saw the way you look at her mom, so don't be giving me that look of what the fuck ever that is because whatever I've got in my head for that girl, it goes double for you and her mom," he tells me.

Fuck, that kid has an expert eye. I'm not even going to try to deny that there is something about that woman, but let's be honest, she's grieving for Reaper. I will not push my way in when she has to have time to heal. Reaper gave me the go ahead on his dying breath and I'm going to honor his wishes, but I'm also not going to shit on his memory by trying to take her like this.

Reaper was my best friend, and he didn't talk often about Michelle sober, but when we got a little too much whiskey in us, that's when he opened up. Over the last 22 years, I've heard everything he knew about her, and I felt like I knew her too. I mean, of course I have met her and spent a little time with her while she was here, but Reaper KNEW her in every sense of the word.

# Michelle

Ruger leads me in, and instead of the shock of the carnage, I only see the filth in this man. I hold my hand for a gun, not taking my eyes away from this piece of shit. Out of the corner of my eye, I see it's Ruger who hands me his. I take the gun in my hand and feel it, the weight, the angles, the grip on the palm of my hand. Getting it just right, I feel the comfort in it, the power and strength in it. I look at the man hanging by chains and smile as I flip the gun's safety off with my finger and take aim.

I blow out his kneecap and tell Frodo, "This is for Reaper." Frodo is screaming in agony, but he has no clue how bad it's about to get for him. I pace back and forth around his blood-soaked body, deciding the exact spot I want to be in, like a jaguar going in for the kill. The men are just watching me silently. No one would dare. They can tell by my first shot and not flinching or retching that I know what to do and that I am not walking away from this. I have business to handle with him and I handle my business. I walk over to the side of his body about 15 feet back and aim looking down the sight deciding that it's not quite perfect yet. I take a few more steps to the left and check the sights again, looking at not only the target but the area beyond it. "Yes, that's better," I say in a soft but dark tone.

Remington, the club's enforcer, grins in my direction. "Oh yeah, good checking your surroundings, you've got this," in an encouraging and coaching voice. Oh, I know I've got this, but I nod to him in recognition. I pull the gun up, aiming it at Frodo, and he looks back at me in contempt. He watches me and my hands as he is noticing the gun moving down, down, slow down his body. The target now aimed right at the low life's crotch. His eyes growing wide, and he begs and pleads for mercy, but I don't listen to his bullshit and tell him calmly, "And this is for my daughter!" as the gun goes off and the bullet flies right to his dick. The appendage flies off of his body across the warehouse, bounces off the concrete wall and ricochets, landing on a table of pliers, saws, and other torture devices. As soon as the bullet hits his dick, all the men were grabbing at their own packages, moaning. But when it flies off his body, bouncing off the wall and like Michael Jordan landing like I had purposely and accurately planned the landing all along, they all start busting up laughing. Now seeing me in a whole new light.

Lucky gets down on one knee before pledging his devotion to me, "Marry me?"

"You're cute and all, but I'm almost old enough to be your mother," I answer his proposal.

"Get the fuck up, Lucky. She ain't marrying you," Ruger says a little too possessively.

Lucky crawls across the floor, still on his knees, with his hands in prayer pleading to me, "then will you be my mommy?"

Everyone busts out laughing as I pat his head like a puppy. All but Benelli. I watch this young man walk over to the now unconscious Frodo as he puts a last bullet between his eyes.

## Benelli
## ***Reaper's Funeral***

It's a hot Tuesday, June 10th, to be exact, the day that Reaper is laid to rest. Surrounding the hearse are hundreds of bikes going down the road in a majestic procession. It's easy to see the man was respected, well loved, and admired.

The parade of bikes ride down the highway past cornfields, fishing ponds, the crisp blue sky against the beautiful green earth. We all turn off and cut through to his favorite spot. It's a park and campground along the Mississippi River where he would ride to and then sit to watch the barges going down the river. Along the blacktopped paths, the bikes are all lined up. One would think it was more of a bike show than a funeral. Everyone solemnly walks up to where the urn and easels filled with pictures of Reaper are set up on display. It takes quite a while for everyone to take their pass through and show their respects, but as the line dissipates and the chairs are all filled with close friends and family, the funeral begins. So many people that over half of them are standing behind the rows of chairs. Some of his favorite songs have been playing softly in the background.

Preacher steps up to the front of the crowd and announces that Phoenix, the club secretary of the Unfortunate Souls, New Freedom will come sing *"Freebird" by Lynyrd Skynyrd.* He slowly walks forward and nods towards the urn, tapping his fist to his heart, kisses his fingers and then points them to the sky, looking upward. He turns back to the gatherers, the music starts, and he sings, "If I leave here tomorrow, would you still remember me?" continuing with perfection and emotion, causing all the crowd to shed a tear. Who can't help but get teary-eyed listening to that song? Even me, as I try to be the tough leader that I need to be and wipe it away before it strays beyond my shades. I look over to Elle and realize that all the amazing times I had with him and my father growing up, she never got to have that and now never will. She and her mother are holding each other's hands together, both wearing stylish but not gaudy, black dresses, Elle's head and deep, dark waves of silky hair lean on Michelle's sleeveless shoulders. Michelle takes her arm, bending it and placing her palm on her daughter's hair. She turns her head to kiss her daughter.

Her actions made me think of my own mom. I've missed the comfort and love you get from a mother. I was twenty-two when my mom died and, don't get me wrong, I know she loved us, but she was going through some things when the accident happened. She seemed quieter, more secretive, especially around dad or other club members. We never saw mom and pop arguing around us, but they just weren't like they were when we were young. By that time, Remi and I were living at the clubhouse, so we didn't see what happened at home. I know dad was always loyal and touched none of the club girls, but he was down a lot more that last year she was alive. Mom drank a little more at club functions. That's how she had her accident. We had a big club function with the other charters, and mom had been a little tipsier than usual. Nobody saw it but me, but she was looking at something on her phone and went and grabbed her keys to leave. Dad saw her walking to the lot and tried to stop her by taking them away from her. I couldn't hear what she said but saw her grab them away from him and shove him with one hand and spin and got in her car, spitting rocks from the tire when she left. That's the last time I saw her. She had gone down an embankment and rolled the car several times. Do I think she was having an affair? Probably, even though I didn't want to believe it, but I knew the alcohol was starting to be a big problem for her.

My mind drifted back out of the memory and into the present. I look ahead to my officer, finishing his singing. After Phoenix is done and seated Preacher, another club member, walks up and stands before the crowd again, "Today we lay to rest our brother and honored President and founder, Jonathan Samuel Holmes. Reaper, as most of us know him," speaks Preacher. You can hear snickers throughout the crowd, continuing to get a little louder until someone in the back yells out "John Holmes" which by this time everyone is busting out laughing hysterically. Everyone except Elle, who doesn't get the joke. Even Michelle has a smile on her face. "I can vouch for that," she says under her breath. Elle at this point is so confused and her mom leans over and says she'll explain later.

The funeral goes on the rest of the way without a hitch. People getting up and sharing their memories of Reaper. Some funny, some sad. Most are how he always had your back, and you could always count on him. Elle takes it all in, getting to know him in the only way she will ever be able to now, with the memories of his friends and family.

After the funeral, the procession all heads back to the clubhouse for a lunch and a reunion of sorts.

Elle notices that vast expanse of people at the dinner this time. "Are they all Unfortunate Souls?" she asks me.

"The ones with cuts are. They aren't all in this chapter, though. There are two other chapters besides ours. To think it all started with your dad," I reply.

## Elle

We spend the rest of the afternoon talking and getting to know each other. Benelli also excusing himself every so often, so he talks to everyone. She easily sees why they made him the new president. He has a charisma and an air of confidence about him. I also have other conversations here and there with mom, Sheila, and some of the other old ladies. Occasionally, someone will come up to me and introduce themselves and give me a hug. I don't mind the women, but when the men do it, I stiffen. I can't help it. Benelli is always quick to notice the tension and comes to my side, no matter where he is. He just appears out of nowhere and I am realizing the pattern. He really is a protector; I think to myself.

I am really surprised at how kind and friendly everyone is. Nothing like I would have pictured a bunch of bikers to be. Of course, my only reference is Sons of Anarchy on TV and a photo shoot I did at a bike rally. I smile to myself. Man, was I naïve and sheltered. They really are genuinely good people. Except for the bad ones and remember the Vengeful Demons, and I shudder. At that, I lean over to mom and tell her I'm going to lie down for a while before it's time to pack.

Benelli, seeing me, get up and head to my room at the club and stops me. "You okay hon?"

"I'm just exhausted," trying to pass it off, hoping he doesn't see me about bursting into tears. I get to my room and shut the door. Opening the prescription bottle, I pop a pill they gave me for anxiety and lie on the bed trying to forget all the bad things that I have witnessed and felt in the last week. I curl into a ball and cry myself to sleep.

While I was in my room, Benelli talked to my mom and told her to just stay the night and not to worry about packing and leaving today. He told her I was upset and trying to get some rest. I'm really glad we stayed another night. I slept like a rock the entire night.

# CHAPTER SEVEN

# Elle

It's the day after the funeral and mom and I are each in our rooms packing up to head home. Doc Karen stopped by earlier this morning to let me know all my blood tests came back great, no STD's from the rape and I'm definitely not pregnant, that part I knew. A gentle rap of knuckles on my door makes me look up. "Hey, can we talk?" Benelli asks, with his fists in his pockets.

"Sure," I reply, and he enters the room and leans sideways against the wall, his head laying against it. He is looking down at his feet like a sad little puppy. Maybe he doesn't want me to go. I feel safe around him and I don't want to go, but I don't want to wear out my welcome. Then, without moving his head, his eyes look up at me. HOLY FUCK! That man is just... wow. I never noticed it before. The dark Italian complexion and black hair, those amazing eyes. Now he is running a hand through his thick, black locks and biting his lip. I honestly thought my libido was dead forever. Don't get me wrong, there is no way a man is going to touch me again for a very long time, but I can appreciate that beautiful man in front of me. I need to stop staring at him, right? I need to say something. Would he think it's weird if I tell him not to move and get out my camera? There, I capture us in a moment in time, just staring at each other. Finally, he takes a step towards me

71

and breaks the connection our eyes share. I shake my head slightly to bring myself back to reality.

"Everything ok?" I ask.

"It's just been a long day," he replies, looking back down at the shaggy rug on the hardwood floor. I wonder where he got that reply. I think to myself having lied and told him the same thing yesterday, so I just tilt my head and slightly grin.

I know better than that and feel compelled to get up and walk to him and take his hand in mine and lead him to the edge of the bed. We sit turned towards each other and I reply with, "Yeah, a long ass week," and give him a vast sigh, "but what else is going on? There is something else." Jeez, I don't think I can take much more. What else could it be now? The only thing I want it to be right now is don't make me leave. Part of me is more than ready to go back to Cottonwood, Arizona, away from all this pain, but another part of me feels complete safety around him. I know that if I go back to Arizona, it will not change the fact that Calibar is still out there somewhere.

He stares into my eyes like he's hypnotized, just staying silent and staring. There he goes again, and he doesn't have to say a word. I'll just sit here on the bed and look back at him all day. I don't care. "I don't think you should go yet," he finally lets out. I let out an enormous sigh of relief. "Calibar is still on the loose and I want to protect you." I cringe and pull my knees up to my chest on that last one. "Damn, I'm sorry, Elle. I didn't mean to upset you," he says, running that damn hand through his hair again. That movement right there is it for me. It tells me he cares and even though it's his "tell" of hesitancy and frustration, it's all his "he doesn't want to ever hurt me" look. "I know. I really know nothing about you. I'd really like to get to know you. If you leave, how can I do that?"

he gives me the slightest, sheepish grin as he tilts his head just so.

One deep breath, and start talking. "I just graduated from college, literally. I was planning on finding my father, him taking me in as his daughter immediately and spending the summer with him, getting to know him, before I go back. There is no reason for me to stay now."

I can tell that he didn't want to hear that part when he gets stiff. What did I say wrong and then it hits me. He wants to be my reason for staying. That has to be it? I don't really know him, but I feel drawn to him, protected by him. Instead of letting it get to him too much, he says, "stay, there is no better way to get to know Reaper than staying here with the club. He was this club. I mean, you don't have to stay here. You can stay at my place. I've got a nice house with a huge guest room, a pool, a gym, hell, even a dog," he chuckles to me. "You can hang out here when I'm working and get to know all of your dad's friends."

"I would like you to teach me self-defense," I slowly let out, contemplating his offer. "And I do love animals, especially dogs," I add. "Are you sure I won't be a bother?" when he takes my hands and shakes his head no, I continue, "Well, I had plans to stay in New Freedom this summer. I don't have anywhere to be right now, and I have enough money saved up to support myself this summer, though it would be nice to take some photo jobs though, if I can find some."

"Photography?" he questions. "No kidding, like taking professional pictures and shit?"

"No kidding," I laugh. Just speaking about photography makes my eyes twinkle. I jump off the bed and excitedly go to grab my laptop, plopping back on the bed and opening it up to my photo album with several folders. I pull him over to me excitedly so he can sit next to me and see my work. "Check THIS out," I click on one of the folders named Bikefest/Phoenix.

We are scrolling through the photos, my legs Indian style and he leaning with one arm propped on the bed behind my back. There are photos of people gathered, some of just bikes, but then I show him the fantastic stuff. The pictures I'm super proud of from the motorcycle rally. There are individual pictures of bikers with their bikes, riding frozen in time with their hair blowing in the wind and the amazing red mountains behind them. His mouth drops open. He wipes the palm of his hand across his open mouth. I give him a gigantic smile. "You... you took these?" he asks me in disbelief.

"I love taking photos. It's kind of my obsession," I admit to him.

"I guess so. These are AMAZING!" he tells me.

I blush and say thank you, getting a little shy then. He reaches over and touches my face ever so gently. It's the sweetest thing, "Never get shy about your work, it's, well, it's art what you do," he says. He looks at my lips and slowly leans over to kiss me, but I flinch and jerk my head away. I know he'd never hurt me really and all he's done is be great to me, but it was just a knee jerk reaction. "I'm so sorry," he says and backs up off the bed and stands. "I didn't mean to..."

"No, I know you don't mean me any harm. It's me, my fault. Just broken I guess," a stray tear rolls down my cheek as the flash of Frodo impaling me as Calibar is leaning down, talking in my ear surfaces.

"I'm so sorry, Elle. If we would have just gotten there sooner," he tells me, so truly saddened. I give him a kind look.

"How could you have known? You didn't even know I existed. There is no way you could have known. What happened to me was my fault," I say, getting too choked up to say anymore.

"Don't you EVER say that again, Elle! What happened to you was absolutely not your fault, and I never want to hear you say anything like that again? Do you hear me?" he says angrily and I, for the first time, am scared, seeing so much rage in him. I back myself off the bed and with nowhere to go, I back myself against the furthest wall in the room, my eyes wide with fear. When I take a moment and the words of what he said sinks in instead of the sound of his voice, I realize my stupid reaction to it and slide down the wall and put my head to my knees and cry just saying over and over, "I'm sorry, I'm sorry. I know you didn't... I'm so fucking broken."

Benelli leaves the room and gets a wet washcloth, and hands it to me. I accept it and thank him trying to recover from yet another crying fit. "I feel like I go from being numb to being hysterical. When will I be me again?" I say with frustration. "I'm really not like this," I try to make a joke, so this isn't so awkward.

"No kidding?" he chuckles back. At least we have the same sense of humor to make things less deep. "Listen," he squats down next to me, "I know this isn't you and I know this is going to take a while, but maybe we can work through this together if you let me. Please, just stay for me?" he says seriously but then adds more lightheartedly, "you can stay, and I will teach you how to take down even me. As for your photography, I guarantee when anyone in the club sees your photos, you will have jobs booked up all summer. Hell, you may not even want to leave."

"I'd really like that," I say with a last sniffle, take a deep breath and reach for his hand to pull us up. Hey, that's a big step for me.

I tell my mom I'm not going with her and through the protests, mom looks into my eyes and grabs my cheeks like she always does and sees that I truly need this. "I love you, my baby girl." Even though I know all she wants to do is take me in her arms and hold me like this forever, she continues, "I will not protest on one condition, and I will be by your side the whole time." I look at her in confusion and she holds up a finger and shh's me, reaches in the back of my jeans and takes my phone, "I want you to call Zen and tell her what happened." Before I can protest and say I can't talk about it she shakes her head at me, "No, you can tell her, and you will if you don't want me dragging you home. That's my condition. She's your best friend and you know she would kill you if she found out and you weren't the one telling her." Knowing she is right, I let out a vast sigh and hold my hand out for my phone.

I take in a deep breath and dial her number. It rings and rings and goes to voicemail and I hang up, not leaving her a message. I try to hand the phone back to my mom, but she pushes it back towards me without taking it. "Try again," she says. I groan at her and push the green phone icon again.

It rings, and rings again, and I'm about to hang up when a voice, not Zen's, answers breathlessly, "This is Zen's phone, she has taken a vow of silence and cannot speak but I can give her a message," the Indian voice tells me.

"Um, this is Elle. I really need to talk to her. It's important," I tell the person on the other line. I hear the phone being handed over and the person in the background tells her it's me. The person then shouts and tells me that Zen has the phone. "Zen, something has happened," I say, breaking down.

Immediately, Zen breaks her vow and answers, "What is it, Elle? What's going on?"

I fill her in on what has happened, and she tells me she is booking a flight.

"No hon, you don't have to do that, I will be ok. I'm not making you leave India for me," I tell her.

"Elle, if I was only there, I should have just went with you..." she says, but I stop her.

"No, don't put that on yourself. It isn't your fault," I try to tell her.

"You were there for me when my shit happened, and I am going to be there for you. What's the address?" she asks, and I motion to Benelli for a pen and paper and to write his address on the note and he hands it to me. I repeat what he wrote back to Zen and within just a few minutes she says, "Ok, it's done. The flight is booked. The soonest I can be there is around 58 hours. Can you hold out till then?"

"Yes, I will be ok," I say sniffling.

"Ok, I've got thirty minutes to get packed and tell everyone I'm leaving before my ride gets here and we head to the airport. Hang in there sweetie, I'm on my way," she tells me and ends the call.

"She's packing for the airport. She'll be here in a few days. Oh, Benelli, I'm so sorry, I didn't even ask if this was ok," I say worrying.

He shakes his head and tells me not to give it another thought. "It's totally cool, we can put her in Michelle's room... unless you are going to stay too?" he looks at mom and asks.

"Since we were going to take Elle's car back home and if it's fine with you, I will check the flights and hopefully book mine for around the same time that Zen gets here and we can make one trip to the airport," mom asks him.

I look at him with my hands clasped in a plea that he will say yes, and of course, he does. He's so understanding and awesome, so I jump up to hug him. I tense a little when he hugs me back, but try not to let it show. I think he does because he quickly releases me.

"Okay, how about Elle and I run to the store, and we cook for you guys?" mom says to Benelli to break the tension.

"Yes! What do you like, mom and I can make anything you want," I say getting excited and looking forward to mom and I in that giant kitchen.

I can tell he wanted to tell us not to worry about it but instead said, "There ain't much I won't eat, I'll let you surprise me. I'll have one of the prospects take you to the store." He then takes his phone and sends a text to Toxey, MacGyver, and Fireball. Within moments, Toxey and Fireball are in front of us. "Where's MacGyver?" Benelli asks.

"He's helping Justice rig something up in the garage," Fireball answers and continues with a laugh, "he's kind of scared of her," and nods towards Michelle.

"Mom? He's scared of mom?" I ask and look at her confused and cross my arms, "Mom, what did you do to him?"

"Me? I'm sweet and innocent," she says with a chuckle.

"I call bullshit," Ruger says as he walks up to us with a wink to my mom, "What's going on?"

"Change of plans. Michelle is going to stay a few days and Elle is going to stay until she gets tired of us. Her friend Zen is going to come to stay with us in a few days too," he tells his dad.

"Michelle, you know you are welcome to stay too," Ruger tells her hopefully.

"I appreciate that, but she'll be in excellent hands with Zen. I need to get back home to Cottonwood and my shop in Sedona. Right now, let's get some groceries and cook you kind men up a feast," mom tells him.

"Sounds great to me. I'm starving. I've got the SUV out front with the air on," Fireball says to us, spinning the keyring in his fingers and heads to the door.

Mom and I decide since the Neroni's are Italian that's what we would go with and get the makings for a super cheesy meat lasagna with garlic bread and salad. For dessert we are making a no bake lemon jello cheesecake and some cherry pie filling for the top. We get back to the club kitchen and Fireball and Toxey are carrying in the groceries. We told them we could do it ourselves, but they wouldn't have any part of it. I start on the cheesecake so it will have time to set as mom gets a big skillet and browns the hamburger and ground sausage. We are dancing around the kitchen to the music shuffling on Pandora on mom's phone.

Lucky comes in and spins mom in a circle and dips her, and plants a big kiss on her cheek, "Hey mom, smells amazing, what's for supper?"

I'm holding my hand over my mouth trying not to die laughing at the sight, but I then mouth, "Mom?" questioning and laugh again when she says, "Don't ask" and rolls her eyes.

I answer Lucky by saying, "well, older brother??? We're having lasagna, salad, garlic bread and cheesecake."

Lucky starts rubbing his growling stomach, mouthwatering. "Need any help?" he asks.

Mom, without a beat, hands him a giant stack of plates and shoos him out of the kitchen to set the table.

"Did I miss something?" I ask.

"Let's just say I've had some bonding time with the boys," she tells me.

"Apparently," I laugh.

As the guys gather, she sends them all right back out to work with some setting the silverware out, some with glasses or napkins. She's running this kitchen like she's lived here her whole life.

Four girls I haven't seen before came into the kitchen. One holds her hand out to mom and then me to shake. "I'm Jinx, this is Breezy, Lyric and Goldie. It smells so amazing, or we wouldn't be asking. If you have any leftovers, would you mind..."

Mom stops her from finishing and takes her in a hug. "You girls are welcome to eat with us, there is plenty."

"Ma'am, I didn't mean to join. I mean, um, we um..." Jinx stumbles with how to put they are club girls.

Mom puts one hand in Breezy's and one in Jinx's and looks at them and quietly says, "I know." She then goes on to tell them, "You are part of this club, and you're welcome to eat with us."

The girls weren't used to so much kindness. All three gave mom and me hugs, and then proceed to help carry the food and everything else to the massive dining table.

Ruger, Benelli, and the rest of the men still at the club all come in. Ruger starts to say something to the club girls, but Michelle catches his eye, and she shakes her head no, to not say anything to them.

They all sit down and enjoy the most amazing meal some of them have ever had. Everyone is laughing, telling stories, picking on each other, and getting along like any normal dysfunctional family. I sit back and smile. This is the first time I've really felt happy since I've been here. It's like Sunday dinners back home and it's normal. It's great to feel normal again. I see Ruger mouth thank you to my mom over the jovial chaos, and she smiles and nods back to him. I think he likes her.

# CHAPTER EIGHT

## Elle

The last few days have had its difficulties. Sometimes I am doing just fine and then BAM! I flash back to my time with the Vengeful Demons and break apart. Mom has kept me distracted by cooking for everyone, which magically grows every day. I think word is spreading through the club of the feasts. Every day we have more and more club members here. It started out just the single guys, but now we have the families too and honestly; I love it. It has always just been me and mom until we started Sunday dinner with my friends; I miss it.

We went to an art shop yesterday where she bought painting supplies. She always brings some with her, but with her rush of everything that happened, she didn't, of course. She took us to the spot where I was conceived, and she painted the river, the bridge, and a small island out in the middle of the river. I roamed around with my camera, taking photos. I got extremely close to a doe that was drinking on the bank of the river.

Benelli took me to his house today, and I moved my things in. We drive up this big hill that goes on forever surrounded by woods, and the higher we go, the bigger boulders I see. When we get to the top, the ground levels out and overlooks the river. This house is amazing! It is like a fancy log cabin you see in magazines. It has a huge porch that wraps around the front and one side with some rocking chairs and an over-sized porch swing full of colorful cushions and fluffy pillows, looking entirely too inviting. Around the corner comes the biggest pit bull I've ever seen, with the goofiest smile on her face and tail wagging like crazy. "That's Luna, she's a dork, aren't you girl, aren't you so silly?" he's bending down rubbing all over the dog talking baby talk to her and she's eating up all this attention. I walk over to her and stretch out my hand for her to smell. She sniffs and then forces her head into my palm, so I'll pet her. I show her some love and the next thing I know she's jumped up on me, eye level licking my face. For a split second, it scared me, but I quickly realized she's just a love bug. This big dog actually wrapped its paws around me and hugged me. She almost knocked me to the ground at her size.

"Luna, get down, quit. Yes, she loves you too. Now get down. LUNA!" Benelli says. At the firm voice of her name, Luna gets down and lays down on the ground looking guilty but when she realizes he's not really THAT angry with her she hikes her butt in the air and wiggles it, wagging again with that big smile saying, "dad can I play now? Let's play, come on, throw me a ball." Benelli just shakes his head and leads us up the porch and into the house.

There are high ceilings and beautiful wood. It's an open floor plan with a giant, inviting sectional in the middle of the primary area and a TV on the wall that rivals a theater. Along one wall towards the corner is a bar area done in a western theme. Old rifles, six shooters, horseshoes, and other items on display. There's a gigantic kitchen with a huge island in the middle that has cabinets with even outlets and also a seating area. I'm imagining baking many Christmas goodies spread out all over that island while I see the snow-covered trees overlooking the river. Kids with hot cocoa mustaches reaching their little fingers over the edge to sneak some treats. Benelli sneaking some for himself and them, as I tell the kids they have to wait till after dinner. Wow! Where did THAT come from?

Benelli puts his hand on the small of my back and it brings me back in to the moment. "You good?" he asks me when he sees my mind has drifted off.

"Yeah, I'm good," I say, blushing and tucking my hair behind my ear.

"The bedrooms are up there," he points to the most elaborate staircase I've ever seen with twisted limbs and wood with designs leading the way upstairs, "the gym is downstairs, and the pool is out here," he says as he slides the glass doors open and we walk out to the back. There's an in-ground pool with lots of area to lounge around, a miniature cabin that's a pool house, and an even smaller version that contains a dog bed for Luna. "We should probably get back before we have to get your mom to the airport, I'll give you a better tour tonight," he tells me as he locks the house back up, shows me how to enter the security code and leads me to his bike this time and hands me a helmet. "I thought since we don't have a load now, we could just take the bike instead."

"I've never been on a bike," I say nervously.

"Well then, I think you're way overdue," he says as he plops the helmet on my head and straps it up. He gets on the Harley and starts the beautiful machine. He takes my hand and puts it on his shoulder so that I can swing over. Once settled in the vibrating seat, I wrap my arms around Benelli, grasping tighter and burying my body into his back as we move. The smell of his cologne is driving me crazy. Some kind of musk and spice. I swear it must have some kind of pheromones in it, because all I want to do is to be wrapped around his body, in an even better position, and sniffing him up and down. Apparently, that's exacting what I'm doing because he starts laughing at me.

Ugh! Can I be any more embarrassed? I lift my head and body off of him while still hanging on, trying to regain control of my flaming cheeks and he grabs one of my arms, pulling me in closer and says something, but I can't hear. I, again, lean back into him to try to have him repeat it and he takes my hand and lifts it to his lips and kisses it. "That's better," he says and keeps me tight around him.

## Benelli

There is nothing better than having a beautiful girl pressed against you as you ride down the highway. Okay, maybe a few things, but we'll give that a little time. I can tell she loved the house and Luna and whatever she was daydreaming about in the kitchen that gave her a far-off smile. The feel of her full breasts against my back and her legs firmly against mine made choosing the bike the right thing. I would have faked the truck not starting back up if I had to. I wanted this time and closeness with her. She smells like some exotic perfume that overtakes my brain... both of them. I try to maneuver my jeans to allow for more room and Elle sits up straighter. "Crap, did she notice? I don't think so. Can we just stay like this all day her wrapped around me?"

I glance into the rear-view and see bikes coming up behind us fast, motors revving and roaring past. They pass us without incident, but they are all glaring, the Vengeful Demons. I don't see Calibar in the group, so maybe he's still hiding out, but I know that Elle has noticed their cuts because she's clenching my waist for dear life. We make it back to the clubhouse and I take her in to Michelle and call a quick meeting before we head for the airport.

In church, I tell the men what I saw, and how Calibar wasn't with them. "How are we coming on locating him?" I ask Virus.

"Well, we know he's not anywhere close. Our St Louis chapter spotted him heading to the airport, but by the time they got turned around and inside, they had lost him. They kept a lookout heading out of the airport and he never passed them. Best bet is he flew," Virus replies, adding, "Colt checked in with the prospects and they are almost there."

"Out of the country if he knows what's good for him," Justice states, twisting his fist into his giant palm.

"Just in case, keep your eyes peeled. While we're at it, see who's leading the VD without Chains and his goons around and what their intentions are for the future of their club. I don't want any trouble out of them," I tell my men.

"Any other new business?" I ask and then continue when there isn't any, "We've got a bid in on the Riverboat Casino that's up for sale. We sign the papers on the restaurant in Devil's Backbone tomorrow morning. How's everything going in the finance department?" I ask Lucky, our treasurer.

"Everything's gucci on this end. Dispensaries are making a killing now that weed is legal. I saw people waiting in line for 4 hours the other day! The diner and the donut shop are even making more profits. Great move getting those places last year a few miles down the road. Everybody needs munchies." He laughs and inhales a hit.

"Never say gucci again," Winchester says, smacking Lucky upside the head with his good arm and grabs the joint from him and takes a hit.

"I second that," says Ruger, "but it probably wouldn't hurt to hire a couple new waitresses and an extra cook. It really has been picking up lately."

"I'll get Lyric on it. How's the club been?" I ask Remington.

"Going good there, too. Lyric is interviewing some girls right now, in fact," he says, looking at the time on his phone, "if you're good I need to get over there and supervise."

"You just want to see what kind of new tail you have to choose from," I reply and dismiss church, seeing we have to leave ourselves in a few minutes.

## Remington

I pull up to the club that's divided, entering on the "strip" side and stroll in. I can see Lyric is about to pull her hair out with this group. I walk up to her sitting on the stage and nudge her shoulder with mine. "Rough day?" I ask.

"Are you kidding me? Look at these girls, not one of them has any class. Look at this name," and she hands me one of the applications and I shake my head and laugh, handing it back.

"Ratchet? Is Ratchet here?" she asks in frustration.

"It's Rachette, pronounced Rah-Shay," a dirty blonde speaks up and steps forward.

"Girl, don't even play. Your momma named you Ratchet... Ra-chet. I can't even deal with this. I'm done Remi, they are all yours," she says shoving the stack of applications to me and heading to the back.

87

I try to grab them all without dropping any and tell them, "Um, why don't you girls take a break, go get a drink on me," and I motion for them to head to the bar. Most of them hustle to the bar for a free drink.

I walk into the office in the back and before I can say a word, Lyric has her hand up in a stop sign, "Don't. I'm not going back out there. I've been studying my ass off, taking way more summer classes than I can probably handle just so I can graduate early. I don't have time for this bullshit, Rem."

I slide around the desk and with all my charm touch the back of my fingers to her cheek, she's not buying it and turns her head.

"Don't even try it, Rem. It's not going to work this time," Lyric protests.

"Lyric, nobody can pick the right quality of girls like you. You know what kind of girls we'd probably end up with if I did it," I try pouring on the charm and brush her hair back and nibble on her beautiful brown lobe. At first, I hear a hrmph, but then she moves her head so I have more access to her neck.

"They sent you because they know I have a weakness for you and that long hair, didn't they?" she asks.

"Baby, I volunteered," I moan into her ear, and I can almost hear her purr. She rises out of her chair and melts into my arms, and we kiss, her hands buried and pulling in my long, thick black hair. "You're gonna do the hiring for me right, babe" I take a little lick and whisper into the side of her neck.

She shivers and quietly breathes out, "Uh huh," when I spin her around and smack her on the ass and say,

"Thanks doll," pushing that sweet ass towards the door. Oh, is she mad!

"Remington Neroni! One of these days!" she huffs and stomps towards the stage and picks up the stack of applications again.

"One of these days is right," I say only to myself as I'm walking out of the club and back to my bike.

## Elle

Benelli and Ruger are taking us to the airport to drop off mom and pick up Zen. I hate to see my mom leave, but I can't wait for my bestie to get here. I feel like a part of me has been missing since she left.

I had heard my father say that mom was now Ruger's before he died. I don't get it. He was never in our lives and now he's "giving" mom to another man. Like mom would ever go for something like that. I mean, he's very attractive for an older guy and I see how he looks at her. There is something there, at least for him. They get along and joke around but that's easy to do with mom, she's amazing. I never understood why she's never gotten serious with anyone my entire life. She's dated over the years, but nothing serious. She just told me she'll be with the one when she "feels" it. I just figured she never got over my dad, which breaks my heart because she has so much love to give someone. I look over and see Ruger and mom talking and smiling at each other. Who knows, maybe he's the one she'll feel that spark with. Too bad she's going back home.

We get to the airport and wait for the boarding call. Mom gives a quick hug to Benelli and tells him to take care of her girl. She then gives Ruger a longer one and tells him thanks for everything. Finally, it's my turn, and she gives me a tight hug and then with her hands on my cheeks she tells me, "Oh, baby girl, you will get through this. I promise you. Let Benelli in. He's a good man and you can trust him." With that, she gives me a kiss on the cheek and boards the plane.

We end up going to the airport bar and wait until it's time for Zen's plane to get here. It's a couple hours, so we people watch and have some beers. We make up stories of where they are going and why, and I'm getting a little tipsy, so they're getting a little more outlandish. "That guy, see that guy with the stripey suit, yeah you, I see you and you're going to meet your lover self. He's going to Tuscaloosa to see his Latin lovah." I then sing that dang Soulja Boy TikTok version of "Hey, you there, I see you over there."

"Okay girlie, you're officially cut off," Benelli laughs and shrugs his shoulders at the guy holding her empty beer up for him to see.

"You know what you are? You are cute, you know that, right? You are F I N E fine with your bad self," I tell him. Okay, maybe I'm a little more than tipsy.

"I hate to say this, but we need to get to the terminal with her," Ruger tells Benelli, looking at the time, "neither of us know what this chick looks like and she won't know us either."

"This is what she looks like," I say, shoving my phone in Benelli's face, "she's my bestest friend ever."

"Jesus, she didn't have that much to drink. Did she mix it with those pills the doc gave her?" Ruger asks his son.

"I don't know dad, why don't you ask Michelle," he says, trying to keep me heading in the right direction.

"ZEEENNNNNN!" I call out and take off running like a raging lunatic towards her. She runs into my open arms and laughs, hugging me back.

"Looks like she's been having a good time," Zen tells the men and shakes each of their hands and introduces herself.

"Yeah, but I bet she feels it in the morning," Benelli says.

"I know what you can feel," I drawl out, my palm sliding down his face, thinking I am being way sexier than the reality.

"Okay, let's get this party girl home," Zen tells them, grabbing her bags off of the carousel only to have them taken away from her by Ruger.

By the time we get back to Benelli's house to drop us all off before I pass out, Ruger confirms to them that yes, I did take an anxiety pill before leaving for the airport, per Michelle's text. Benelli carries me upstairs and pours me into my bed and tells Zen to just crash here with me for the night. He takes off my shoes and tucks me in clothes and all and kisses me on the forehead, but I grab him and pull him in for the biggest, most passionate kiss I can muster in my drunken state. I don't know whose eyes were bigger, his or Zen's, but I pass out before I can guess.

I wake the next morning with the worst hangover I've ever had in my life. I roll over and look at my overly happy hippy best friend that's smiling at me over a big cup of coffee. I groan in agony and grab my head. "What did I do? I don't even remember picking you up at the airport, and that was early in the afternoon. Did we spend ANY time together?" I ask as she hands me a big glass of water and some Excedrin Migraine.

"Your man dropped these off for you," she tells me in a slight giggle, meaning the pills and water. "You were pretty drunk at the airport; you passed out right after he put you in bed and you kissed him."

"I did NOT!" I am asking more than I'm telling in horror. "What did he do?"

"You did! Well, needless to say, he was as shocked as I was, but I think I saw a cocky grin as he was leaving," she tells me.

"What about you? What did you do all evening? I'm sorry about that by the way" I say as I steal her coffee and the toast, she was munching on for myself, but Zen and I are good that way, we understand that we aren't always going to be the perfect host or spot on friend. Sometimes we don't have to talk at all, and we are just... good.

"Well, after you passed out, I went downstairs and hung out with Benelli. What a house, by the way," she says, and I interrupt with "I know right," before letting her continue. "Some of the guys came over and hung out, Remington, Justice, Virus, Lucky and Phoenix. They ordered pizza and we just ate and talked and holy shit Elle, these men are fine as hell! You got Remi with his long black hair and tribal tattoo on his arm and shoulder. Justice is this giant, muscular mass of dark yumminess, Virus and his colorful tats and that V shaped body that's all-broad shoulders, mmmmmmm. Virus has this sexy CSI nerdiness about him. You know how they start out all cute and geeky, but by the end of the series, you have a lady boner for them? Oh, and there's Phoenix, he's got this funny side but also this tortured, broody side all thick and juicy Gemini." she's wiping the corner of her mouth like she just finished swallowing.

"And there is no question in my mind which one you have an eye for," I laugh. "You never were one for the pretty boys or the jocks."

"I can't help it. I like my men with some meat with their muscle. I only want one bone poking me when we're spooning... or forking. He rode me on his bike out to the clubhouse last night," she pauses her story as she closes my mouth with her hand, "Yes, he gave me a ride and no, not that kind of ride. He was just showing me around and to meet some of the other club members."

"Mhmmmm, I bet Phoenix could show you all kinds of things," I say.

"What is it with this club, anyway?" she asks me in all seriousness.

"What do you mean?" I ask in concern.

"They are all good looking. Like every man, woman, and child in this club. Not one ogre in the bunch. Seriously, do they check you out before they let you in and if you're homely, you can't join? I feel like I'm in some MC romance book, alternate universe shit where they have every shape and size you could desire, and they are all beautiful."

I laugh at her comment. "I mean, you have a point. I've been here a couple weeks almost and I haven't seen an ogre yet and I've even seen hundreds of them! Maybe we're dreaming?" and I give her a little pinch.

"Owww, dang Elle." And she swipes me with a pillow.

"Just checking," I laugh and jump off the bed before she can get even. "Hey, I'm going to hop in the shower," I call back to her. "We can figure out what we're doing for the day when I get out."

I'm in the shower scrubbing away, happy to have my friend here when someone steps in the shower with me. I stiffen and I turn my head and scream. Benelli jumps, startled also, dropping the towel half in, half out of the water. I look at him and he's looking at me but still standing there. Finally, I yell, "Get OUT!!" and he backs out of the shower, apologizing. I may have kissed him last night, which I don't remember, but he better not think... but then I think. I think about those men and the car hood, and I just stand there for what must be a long time because the water is now cold and Zen comes in and leads me out, wrapping me in a big, warm, out of dryer towel.

# CHAPTER NINE

# Colt

Toxey, Mac and I left to search for Calibar, and the trail sent us towards St. Louis, Missouri. Kind of stupid on his part, considering we have a chapter there. The Vengeful Demons were evil as they come, but brains never were their forte. We lose his trail close to the airport, so I'm betting he left the country. I would much rather I kill the bastard, but if he left, we will have to wait till Virus gets me another lead. In the meantime, we are going to stay with the Unfortunate Souls- St. Louis chapter and go see my little sister Pistol at STLCOP, St Louis College of Pharmacy.

We need to get to know Mac and Toxey before we make them patched members. I asked Toxey to go with me and MacGyver immediately volunteered, too. That's a big check mark in his favor. We head to the clubhouse to get settled in before we go see sis at her sorority. I have got to make sure I keep these two in line with all the college girls.

We are greeted outside by Lerch, the club president, "Colt, good to see ya man," the massively tall man says as he shakes my hand and pulls me into a bro hug, "who've you go with ya?"

"This is MacGyver and Toxey, two of our prospects. Thought I'd bring them with me and see if they're patch worthy," I tell Lerch, and he shakes their hands as well.

"Well, let's get in there and get a drink, and then get you guys settled," Lerch tells us.

We go into his clubhouse and go straight to the bar where one of the girls serves us up beers. We walk over to one of the tables and take a seat. This branch is a little wilder than ours, with far more scantily clad girls running around. A couple of them come over to the table and are trying to be all up on Toxey and Mac, but they completely ignore them. Eventually, they take the hint and are all over me. "I appreciate it, ladies, but we're here on business. Party time is going to have to wait," I inform them. I like the fact my men aren't giving in to these girls and taking their job seriously. They have a good head on their shoulders, another check in their favor.

Lerch and I fill each other in on what we know, and when we are done with our beers, he's taking us to some rooms. "Sorry guys, we only have two empty ones. Two of you are going to make it sharing."

"No problem, we're low on the totem pole. We can bunk together," Toxey tells him. We get our packs in our two rooms and head out to go visit Pistol.

We arrive at her sorority house on our bikes and she's running out and jumps in my arms, wrapping her legs around me. "Colt! What are you doing here! I can't believe you're here!" says my brown-eyed, chestnut-haired sister.

"I couldn't go to St Louis without seeing my favorite sister," I tell her, placing her down.

"Your only sister," she elbows me in the ribs.

"Oh hey, this is Toxey and Mac, two of our prospects," I point towards the two men, and they step forward, reaching out their hands to shake, but my sister tells them how it is.

"Well, if you're an Unfortunate Soul, your family, give me a hug," Pistol says as she grabs each and hugs them. I look over and see the two men look at my sister and then smile at each other. Great, that's all I need is to lose two good prospects fighting over my kid sister. Yeah, she's too pretty for her own good, but I don't need them fighting over her. I decide to just observe and see how this plays out. We're only going to be in town one maybe two days tops before we either head back to New Freedom or travel on if we get a good lead on the guy we're looking for.

We decide to take her and her roommate, Mia, to get pizza and catch up. Mia keeps calling her Amari, which is so foreign to me since I've only ever called her Pistol. The five of us are having a great time and so far, there is no rivalry or weirdness between the two men, so I decide I have nothing to worry about. Mia is definitely the tamer of the two girls. She's definitely someone I'd like to get to know better. She's got an outstanding personality, funny, seems to have her head on straight. I have a sneaking feeling my sister has gone buck ass wild away at college. It was hard for me to get away with anything in a small town full of eyes reporting back to mom and dad; I am sure it was even harder for her being a girl. They decide to go out bar hopping tonight and I'm just not up for it, but I tell Mac and Toxey to tag along to keep an eye out and don't get wasted. I'm just going to head back to the club and see what the plan is. I give my sis an enormous hug and tell her we may be heading out in the morning and to not get my men in any trouble. She laughs and promises to be good, yeah right.

2:05am and I'm pacing the floor, wondering where the fuck they are. They come strolling in all smiles until they see me. "Where the fuck have you two been? Is she okay?

Is she drunk? Are you drunk?" I'm fuming! Now I know how my parents felt.

"She's home, along with Mia and they are tipsy but far from drunk," Mac assures me, well he sounds completely sober. Another check.

"Why are you so late then?" I demand from Toxey.

"The girls, well, the girls wanted to go to a drag show. She was pretty persistent, and before you ask, I only had one drink. We took an Uber and left the bikes at her house. When we got them home and got back on the Harleys to head back here, we ended up taking a wrong exit," Toxey explains.

"Okay guys, sorry. Thanks for taking care of her. No leads, so we are heading back to New Freedom in the morning. Seriously guys, sorry I wigged out. It's just, she's my kid sister, ya know? Thanks," I tell them and head to my room. I turn an add, "She really made you guys go to a drag show?" I chuckle and shut my door, shaking my head.

## Benelli

I get a call late that evening of the shower incident with Elle, that Colt and the prospects will head back in the morning. All day I've been avoiding her. I tell myself it's so she can catch up with her friend, but the reality is she's got my head all twisted.

From the time I've met her she runs to me to save her, then flinches when I touch her, then excited to tell me about photography, then flinching when I touch her, then getting drunk and kissing me and wow what a kiss, then screaming at me and then getting catatonic when I accidentally get in the shower with her. I mean, I know what she went through was traumatic and she's going to need time, but I have no clue what to do here.

Michelle told me that Zen had been through some shit too and that Elle was there for her and that it's Zen's story to tell. She also told me that Zen has a degree in psychology or therapy or some shit, so maybe she can help her... or help me. I don't know what to do and, in frustration, I pace and rake my fingers through my hair, pulling at it. I pass by the window and see Zen outside on her cell. She hangs up and heads back towards the house. I try to catch her before she reaches Elle and makes it to the door, but I'm too late. I pass Elle as she bounds down the stairs with her purse and keys in hand. She stops in her tracks and looks at me, all guilty.

"Hey," she whispers.

"Hey," I say back, not knowing what else to say.

"Listen, I'm really sorry for, uh, freaking out yesterday," she says.

"Seriously, it's ok, I should have knocked first. I'm not used to company, I guess," I reply. "You two off somewhere?"

"Yeah, we're going to the clubhouse, I told Sheila and some of the other ladies I'd show them how to make pasta from scratch," she pauses, "guess what we're having for lunch?" she says and gives me a slight grin.

"I'm going to go with pasta," I tell her, chuckling. We look into each other's eyes and it's like I see a need in them, but I'm afraid to say or do anything wrong and have her go back into her shell. I've never been like this with a woman before. Dominant alpha mode, yeah. She doesn't need that right now, though. I know what I want, and I easily get it. I'm softer with her. Hell, if it was anyone else, I would have had her in my bed by now, but she's different and what she's been through makes her even more so.

After what seems like several minutes of just staring at each other, but it's probably less than one, she says, "Um, well, okay, I'll see you at lunch then?"

"It's a promise," I softly tell her, and she heads out the door to her car, meeting her friend there. They get in and take off down the hill.

"Arrrrghh!" I growl loudly, grabbing at my hair again. What the hell is it with this girl? What has she done to me?

Later that morning, I show up to the club and notice Zen in the garage sitting on a bike with Phoenix adjusting something under her. Now's my chance. "Hey guys, what's up?" I ask.

"I'm helping Phoenix adjust the shocks? Bumper?" she looks at Phoenix is question.

"Shocks and sag," he smiles up at her and says. "That way when you go riding with me it'll be more comfortable," he winks at her.

Ok, that's something new, I think to myself. Phoenix actually likes someone, hmmmm. He's never dated anyone that I know of. Phoenix has always stuck strictly to the club girls or maybe one of the strippers or bartenders at Fisherman's Pole, the strip club we own. He's the quietest man in the club. You couldn't find someone more loyal, but if you're wanting someone talkative, he is not the one you go to. Something happened to him before he came here, and he's never talked to anyone about it that I know of. Hell, it could have been from childhood, but I figure he'll talk when he's ready.

"Hey Zen, if he's about done with you, can I steal you away before lunch?" I ask.

"Sure, we good?" she looks down at Phoenix and when he nods, he's good. She slowly gets off the bike. As we are walking away from the garage out of earshot, she links arms with me and says, "Everything you've always wanted to know about Elle and how to win her heart, right?"

"Is it that obvious?" I ask.

"Only to a professional," she replies and winks. Just then we hear two loud crashes in the garage and swing around to see Phoenix hopping around on one foot and he's holding his fist, cussing like a sailor.

"What the..." I say and head back, but Zen merely pats me on the chest and smiles some kind of chick knowing look and leads us to continue forward. We stop and grab a couple drinks from Breezy at the bar who scowls at Zen, but it doesn't even phase her, and we head back outside for a walk down by a little fishing pond we have back behind everything. There's an old gazebo out there that Reaper, Uncle Win, dad, and Brick built like 20 some odd years ago. Reaper just had to have it built. I never knew why because no one ever used it for anything special that I can remember. Oh well, we sit down in the gazebo and stare at the pond, and I start. "I don't know what to do," I tell her. "I have feelings for her. I want to be there for her, but every time I get close, she pulls back."

"She's going to be that way for a while, I'm afraid. It's just how it is, but if you REALLY want to be there for her, you'll find a way and wait," she tells me. "Just keep being there for her, okay? Right now, all men scare her, and it has nothing to do with you and I know that's killing you," and before I can protest, she places her hand on top of mine that's sitting on my leg, "she trusts you as much as she can right now, I see it. She'll get there."

"What can I do? Can you tell me about her, you know, from a best friend's perspective?" I ask slowly.

Zen smiles up at me, "Elle is amazing! She's bold and bright, like a star. She's the type of person who would give you the shirt off of her back, really. One time we went swimming at this place called Slide Rock, it's like a water slide with naturally grooved, smoothed rock out in the water. We had our clothes laid on some rocks and while I was changing, some boys ran off with all my clothes, my swimsuit I just took off and some of hers too. All we had left was one bikini bottom, one shirt and a bandana she had on her wrist. She gave me the long T-shirt, she wore the bottoms and tied the bandana around her as a top."

"She roots for the underdog, and she hates bullies. Elle's also a born leader. She was class president, and her platform was anti-bullying and of course changing up the menu in the cafeteria," she says laughing and goes on to say how she loves to cook with her mom, how amazing it was and how they would host meals on Sundays.

"She loves photography, as I know she's told you, and she wants to open her own shop up some day, called Picture This Moment by Elle. Between you and me, her dream is to see her photos in a gallery showing. She easily could ya know, she's just that good," she tells me dreamily, which shows me just how close they truly are.

"She loves music, all kinds, and she's a brilliant singer. Karaoke, she's all in. Me? I couldn't carry a tune if I had a basket to put it in," she laughs and I join her, telling her I'm the same.

This is giving me a few ideas. I love hearing about Elle. She sounds exactly like the kind of woman I'm looking for in a wife. Wait, what the fuck am I thinking? We've only had one kiss and I really doubt she remembers it.

"I know you care for her and I'm so glad that you do. You're good for her," Zen states when she notices my face.

"Do you read minds on top of everything else?" I ask her. She gives a suspicious grin and shrugs, maybe.

We continue talking and finish our beers. I tell her thanks, and we walk back to the clubhouse because I'm sure Elle will be looking for us soon for lunch. Here's hoping both Elle and Zen decide to stick around the area. I've convinced Elle she should recover here with me and that it's safer, but I don't want her to leave after that. They both fit in great with the other members of the club and are liked by all, well, all except maybe Breezy and I'm sure that it's just her getting a little less cock than she used to, she still has plenty of men to choose from.

We head in to meet Elle and eat lunch. She is one hell of a cook and the ladies apparently kicked ass at the fresh pasta lesson. Over lunch, we agree that today is as good as any to start her self-defense lessons. After they clean everything up, I follow her in her car back to the house. Zen said she would get a ride from Phoenix later. We get back to the house to change and I head downstairs to the gym to get ready for her lesson. She comes down the stairs and DAMN she is fucking hot in her black leggings and sports bra with a loose fitting, cropped pink T-shirt hanging off one shoulder. Curvy in all the right places, and I love every inch. She seems to be in a really good mood today. I walk over to the stereo system and ask, "do you want to hear some music while we workout?"

"Yeah, that would be great!" she replies enthusiastically as she bounces over to where I am. "May I?"

I step back and let her at it. The next thing I know I hear Slipknot-Nero Forte blaring through the speakers, and I just look at her in shock, she laughs and shrugs her shoulders, "What can I say, I like a little bit of everything when it comes to music."

"Whatever you want, doll, it's your workout," I reply, and we go to the mat. "Now, you know with learning these moves, I'm going to have to touch you and pretend to attack you. Just remember, I'm not really going to hurt you. I'm here to teach you to protect yourself. You're safe with me, OK?"

"Okay," she tells me and takes a deep breath, releases it with a sigh and nods her head. She's ready. At first, she freezes and tenses, but then she remembers it's me and focuses on the moves she needs to make. We continue and concentrate on one take down at a time till she has it mastered. We started with just two different things today, working on each till they were perfect, and then we did some core exercises and finally the punching bag. When she rolls her head and neck, I know she's done for the day.

"Sore?" I ask.

"Yeah, I know it's because I kept tensing up when you were attacking me," she says as she tries to rub the muscles out, "I am doing better though, I think."

I have her sit on a bench and ask, "May I?" and she's not sure and pauses, but then she says yes. I sit behind her and move her hair over to the side and at that point, she shuts down. "Elle, it's me. It's just me," I say as I move around to face her. "Look at me Elle, come on babe, look at me." She opens her eyes and looks into mine, tears falling down her cheeks. "He did that, didn't he? Moved your hair away from behind?" I feel like an ass when she nods yes. I take a deep breath and tell her, "Ok, let's try this from the front," and I ever so slowly reach my hands up to her neck and shoulders to massage them from the front. She keeps her eyes focused on me and allows me to keep going. Okay, progress, yes!

"Okay Elle, here's what we are going to do. I'm going to let you be in control of this. I like you, but I will not touch you unless you want me to and tell me to, alright?" She nods without saying a word. "I can tell how tight your muscles are that you're probably going to need a massage after each workout, so you don't get tension headaches. Plus, I think that touching and getting used to be touched should also be part of your healing process. Do you agree?" again she nods without saying a word. "Elle, I need you to talk to me."

"You're right, I know you are, but it's really scary for me and I don't want you to get frustrated and ditch me when I'm too much to handle," she tells me. "I, I like you too but I'm just not, I just can't yet, is that ok?"

"Babe, of course it's okay. We'll take this, the training and everything, and this," I take her hand and put it to her heart then mine, "as slow as you need, I promise, I'm not going to run."

# CHAPTER TEN

# **Benelli**

It's been about a month of working out and she has good days and bad days, but I see improvement. Not as fast as I want it, but I did promise I'd stick it out with her. She's really kicking ass at the take downs and me grabbing her when it comes to self-defense. I don't know if she loses herself in the music or she is feeling more powerful or both, but she is getting more self-confidence. She hasn't attempted to kiss me or touch me other than that, though. Outside of the gym there is nothing physical, and I told her it was in her hands, and I meant it. As much as I want to touch her face, to kiss her, to wrap my arms around her and make love to her, I have made no attempts. I'm waiting for her and it's driving me crazy. How can she make so much progress in the self-defense and it not spill over to her, and I is a question that I don't have an answer for, but I so wish I did?

I spend my time running the club, checking on our businesses and leading the men every day, so I'm not tempted to grab her and kiss her. I know when she opens up and lets me in, I'm going to have to be gentle, to let her know that sex isn't what those assholes have put in her head. Don't get me wrong, I know she's not a virgin, but since this, I'm going to have to treat her like it's her first time and there is no way I'm going to make this first time with her anything more than perfect.

Our normal routine, she gets up before I do most days and makes breakfast, has a cup of coffee ready for me when I get out of the shower and head downstairs. She's already let Luna out who has been a traitor and sleeps with her snuggled up every night. Oh, how I wish I were that dog. I know it's wrong, but I took the spark plug out of her car so that she has to ride the bike wrapped around me to and from the club. Yes, I'm an asshole, I'll admit it.

She spends Tuesdays and Thursdays cooking with the ladies, helping them shop for the club, hanging out with Zen or whatever else that comes up. She has one hour each of those days set up for "real talk" as she calls it, where Zen gets to use her degree on her, and she can't complain about it. That's what Zen tells her, anyway. Monday, she works on her landscape and nature portfolio, taking pictures. Wednesdays and Fridays is usually booked with photo shoots, which is pretty impressive since she hasn't been here that long. The weekends she spends several hours editing and having them sent off to get prints.

She doesn't know it but while we are at the club I've had Brick, our construction expert, fixing her up a studio with her own darkroom, areas for shoots, an area to show the pictures to customers and whatever else she needs (thanks to dad calling Michelle and asking what it is she needs for a studio) and I'm going to surprise her with it for her birthday coming up September 3rd. I know she's going to say it's too much because that's just how she is, but honestly, the club already owned the shop and wasn't doing anything with it so I had a meeting and they agreed I could buy it from the club, and they wouldn't take much for it. I tried to fight them on that and offered what it's worth, but they wouldn't have it since it wasn't making us money, anyway.

Zen is helping me with the party and Michelle is coming to town for that weekend, Elle doesn't know yet. Dad seems happier lately knowing that she'll be here, but denies it when I give him hell on it. Zen has Phoenix in charge of setting up the music and making sure Elle has karaoke also that night. We went out for karaoke for Zen's birthday, June 30th, shortly after she got here, but Elle wouldn't get up and sing that night. I hear her sometimes in the shower and can't wait to hear her for real. Aunt Sheila and the other ladies were in charge of the buffet. There's a big rodeo that day in Sikeston, and I've talked Elle into going and taking pictures so that she suspects nothing.

Today is a Thursday and I'm waiting around doing the books and getting payroll done for the checks in the morning while Elle to having with her "real talk" with Zen. I've taken her out to eat at a new restaurant the club just purchased instead of our normal self-defense. I told her we could skip tonight and do it tomorrow.

## Elle

"So, tell me how things are going. How's the self-defense?" Zen asks me.

"I think I'm doing great. I don't flinch anymore when he grabs me and I even flipped him the other day," I tell her.

"That's fantastic! I'm so proud of you," she tells me, "how's the personal stuff going?"

"We get along great. He's patient and caring. I love spending time with him," then I pause.

"But you haven't touched him in a physical attraction way," she says, and I lower my head and shake no. "So, what do you think is making you not do that?"

"I don't know. I want to touch him. I do. I want him to touch me and kiss me. I'm just scared to make the move," I tell her, trying to explain.

"Before the attack," I cringe as she says the words, "I know you had no problems making the first move, you were strong Elle, you were fierce, you had control of your life and your body and you did what you wanted and never let anyone take that control away from you, where is that Elle?"

"I don't know..." I reply with a shrug.

"You do Elle, you let those monsters take it from you, between that and your dad's murder you let that club take it away," she tells me, "you know they won't harm you again, they're all dead but one."

"It's that one that terrifies me," I tell her.

"Let's go back to the self-defense. You said you've gotten so good that you don't freeze when someone comes up behind you to attack you. You've also said that you flipped Benelli onto the mat, right?"

"Well, yeah, but it was Benelli. I knew he wouldn't hurt me," I say.

"No, you could physically flip an attacker that was much larger and more muscular than you, correct?" she asks with some demand in her voice.

"Yes," I reply.

"Yes, what?" she asks again.

"Yes, I could flip a bigger, stronger man than the one that is still out there."

"There you go. You have enough strength and power to overtake the man you fear," Zen says, "he can't control you anymore, say it."

"I have enough strength and power and he can't control me anymore," I say, but not believable.

"What was that? I didn't hear you," she says with her hand cupping her ear.

"I HAVE ENOUGH STRENGTH AND POWER AND HE CAN'T CONTROL ME OR TAKE ANYTHING FROM ME ANYMORE!" I say with a bit of power, filling me inside.

"You are in control of your life," she says, still cupping her ear.

"I AM IN CONTROL OF MY LIFE," I repeat, believing it and stand to my feet.

"Now, as your friend, I'm telling you, go out there and for the love of God and make a move on that yummy man that is dying for some attention," she says and swats me on the ass like I'm going out to make the winning touchdown for the team or something.

I head out of her room at the club and walk straight to Benelli's office where he's normally waiting for me chanting to myself, "I've got this, I can do this, I've got this, yep, gonna grab him and kiss him. He won't know what's coming." I march right up to his office and open the door without knocking. "Benelli Neroni, get over here!" He has this look of "Oh shit, what did I do now" but comes to me all hot in a brand-new pair of jeans and a snug fitting dress shirt that shows off his muscles. I've never seen him dressed like this, but I've got to keep my mind on the prize. I grab his face with my two hands and plaster a fiery kiss on his lips. Oh, the taste of his mouth sends shivers through my lady parts, his lips fitting perfectly against mine like we were made to be kissing each other.

He pulls me back far enough to look into my face. "Are you sure?" he asks hopefully.

"Yes, I'm sure," I reply, and I barely get those words out of my mouth when he's crashing back down on to mine, kissing me passionately and without control. Our lips and tongues intertwining, doing a dance that only we know. His hands grasping my hips, pulling me so close I don't know where I start, and he stops. He's the best kisser I've ever had in my life, and now that we've started, I don't want it to stop. We grope and paw at each other like a couple of teenagers experiencing the touch of another for the first time. We stop for a moment, both panting like we have run a marathon, his forehead down on mine, a need deep down inside of me, my stomach fluttering around. "So, this is what it feels like," I breathlessly say.

"What?" he asks, still breathing just as fast, still resting his forehead on mine.

"Butterflies, my mom always said if I got butterflies, I'd just... know," I say and lean my head back, looking into his beautiful caramel brown eyes hoping he felt them too.

"Yeah, I know what you mean, I have this weird, crazy feeling," he places his hand on his stomach, "it's a weird feeling, I mean good, but weird, I've never felt it before, I don't know how to explain it, I'm thirty years old, and have never," he shakes his head and looks up at me cupping the back on my head with his hand, "never" and he kisses me in this sweet, soft kiss. Just then his alarm goes off on his phone and I look at him questioning. "Alarm, I made reservations," he says, turning it off.

"Well, I guess we better go eat then," I say and kiss him one last time for good measure. We walk out of his office holding hands and Lucky and Remington see us and start applauding and whistling. He puts his arm around my waist and has his other arm raised, giving them the middle finger as we walk out.

We take the bike again because my car is "broke" down. At least he wants me to think that. I know he took the spark plug out so I could be close to him. He can have that. I have my arms wrapped snuggly around him and have my head on his shoulder as we travel down the road to the restaurant. We get there and I see it's a really cool place. It's a steakhouse where all the staff are dressed in gangster and flapper clothing from the 1920s. We can't decide on appetizers, so he orders deep fried avocados called Spent Shells and something called Blazin' Bullets. He ordered us steaks with a side of bacon wrapped asparagus and salad. We laughed and talked, and it was so different now with us. I mean, I've always had a good time with him, but there's an easiness even more so now. We even had our waiter take some pics of us posed in front of an old car with Tommy guns like Bonnie and Clyde.

After dinner, we walked to this bar that had country dancing and he swung me around the dance floor. Swinging and what was it called, the pretzel?, was not what I'd ever done, so we would get all tangled up and I just laughed. I laughed until my side hurt and we had to take a break. He taught me how to two step and the slow dances; oh he is so sexy on the dance floor. There is nothing sexier than a man that can dance. We ended up dancing until it was closing time.

We left the bar and walked back to get the bike hand in hand. He handed me the helmet and told me he wanted to take me somewhere. We rode for maybe an hour, and we end up taking this road in the middle of nowhere. The headlight, as we stop, is shining on this really cool spillway waterfall. He takes off shoes and socks, rolls up his jeans and then slides my shoes off of me and we wade through the path that's about three inches underwater from the rain and climb up to the top. The place is deserted since it's now around 3am. He stares into my eyes to make sure I'm still alright and for once I completely am. I'm in the moment with the man of my dreams and I don't want to be anywhere but here with him.

We walk across the rocks that are sitting above the rushing water and he stops me in front of a flat rock right in the middle and he stares into my eyes. I know what he wants. He wants to know if I'm ok with this. If I want this as badly as he does and I do, oh how I want this. I look back at him and my answer is in my actions. I slowly lower the straps down from my dress and it falls to the rocks at our feet. That's all the answer he needs. He picks up the dress and lays it across the flat rock behind us, waist high. Benelli picks me up and sets me down on it. It's at such a perfect height for lovemaking I feel as if it had to have been man made for that exact purpose.

He looks at me in the moonlight, "you are so fucking beautiful Elle." I unbutton his shirt, my hands sliding across his chest as I do so. Without taking his eyes off mine, he unzips his jeans and removing them. In the moonlight I see the massive bulge begging to be released completely from his red boxer briefs and when he's completely naked my breath hitches. It's much bigger than what I imagined it would be. Much more than I've ever had before. He pulls me in and kisses me.

I slowly take my fingers, tracing the muscles in his arms across his chest, raking my fingers through the patch of curls on it, my tongue teasingly nipping and gently sucking at his neck. I wrap my hand around his engorged cock and between his neck and my stroking. He groans in absolute pleasure. He leans into me and kisses me slowly, going down my body with each kiss until he reaches my breasts where he takes my nipple in his mouth and swirls his tongue around it and gently sucking. I don't know how it's so different from what I've ever had before, but I'm arching my back at the pleasure of it. Some men bite and sometimes too hard, but he savors it in a way that I've never felt before. It's amazing and I feel myself getting wetter and wetter.

With the falls rushing around my body like it's another stone in its path, it cascades around my body, and I come. He hasn't even entered me yet and I come. He watches my reaction, and he smiles. "Yes, baby, come for me." He takes my mouth in his. His tongue invading me as he presses his body closer to mine. He reached for his pants, laying on a rock to grab a condom and stares into my face for approval. As a natural reaction, I spread my legs further apart for him to enter me and he immediately puts it on. When he enters me, I moan with the feel of him, the perfect fullness that I didn't know how badly I needed.

I wrap my legs around his body, and I rock with him back and forth as he pushes in and out of me as we kiss, his fingers firm in my hair. It's slow and so sensual and exactly what I need at first, but then it builds in us both. I can tell he's as close as I am, and we need that release. I need it as bad as the air I breathe. The need to come again is strong, and I need to for him to as well. I wanted to tell him that all my tests came back clear, and I was on the pill, but it seemed awkward at the time. He adjusts me so quick I don't know how he did it but my legs are in another position and he's hitting my g-spot so fast and perfect that I explode again my pussy pulsing against his cock, milking it, it's so hard and deep inside me, "Oh God baby, yeah, so good," and then he groans this manly grunt and fills me completely and we fall into each other, the falling of the water enveloping around us.

Once we regain our jagged breath and composure, he raises my bottom up and grabs my soaking wet dress and slips it back over my head; it clinging against my body like a second skin, the outline of my hard nipples clearly evident. It was in just a nick of time because a spotlight is shined upon us. The police officer says over a loudspeaker, "Okay kids, the area isn't open until 7am, I'm going to need you to leave right now."

Well, at least I have my dress on when the light hits. Benelli is still naked trying to cover up his package with his pants and I bust out laughing. I am laughing so hard at him, at the police, at the whole situation. I can't seem to stop. When I snort and then laugh harder, Benelli laughs too and throws his pants at me. The officer had turned off his light when he saw me stand and walk off with Benelli's pants. What does this guy do? He decides fuck it, whoever it is has already seen his bare ass and probably more. He turns around and shakes his ass, twerking like the rent is due. It's more than I can take, and more snorts and laughter and I hop back over to him and hold his pants out to put back on. I can't. It's just too damn hilarious. Once we are dressed, he leads me back to the path and to the bike, where the officer just shakes his head at us and pulls off. Then he kisses me once more before we climb on soaked to the bone and we ride back to the house and I'm in utter bliss.

By the time we get home, it's almost daylight. I don't have any photo shoots until late afternoon, so he leads me to his room, to his king-size bed with flannel sheets and thick, cozy comforter and thick down pillows your head just sinks perfectly into, and we quickly fall asleep wrapped in each other's arms.

# CHAPTER ELEVEN

# **Elle**

Calibar is on top of me, straddling me in the bed, his filthy hand covering my mouth so I cannot scream. I am pinned beneath him. In his other hand, he holds a knife that glistens slightly in the moonlight shining through the big window as he tells me a psychotic "shhh" sound holding it in front of his face. I am scared and frantic, wondering where the hell I am and how he got to me. All I can think of is I'm in a bed, but where?

Benelli! I was in Benelli's bed when we got home this morning. I remember we laid down together and fell asleep in his bed. Where is he? Why isn't he protecting me, I think. He promised me he would always keep me safe? Calibar sees it in my eyes. He knows what I'm thinking. "He couldn't protect you from me, could he? Thought he was so superior. Did he really think he could stop me from getting to you? Well, he's definitely not going to do it now, my dirty, little cunt."

Why is he using past tense, "he thought?" He grabs my face so hard it leaves bruising fingerprints on my cheeks and forces my head to the side. I try to force my face back because if I don't look, if I don't see it for myself, nothing bad happened, right? It's no use. He's so much stronger than me.

"NOOOOOOOO!!!" I scream and then I feel the whack of the back of his hand hard across my face, jerking it to turn to the opposite side of the room. I want to run to him, my Benelli, but I can't. He still has me pinned down. I turn my head towards him again, hoping against hope that I won't see the horror I just saw, trying to convince myself that it's not real. But as I open my eyes, it is real, all too real. Benelli, who I finally gave myself to last night and allowed myself to feel again, is there, half on the leather chair, half off, with his throat slit and blood running down his body. His eyes are still focused on me, giving me a look like, "why did I ever love you?"

He's right, if he hadn't had held me that first time in the Old Tin Barn, if he hadn't been there for me, if he hadn't taken me in and patiently waited for me to give my body, my mind, my soul to him. He'd still be alive right now. I loved him and he was killed because of it. Just like my dad. I loved him. I do love him.

The next thing I know he is holding my sweaty body, my voice screaming incoherently, and he's shaking me and trying to get me to wake up, "Elle, wake up baby, it's just a dream, come on honey, wake up," and then I do, scratching and clawing trying to get away from Calibar. He holds me slightly away from him to defend himself, and I finally come to my senses. "Benelli?" is all I can say, and I grab him as fiercely as I can, glad that everything I had seen before was just a nightmare and not my new reality.

"Yes, baby, it's me. It was just a bad dream," Benelli tells me, and we hold each other in a tight embrace, and we don't want to let each other go.

"I'm so sorry. It's all my fault. If you didn't love me, then he wouldn't have killed you," I say, still a little dazed from the all too realistic dream.

"Hush that talk, enough of that. He's not going to kill me or you for how we feel about each other, I promise Elle," he tells me, holding my head against his chest as he strokes my hair.

A couple of weeks go by, and my mind betrays me with three more night-terrors. They have me still fucked up, and I know I am. I don't even think Zen and her degree can save me anymore. I'm no longer scared to have Benelli touch me like before. In fact, I find it difficult to be out of his sight, which I know makes it hard for him trying to run a club and a bunch of businesses with me following him like a scared puppy. I'm looking over my shoulder everywhere I go, even if he is with me or not.

Just out of the blue, I will start getting cold sweats. My heart starts pounding. I can't breathe. I am constantly waiting for Calibar to appear out of nowhere, and it's making my life a living hell. I have talked to my best friend about it, and we've already had a few "real talks" but she didn't get too real with me, see she even thinks I'm a basket case with no hope. Okay, I know that's not true, but just when I think I can get over it, I have another nightmare.

Strangely enough, I have found a really good friend in Phoenix. He used to have nightmares and panic attacks all the time and knows what I'm going through. Phoenix reached out to me one day when I was doing dishes at the club, looking out the window with my mind so far from where I was in reality. He made sure he got my attention without touching me or being too close.

Once he got my attention, he leaned with his back to the countertop and began, "Listen, I know what you're going through. The nightmares, the cold sweats, the panic attacks... I, uhm, I know what it's like. If you ever need someone to talk to that, you know, actually gets what you're going through, you come see me okay?" That's all he said to me that day and walked away. He spends a lot of time in the garage building bikes, so that's where I find him.

"Hey," I say as I hesitantly walk up to Phoenix and Zen talking.

"Hey sweetie," Zen says and places her hands on my upper arms, "how are you holding up?"

"I'm... ok, I guess," I say and look at my friend, who knows I'm lying my ass off right now. I try to change the subject by squatting next to Phoenix, "so what's this project?" even though I won't have a clue what he's talking about.

"I'm restoring this baby," he says proudly. "It's an ultralow Screaming Eagle Edition. It was your dad's pet project." Then he realized he mentioned my dad, "sorry Elle."

"No, don't be sorry. I want to know all about him. Do you care if I hang out here and watch for a while?" I ask.

"Sure, you're welcome to. Maybe you'd like to help me?" Phoenix replies.

"I don't know what to do, but yeah, that would be great!" I tell him eagerly.

"Well, I'm going to leave you to it," Zen tells us.

"Oh, sorry Zen, I didn't mean to..." I say to her, but she stops me and tells me it's totally cool. She has errands to run, anyway.

# Benelli

I am so worried about Elle, and I don't know what to do. The girls are in the garage on my way to the clubhouse. I'm glad she feels comfortable around here, and that she is making friends with everyone. I'm about to go in when I hear Zen call for me, "Benelli, got a minute?"

"Yeah, sure, the office good?" I ask.

"Sure," she tells me, and we head to my office, and she sits in the chair across the desk from me.

"What do I need to do, Zen? I'm at a loss here. I'll do anything you tell me," I ask her, slouching in my chair, my folded hands in my lap.

"I have this idea, well, it's a two-part idea, granted, it's not professional but, as her friend, I think this will work," she says, and I lean forward eager to find out anything that could bring her back to me. One night, having her complete with me just wasn't enough.

She tells me she's going to talk with her and that she wants one of the guys to "mock" grab her and see what happens. We both agree that instinct will kick in and she will successfully defend herself, therefore, giving her confidence. Her other idea is letting her beat the pity, the hurt, the anger out of either me or the punching bag in the gym. Maybe it's just me, but I'm going to go with the bag. The rest of our discussion is making the final arrangements for the surprise birthday party plans. We started the surprise with her closer friends in the club and her mom hiding out in the studio. After we shock the hell out of her, there we will move it to the clubhouse where hopefully she will be surprised again, thinking the studio is the whole thing. I gave Zen the cash for all the decorations and anything else she may need for the party, and I headed out to meet my girl for some sugar before she meets up with Zen.

While she's in with her friend, I have to try to talk someone into attacking Elle when she doesn't expect it. Yeah, this is going to go over great, not. I don't want someone too big and too tall, so Justice and Remington are definitely out. Lucky does body building competitions, so I'm going to go with no from him. I think he'd do it, but I want someone I think she'll successfully destroy and prefer someone that's closer to Calibar's size, hoping she's going to feel like if she can conquer "this guy" she can conquer him if needed. I've got it! I open my phone and start dialing.

"Virus, hey man, how's it going?" I ask.

"What do you want?" Virus asks me.

"What do you mean? How do you know I want something?" I question.

"Out with it. I know you need a favor," he says. "Okay, okay, I need you to attack Elle," I say.

"What in the hell are you talking about?" Virus asks.

"Not like, for real, I just need her to think she's being attacked by a stranger and see how she reacts," I say.

"Nope, no way, no how, not happening man," he replies, "that's what prospects are for."

"Fuck, I completely forgot about them. Mac and Tox don't know they've been voted in yet, one last time, to fuck with them. Great idea brother," I tell him.

"Glad I could help," he chuckles, and we hang up.

I send a group text to Mac and Toxey to meet me in my office. They meet me in there and I tell them the plan and let's just say they are less than enthused to do this. "You are the prospects; I am the president. You will do what I say if you want to ever be patched in, got it?" I say and they both lower their heads and nod yes to me. I'm on edge whether this will work or drive her further down that dark road, but if Zen thinks it's going to work, she's the pro on this feeling shit.

We get it all set up. She's going to come looking for me at the office and Lucky will tell her I went down by the pond. When she heads that way, Mac and Tox will have masks on and come around the building and one will scare her and the other grab her.

## Elle

Zen has given me an all-time high, woman power, Xena, warrior princess, confidence boost. I am not my nightmares; I am not the victim; I am strong and fierce. She always has a way to get my head out of it. I head to Benelli's office to meet him, but he's not answering his door. Weird, he's always there.

"If you're looking for my brother, he went down by the pond to the gazebo," Remington tells me.

"Oh, okay, I'll just wait for him here," I tell him, knowing my birthday is coming up and thinking maybe he's planning something there and I don't want to blow his surprise.

"No, you have to go, I mean, he said if we saw you to have you meet him down there," Lucky tells me really suspiciously. Remington elbows him in the ribs, and he doubles over.

123

"Uhm, what's going on, guys? You guys are acting really weird," I tell them.

"Don't mind Lucky," but when he sees the glare in my eyes knowing I'm not buying it he continues, "Benelli has a surprise for you okay, we weren't supposed to say anything, so act surprised."

"Really?" I say giddy.

"Yeaaaah, a surprise," Lucky says, trying not to chuckle, and he gets a punch in the gut this time by Remi.

"Okay, I promise to act surprised. Thanks guys," I tell them and head out the door and around the back of the building, all excited. As I make it around the building, a man in a ski mask jumps out at me, ready to grab me, and I scream. Right before I'm grabbed by a second guy, I take my palm and punch upwards into the first guy's nose, hearing a break, and he goes down. The second man that had successfully grabbed me is trying to hold on as I try to wriggle free. I grab one of his hands and bend it backwards and while doing so I spin around, still holding the hand and use the weight of my body to flip him over and slam him to the ground; I kick him for good measure and then run as both are laying on the ground. Before I can get too far, I'm grabbed by Benelli and attack him, but then realize who it is and wrap myself around him.

The next thing I know, the whole club is out there laughing their asses off, pointing at the two men on the ground. What the hell is going on? I stare at the men on the ground and then shift to the club. Lucky is literally lying on the ground holding his stomach, laughing his ass off. I look up at Benelli in confusion.

"Tell me we got that on video, Virus?" Colt asks.

124

"Oh yeah, we got the whole thing," Virus replies. The men on the ground are pulling their masks off and it's MacGyver and Toxey!!!

"Okay, what the hell is going on?" I cross my arms and ask, getting extremely pissed off.

"Before you get too mad, it was your best friend's idea," Benelli tells me, pointing at Zen. I look at her now, FUMING!

"Hear me out, I just thought since you were kicking ass on your self-defense with Benelli that it might benefit you to see that you CAN do it in a real-life situation," Zen tells me.

"What the ever-loving fuck, Zen!" I exclaim.

"But look at these guys, you did do it," she tries to explain.

"Uhm, guys, broken nose here," Mac says as he's holding the ski mask up to Toxey's nose, trying to catch all the blood.

"Doc's on his way, keep your panties on," Justice says still chuckling at the entire show. The men from the club get the guys picked up and walk their limping bodies back inside. Benelli and Zen stay behind with me, my arms still crossed and tapping my foot.

"Before you yell at us, just stop, and think, did we have the prospects sneak up on you when you weren't expecting it? Yes. Did you kick BOTH their asses when they jumped you? Yes. You did it with no help from anyone. You, Elle Burrow, saved yourself. Just think about that for a minute," Zen pleads. Okay, I'll admit, she makes a good point. I did kick their asses.

"Oh, my God! I broke Toxey's nose!" covering my mouth with my hands, "those poor guys!" I exclaim and then slap Benelli in the chest. "You are so evil!"

He grabs my hand and puts it to his lips and kisses it. "But it worked, right?" he asks hopefully.

"Okay, yeah, it works. I can defend myself if it ever came down to it. Now can we go check on the boys?" I say and start heading to the building ahead of the two of them. I turn my head back towards my man, "Oh, and by the way, I think they earned that patch, mister."

"Already taken care of, my dear," he tells me, and we head into the club. In the bar area of the club, a giant TV is on the opposite wall of the bar and on it is a constant loop of the attack being played over and over and the club can't get enough.

## Benelli

I walk up to Justice, his arms crossed and leaning against the wall. I lean up next to him, crossing mine and discretely take the patches from him. It's time. We've already had the vote and if anyone deserves to be patched in for their loyalty to the club, it's them.

Doc has finished up bandaging the guys and they're all sitting at the bar drinking bottles of beer, trying to ignore the harassing jokes from the others and facing the bar so they don't have to see the footage. I walk to the center of the bar and take my thumb across my neck in a motion to tell them to cut the video and give me attention.

"Mac, Toxey..." I say, and they turn to look at me. I motion for Colt to have his mom, Tequila Sheila, and Rivet's old lady Aqua Net to come out of the kitchen carrying the giant cake. Our club's emblem and patches with MacGyver and

Toxey's name on them. They look at the cake and then at me. "You have been prospects for over a year now and whether it came to grunt work, searching with Colt, or well... getting your ass kicked by my girl," I look over to Elle then back to them, "you have proven your loyalty to the club and the willingness to do anything we ask of you. For all your service, we'd like to present you with your patches. You, Mac and Toxey are officially Unfortunate Souls."

The clubhouse erupts with whoops and hollers, whistles, boots stomping on the floor, bottles and fists hitting the table. Mac and Toxey help each other up off the bar stools and limp towards me to accept the patches and thank me. As soon as they have them in their hands, the club surrounds them to pat them on the back and congratulate them.

Elle walks towards them shyly to give them both hugs, guilty of the pain she inflicted. "I'm sorry guys, I didn't know. But congratulations," she says, shrugging her shoulders then holding out her arms for a hug.

"No offense, Xena, but I'm afraid to have you touch me," Toxey tells her.

"Same," Mac says, "but no hard feelings, you didn't know. You're really fucking tough."

Xena, I think to myself; I like it. That's exactly what she has become, a warrior princess, my warrior. Now, if I can just 100% convince her of that.

Later that day, Elle and I stand in the gym. I want her, no, NEEDED her to let it all go. Let go of watching her father she had just met get murdered. Let go of the rape. Let go of all the pain and fear. Not only for herself, but for me. I want her so badly. I've been patient, and I've been kind.

My mind going over and over everything that has
happened since we met. Her running into my arms. But
she's got to get past this. She seriously kicked the asses of
Mac and Toxey so she knows she can defend herself. Now
is the last step in putting it behind her. She's got this.

"Ok, we're going to do the punching bag today," I tell her.
"I'll hold the bag and you hit it." Elle hits the bag. "Like
this," as I take her fists in my hand, "or you will end up
with a broken thumb." I adjust her fists and she hits the
bag again. "Harder! I know you've got more in you than
that," I chuckle. She focuses and hits harder. "Picture
them, babe," I softly say. Something snaps. She gets so
much anger and starts beating the bag even harder.
"There you go, better. You've got this. See, picturing them
is working. Just let it go," I encourage.

"I'm picturing you, you asshat! I have been letting go, I
have been getting better!" and gives the bag her hardest
punches yet, even pushing me back a little while I'm
holding the bag. Unsure whether to be insulted, pissed or
laugh. She has never just opened up like that yet. It's
pretty sexy.

"Asshat?" I question her with a smirk and chuckle.

"Yeah, asshat!" she's trying to be mean, but I do that look
on my face with my head tilted down and I make those
eyes at her where I look up and then grin. I know it's her
weakness and I pull that fucker out as often as I need to.

I know her and she's thinking, "that fucking cocky ass
grin." She starts laughing, and that gets me to laughing. So
far, we can't seem to stay mad long, and I hope it stays
that way. When the laugher lulls, I take this opportunity,

"Please, just listen to me, Elle. Hear me out. When I'm
mad, sad, pissed, any emotion that has taken me over, I

come here. I work it out of me. I put it all into this gym and release it and let it go. I'm telling you to give it a try. Focus on it. Let it build up, and then let it go. It works for me. And I'm a well-adjusted human being, right?" I chuckle.

"Okay, okay. I'll try it your way, Mr. Machoman." She focuses on the bag, she's letting it build up, it's not that hard to tell what she's thinking. It's about the two men that raped her and about watching her dad get killed. She is thinking about the fact that she finally got to meet her father, who turned out to be a great guy, only to get shot and die in front of her and she'll never get to know him and never get to have conversations with him. She's hitting the bag as hard as she can. Punching at first, then beating the complete shit out of the bag. She's punching and kicking and fierce, and it's all I can do to hold on to it. But this is it she's finally doing it. I can see the change in her. The switch, so to speak.

"That's it, Xena, the warrior princess! Beat the shit out of it. Be that badass I know you can be. You're doing great," I coach and cheer her on.

## Elle

With that, I let it go, let it all go. I couldn't be meek little Elle anymore. I wasn't that person any longer. Now new, I felt stronger, bolder, more in tune with my power and self than ever before. "That's fucking right," I boost myself aloud, "I AM fucking Xena! No one is ever going to hurt me like that again! I'm not this ball of mush that weeps all the time! I'm a fucking bad ass and I'm going to live the rest of my life a bad ass biker bitch and no one is going to fuck with me or my family again!" and with one last kick I fall to the floor exhausted.

"Bad ass biker bitch, eh?" Benelli lowers himself to the floor next to me. "Does that mean you need an even more bad-ass biker by your side?" he questions.

"Yeah, I thought I'd see if I could tame Lucky and his charms down." I laugh hysterically.

"I don't think so, Xena. You're mine. You've always been mine. I just had to wait until you became the woman that you needed to be," he states matter-of-factly as he climbs over me and pins me to the floor, "and now that you're Xena,

I'm staking my claim on you. You're my woman and your heart belongs to only me." When he says that, I feel the strongest pull in my heart and the heat between my legs is scorching. I feel that tingly, pulsing throb and it shows on my face. The undeniable need, and he takes it. He smashes his mouth down on mine and he kisses me with the intensity of two teenagers in the back of a car, way past curfew, but they can't stop. His kisses are so full of fury and I'm taking it all in. My panties soaking with the pleasure. "Can I come from kissing?" she questions herself. Then at that moment he maneuvers his tongue in such a way that I came, and I came hard. He sees it in my face. He knows what he's done to me.

He then quickly starts undressing me. "If you think that's good baby, just wait," he tells me with a cocky arrogance.

"Oh hell, I've created a monster," I laugh and then suck in a breath as he sucks and licks on my nipples.

It's so foreign to me that no one has ever touched me, kissed me, or made love to me like this before and my senses are through the roof. His lips lower to my stomach, where he kisses all around my navel. It's sending volts of electricity through me. I weave my fingers through his dark curls as he keeps going lower and lower down my body. His palms grasp my thighs and lift and spread them further apart as his delectable tongue tortures my throbbing pussy. He licks and sucks at my swollen clit and right before I am about to explode; he takes his tongue across my entire entrance in a lapping, teasing way, slowing his pace. I moan in both pleasure and agony at him not letting me come yet.

He just looks up at me and grins the cockiest smile. "Not yet, baby, not yet," is what he tells me as he plants kisses on my inner thighs.

"Benelli, please! I can't take it!" I beg.

"Tell me you love me, Xena," he demands.

"I, I love you Benelli, I love you so much," I say breathlessly and at that he dives his tongue and lips onto my clit and sticks his thick finger inside me thrusting in and out, his thumb massaging against the entrance to my ass. Between all the different stimulations, my mind, and my body shatters, and I completely lose it coming harder than I ever have in my life. The rush is so intense that I become weak, and my legs shake uncontrollably. I can't get them to stop. Holy fuck, what has this man done to me?

# CHAPTER TWELVE

## Ruger

I'm waiting for her at the airport with one of those signs saying her name, "Michelle Burrow." I see the crowd thin out and then I see her shaking her head at me and smiling. Her gorgeous, shoulder length hair bouncing as she walked swiftly towards me. She's colored it since I've seen her last, now a warm honey brown with highlights throughout. The light from the gigantic windows of the airport shining down on it causing a halo effect around her. She's wearing slim fitting jeans, tapered at the ankle. I have always thought that was sexy as hell on a woman, kind of like at the end of Grease, when Sandy comes out all dressed in black.

Well, looky there, I think she has on the same tempting red heels as Sandy, and I lick my lips at the thought. Too bad she wasn't sporting the same leather top. Now that would be a fantasy come true, but hey, that red lacy number clinging to her body will do nicely. I can't help but smile as she reaches her arms out to me for a hug and I take her in a friendly embrace. I don't want to show how truly interested I am with her until I know she's ready and then it's game on.

"Ruger! Thanks for picking me up? How's it going?" she asks and then adds, "How's my girl?"

"Elle is doing much better. She kicked the prospect's asses so hard we had to promote them. Oh, and we call her Xena now," I laugh, remembering the incident that got her that name.

"Please tell me someone recorded that," she pleads, laughing along with me, "Xena? As in Warrior Princess?"

"The one and only and yes, I even made you a copy of it to take home with you," I tell her, and she gives me a high five and then pumps her fist and elbow towards her raising knee.

"Score! That's my girl! So, fill me in on everything. How is the party coming along? Can we stop by her studio on the way home?" she pounds me with questions.

"Slow down, Stacks, one question at a time. She's doing well, really. Xena has had some rough patches, but I've seen a dramatic improvement in the last couple of weeks. Her nightmares had her pretty fucked up, but Zen and Benelli have really helped her come along. I've noticed she hasn't been flinching if one of the guys bumps into her or touches her arm in passing. Of course, Mac is still scared shitless of both of you now," I chuckle, "Between you getting all feisty and Xena breaking his nose, it's going to be awhile before he gets anywhere near the Burrow women."

"She broke his nose?" she exclaimed and clasps hers with both her hands.

"Yep, broke it good," I tell her.

As we step up to the truck, I load her luggage into the back and open the passenger door, my arm raised and my hand holding the upper part of the window, "You called me Stacks earlier... why Stacks?" she asks so close I can smell the seductive scent of perfume on her neck.

I lean into her neck not being able to resist the smell of her intriguing flesh and smile then lean back, my eyes hungrily looking her up and down and I slowly lick my bottom lip, "Because you're... well, you're nicely stacked." A blush forms on her face and she shyly tucks her hair behind her ear and looks down and I want nothing more than to take her lobe into my mouth and swirl my tongue around that diamond stud glistening in her ear. A tightness forms in my gut and in my jeans.

Her breath hitches, and she slowly looks up at me with the slightest grin. She places a hand upon my cheek and then kisses the other side ever so gently. "Thanks," she says, and climbs into the truck.

"For what?" I have to ask, clueless.

"For making me feel again, it's been a minute," she sighs, and I shut the door of the extended cab truck and head over to the driver's side and get in, turning on the ignition, I let out a deep breath as I look forward, yeah, that woman does something to me. We head down the road and I catch her up on the happenings with her daughter, my son, Zen, and the rest of the club. Our conversations are easy, like we've always known each other without the twenty-two years since we've hung out together. Granted, I was married to Barbie and her with Reaper, but we became good friends that summer. Reaper wasn't the only one sad to see her go. We stop by so I can show her the new shop, Picture This Moment by Elle, and she is floored at the work we've done on the place. I open the truck door again to let her back in, and this time I can't help myself and touch her ass to help boost her up. "Ahem, what was that Mr. Neroni?"

"I thought you could use a little boost is all," I tell her innocently and give her a wink.

"Mhmm, I bet," she calls me out.

I flip on the radio to an 80s station as we head back to my place. We agreed she needs to stay hidden until the party, even though she will be in a spare bedroom. Just then, Bryan Adams comes on the radio singing Run To You and we both reach for the volume at the same time, our hands touching each other. We look at each other and both laugh, and I let her be in control of the volume. She cranks it up and we both start singing, both slightly off key, but we don't care because we are in the moment. More 80s songs play, and she seems to know every word. "I'm impressed. How do you know all these songs that were before your time? I grew up with that music. What's your excuse?" I ask.

"Older sister and brother, one born in sixty-nine and one in nineteen seventy. I was an oops they thought they were done having babies," she laughs.

"Winchester and I would work on our cars jamming to this and all the hair bands, of course," I tell her. "Are you close to your brother and sister?" I ask because I honestly don't remember hearing anything about them before, but before she can answer, she spots her daughter and sinks down

135

into the floorboard. I laugh at her short little self, crouched down there and yeah, I could have told her the coast was clear sooner, but I was getting a kick out of it. When she realized that the coast had been clear for a while, she slapped my leg and got back into her seat. We continued joking and chatting the rest of the trip until we got to my place.

# Benelli

It's the night before her birthday and after a fantastic evening of lovemaking, I wait until she was completely asleep before sneaking out of bed. I head down to the kitchen, and I am attempting to make her a birthday cake. It can't be that hard, right? Wrong, so wrong. There is flour, eggshells, and everything else all over the place. I got the damn thing in the oven and lost track of time trying to clean my mess up; I smell something burning, open the oven, the smoke detector goes off making the loudest freaking noise and I'm waving a dish towel around it trying to get it to shut up. Elle sleepily walks into the kitchen and gives me the sweetest smile. "I'm so sorry baby, I tried making you a birthday cake," I say.

"I see that," she chuckles and walks over to me and wraps her arms around me planting a big kiss on me, "Benelli, that's the sweetest thing anyone has ever done for me. Let me help you clean this up and show you just how pleased I am."

"Babe, it's your birthday, I'll clean this up, you go back to bed," I tell her.

"Do you want to know what I really want for my birthday," she says seductively while pulling on my pajama pants I had put on when I got up.

"Oh yeah? What's that?" I say in a low growl, loving the way she's taking control. She maneuvers me over to the couch, slides down my loose-fitting pants and pushes me against the couch, where I fall to a sitting position. She gets down to her knees and firmly grabs my length, stroking. Elle looks up at me with those big, beautiful eyes and I let out a breath I didn't know I was holding. She gives me this grin that I've never seen before and starts licking the tip all around but not putting it in her mouth, all while her eyes are still on me.

She wets her lips, and they are glistening with her saliva as she takes me in just to the top of her hand, still surrounding and pumping me. Her motions get faster as her hand glides up and down as quickly as her mouth, each time her releasing a finger and going deeper with that amazing tongue until she takes all of me and makes a gagging noise on my cock, that beautiful temptress is still looking at me in the eyes and it's all I can take. She can tell I'm getting close and prepares herself for the load. I come and she is pumping her mouth and swallowing every drop until I have nothing left to give. "I thought it was your birthday, not mine," I say, out of breath. "Damn, you are good at that woman!"

I gave her orders to go upstairs, and I finish cleaning the kitchen before I join her. We get up late the next morning and I decide, though I can cook breakfast, that I would take her out. She walks downstairs and damn, she's wearing cowboy boots and blue jean shorts looking finer than I deserve, her camera bag over her shoulder. I hand her a cup of coffee and slap that pretty little ass and she jumps, "Girl, you look like that. We ain't going to make it to the rodeo."

She fans her face like a southern belle, "why Benelli Neroni, I don't know ever what you're talking about."

I grab her around the waist and pull her toward me, planting a fierce kiss upon her lips and she melts into me. Damn, I want nothing more than to throw her over my shoulder and carry her back upstairs, but I've got to get her out-of-town so everyone can get to work on her surprises. "There's a restaurant in Sikeston that throws rolls at you. Do you want to wait the hour and a half and eat there or grab breakfast?"

"Hells yeah, I'm all about some homemade rolls. Are we there yet?" she says, laughing. We let Luna out one last time and get on our way. Ninety minutes later, we pull up to the restaurant and it's huge with Lambert's across the front. We get there shortly after they've opened and stuff our faces on top of all the extras they walk around and pass out like fried potatoes, black-eyed peas, fried okra and had a blast catching an eating the rolls they threw to us from across the room. It's a sight to see, hot rolls flying through the air as we ate. When we couldn't force another bite down, we headed for the rodeo. It's a pretty big deal there, and Elle took photo after photo. After a good majority of the day, we headed back. She said she was hot and sweaty and smelled like a cow and wanted to take a shower. I'm not stupid. I know she is thinking there is a party, but she has no idea. We get home and we hop in the tub, and I act like we have all the time in the world and no plans, anyway. She's getting ancy. "Sooooo, do we have any plans for tonight?"

"I hadn't planned on it. I figured you were tired after all day in Missouri," I say, trying to be serious.

"Oh, okay, I mean, we really aren't going anywhere?" she asks, a little disappointed.

"I guess we can go for a ride if you want." It's all I can do to hold it back.

She perks up, "Yeah, let's go for a ride!" and she rushes around getting ready.

"You're fixing your hair and putting on makeup for a bike ride?" I question.

"Well, I just thought I'd look pretty for you," Elle says, trying to come up with a reason.

"Babe, you look beautiful without makeup, but if it will make you happy, go ahead," I tell her. I ease her hair to the side, so I don't mess it up and start kissing and nibbling on her neck. I glance into the mirror and see her eyes close, and she leans her head to the side for more. It's not long before she's stripping her jeans back off, telling me she has to have me inside her and she wants a quickie. Who am I to deny her that? "Well, only because it's your birthday," I tease.

I quickly whip her around and pick her up, setting her on the dresser. She sinks her fingers into my hair and pulls me in, kissing me feverishly. I unbutton and unzip my jeans, and quickly sink into her. I love the feel of this woman! We fit like we were made for each other. I thrust in and out while my thumb maneuvers around, sending her quickly over the edge. When I know she has had her release, I go over the edge too. I rest my forehead to hers and she looks at me and smiles. I return the look and she giggles, "guess I better get cleaned up again." I go into the bathroom and get her a warm, wet cloth and wash her up.

When I'm done, she hops off the dresser, and she makes fast work of getting ready again. It doesn't take her long, and we are on the bike heading down the hill. When we get into town, it's dusk and they have the sign covered at the shop. "Hey, I need to stop by here and check on this place. We are talking about buying it."

"Sure," she says, confused by the building in the middle of town that she's seen empty since she's been in town. I pretend to unlock the door and I push it open and flip on the light switch.

## Elle

When the light comes on, everyone jumps out and yells "HAPPY BIRTHDAY". I am surprised because I was beginning to think we really were just out for a ride. Damn, I'm glad I did my makeup and hair, just in case. I was so distracted by seeing all my friends and MOM! Running to her, I grab her. "I've missed you so much!" She finally pulls me back and looks at me and then turns my face to look around the room.

My mouth drops open. It's a studio! Everyone spreads out so I can look around. My eyes fill with tears, and Benelli takes my hand and shows me around. "This room is the waiting area, back here is for editing with the best software there is, back here are different prop areas, over here is a dark room for when you use film," he explains to me, "Brick did the majority of the building but the rest of us all pitched in," he continued, and I gave Brick a big hug.

"This is too much, it's just too much," I say, telling Benelli, it's amazing and something that I've dreamed of, but I can't take something that expensive.

"It's too late babe, your names already on it and the sign is already hung," he tells me and hands me the keys and kisses me.

"The sign?" I ask confused. I didn't see one on the way in.

We all head outside and when everyone is out, there Ruger pulls down the cloth covering the sign and someone flips on the light, Picture This Moment by Elle shines brightly above our heads, and I break down again. "Alright, stop that or you're going to have us all doing it," Zen says teary eyed herself, "The cake is back at the clubhouse, let's go celebrate!"

We all pile on our bikes, which the others had hidden in the back lot, and head to the clubhouse. When we arrive, I see triple the amount of people that were at the studio. It's a massive celebration with a giant cake, a band was playing, there was food galore, so many people having a good time that came to celebrate with me. I couldn't have asked for a more perfect day. Benelli had me slow dancing out on the dance floor and was smiling from ear to ear. "Do you know how much I love you?" I tell him, "I can't believe you've done all this for me! If there is anything you ever want, name it, it's yours."

"I love you too, with all my heart, and I do want two things from you, and you said anything," he tells me, scheming. He nods to Phoenix up on stage.

Phoenix stops the music and announces, "Xena, come on birthday girl, get your ass up here and sing for us." My mouth drops open as I look at the stage and then back at the man holding me in his arms.

"Hey, you promised me anything," Benelli tells me and leads me towards the stage.

"Yeah, but I didn't think I'd have to pay up right now," I straight-faced tell him, but step up to the stage, anyway. I whisper to Phoenix, "I don't even know what to sing."

"You pick the song, we have the karaoke set up so if the band doesn't know it, I've still got you covered," he tells me.

I look out to the crowd and spot Benelli, and it hits me; turning to Phoenix and whispering what song I want, and he turns to the band and they nod. I slowly step up to the mic and the music begins:

*Something in your eyes makes me want to lose myself*

*Makes me want to lose myself in your arms*

My eyes are focused on this man, my man. I pour my heart out in the lyrics and couples are holding each other in their arms. When I get to the chorus, everyone joins in with me.

I'm finishing up the song and Benelli walks up on stage and gets down on one knee and opens a box with a beautiful diamond ring that shines in the stage's light is in it. "Elle, you're my friend, my lover, my world. I can't picture a day without you in it, and you, Elle Burrow. are my home. Will you marry me?" he asks.

Tears fill my eyes and I run over to him and grab him. "Yes, yes, a million times, yes! I love you! Yes, I will marry you!" and I kiss him over and over, and we fall over on the stage in a pile kissing. He puts the ring on my finger and it's so beautiful. We come back from our own little world when we hear 100 people cheering at us. People wanting to congratulate us pull us down from the stage, most of all my mom, Zen, Ruger, Remington and the rest of the family, my family, I think. I finally get the enormous family that I've always dreamed of. Did I say this birthday couldn't get better? Well, it did!

# CHAPTER THIRTEEN

## Elle

My studio has really taken off. I am so grateful for Benelli getting it for me and for the club doing all that work. I have shoots booked pretty much every day and even some weddings. We haven't set a date yet, but I can't wait to plan ours. They have some incredible ideas. I just did one with a fall theme, all the reds, oranges, and golds. It was so beautiful. What season we should pick? I wonder if bikers do big, ornate weddings? Can I get Benelli in a tux? My mind is all over the place. Focus Elle, focus. I have tons of photos to edit before my next shoot comes in.

Coffee, that's what I need. Benelli kept me up late last night, or should I say I kept him "up". I run next door to Common Grounds to get my large frozen white chocolate mocha fix and have them put an extra shot in for me. I need the boost. Yes! Caffeine bliss! I get back to the shop and realize I forgot to lock the door. Crap!

I open the door to the shop to realize there is someone in there, or at least there was. Some photos I had sitting on the counter are on the floor. Damn, why haven't I had Benelli get me a gun and teach me to shoot? I slowly back out the way I came and dial him up. "Hey Xena, how's my girl?"

My words are shaky, "I, I think someone is in the shop. I don't know. There are pictures on the floor. I went to get coffee and forgot to lock up. I went outside to call you."

"Fuck! Don't move. I had to make a run to see Lerch. I'm three hours away. I'll get Justice to come check it out. Do not go back in there! Fuck!" he tells me frantically.

"I'm safe. I'm in the coffee shop next door. It's probably nothing babe," I try to calm him down, but I'm still a little jumpy myself.

"I swear when I get back home, I'm getting you a gun and you're learning to shoot!" he says.

I chuckle, trying to continue to make him not as anxious. "I was just saying that to myself. I swear I'm okay."

"Okay babe, promise me to stay put. I'm going to get off here and call Justice just to be safe," he says, a little calmer.

If it was someone trying to hurt me, they would have done it when I backed out of the door, right? They would have already come after me, I try to convince myself. I keep an eye out for Justice and for my next client so I can catch them before they enter. I hear a motorcycle and relief washes over me. That is, until I realize it's not Justice, it's a Vengeful Demon. I don't recognize him and luckily; he doesn't see me but he's going slow and looking for something, or someone. He continues down the street until I can no longer see or hear him. I breathe out a long sigh of relief.

The girl at the counter has been noticing how sketchy I've been acting and saunters up to me. "Are you ok? You own the photography studio next door, right? You came in here, well, freaked out, and I notice you duck in the chair when that bike came by."

"Yeah, that's me, sorry," I reach out my hand to shake hers, "I'm Elle. It's just me being a worrier, I'm sure. I thought someone was in the shop when I left here with my coffee. I'm sure I'm just being paranoid, but someone is going to come check for me to be safe."

"There's no reason to take chances when you don't need to. You stay here as long as you need to. I'm Jackie," she says, shaking my hand. "That's Jamie over there. If you need anything, let one of us know." She turns to head back to the counter and the bell over the door chimes.

A woman walks over to the counter. "I tried opening the door next door, but it's locked. Any chance you would know anything about the photography studio next door? I have an appointment, but I guess no one is there."

Shoot, I guess I got distracted watching out for her to show when I was talking to Jackie. "Hi, sorry, I meant to catch you, I'm Elle," I jump up from my seat to greet her.

"Do we still have an appointment?" she asks, confused.

"Yes, of course, just needed a coffee fix," I say, trying to play it off. "Can I get you one too?"

Relaxing, the woman says sure and gives the girl with long brown hair her order and I pay for it, then we head back to the table.

"I'm really sorry about not being there, I hope you don't mind if we can have the meeting part of it here for now," not knowing what else to say since I can't exactly take her over there until Justice gives the all-clear. Just then, I hear his bike pull up and turn off. The bell to the coffee shop dings again and in he walks. "I'm so sorry. Will you excuse me?" The woman doesn't say a word and just nods with her mouth open. Strange, I think.

"You okay?" he asks.

"Yeah, I'm fine. If you can just run through and tell me it's all clear, that would be awesome. Wait, I know I left it unlocked and the woman at my table just told me she couldn't go in because it was locked. What the hell Justice!" I say, freaking out again.

"Do you have the key?" he asks, reaching out his hand. I go back to the table and get it out of my purse. Thank God I at least remembered to grab that. I hand him the key and he heads back out to go next door. My nerves are shot, and how the hell am I going to explain all this to my client? I walk back to the table and notice she's still there with her mouth open but both Jackie and Jamie are cleaning already spotless tables near me, both staring at the door Justice just walked out of. I turn to look at the three of them.

"Did you see how tall he was, and those muscles?" Jamie asks Jackie in a low voice.

"Did you see how smooth, dark, and creamy his skin was? And that voice, dayyumm" Jackie replies.

"Did you see those light green eyes?" the client asks, and the other two reply with a dreamy "mmmmmhhhhmmmm."

I smile, realizing that they are all mesmerized. "That's my friend Justice."

"Justice," they all repeat in their hypnotized state like a bunch of schoolgirls. I can't help but laugh. Realizing he hasn't come back as fast as he would and not hearing any loud noises, I excuse myself to run over there and check on him. Like I can do anything, but hey, I was only thinking that I hope he's okay.

"I'm going to run next door and make sure he found what he was looking for and make sure he's fine," I tell them.

"Oh, he's fine alright," the older client says, and I head next door.

I open the door to my shop, and it triggers the bell that alerts me to the back when I'm editing. The next thing I know Justice comes out front with his gun drawn on me but in seconds he realizes it's me and lowers it, "Z, you might want to come back here, but lock the door first." He has been calling me that instead of Xena when that nickname got hold. I lock the door wondering what the hell is going on but when I hear the dead bold click, I head back to where he is and stop in my tracks when I see a filthy and scared young girl huddled in the corner at the back of the shop. She can't be more than ten or eleven.

148

I squat down next to her and try to reach out to touch her, but she flinches away, curling in a tighter ball. "It's okay sweetie, no one here is going to hurt you," I tell her softly. She looks up to me and then to Justice and I can tell she fears his size and I'm guessing the cut since I piece together the Vengeful Demon looking around and with her hiding in my shop. I tell her I will be right back and pull him to the other room and fill him in on the VD going by and tell him what I think. I ask him to wait out in the lobby to make the little girl a little less frightened.

I go back to her and kneel beside her. "I'm Elle. Can you tell me your name?" She looks up at me, then over my shoulder to see if Justice is still there.

"Where did the bad guy go?" she asks.

"That's Justice honey. I promise you he's not a bad guy," I tell her.

"He has on a black vest like the bad men that took me," she says matter-of-factly.

"Oh baby, he's not with those evil men, I swear. Those bad men with the black vests took you away? Were they on motorcycles?" and she nods, crying again.

"The men that took me were in a van, but they met up with other guys that were on motorcycles. I was walking home from school, and I was almost home. Only two blocks from my house when they pulled up and grabbed me. I tried to get away, I did, but they were stronger than me," she tells me, sniffling. "They put me in this silo where there were other girls and there were dead people in there." I clasp my hands over my mouth, and flash back to the VD clubhouse and them saying something about putting Lilith in a silo to die. I've got to tell Justice so he can get the men on this. Shoot, I just remembered the client at the coffee shop. I reach for her hand and luckily, she takes it.

"Honey, I need to go talk to my friend so he can take care of the bad people. Will you sit on this couch until I can get back? I'm just going up front. You can come with me if you want to," I tell her softly.

"I'll, I'll just sit here if it's okay. Can he come to you? I don't want you to leave me," she pleads.

"Okay sweetie," I tell her and call out, "Justice... can you come back here?"

I meet him at the doorway and talk in a hushed voice, "Yeah, the VD definitely took her. I've got more to the story, but I don't want to say in front of her. Can you please go to the coffee shop and tell my client something came up and I need to reschedule? Throw out that deep, Barry White, sexy voice for good measure and throw on the charm? I can't leave her. I'm going to get her name, and can you call the police and have them meet us here? We need to get her back with her family, and they need to know what's going on."

"Barry White and charm, huh? I think I can handle that. As for the police, let me think about it while you get her name. We may want to handle this ourselves if you know what I mean," he tells me and walks off, but before he leaves, he gives the little girl a big smile and the sweetest wave, "Everything's going to be okay princess, Uncle Justice is going to get you back to your family and take care of those mean men," and then walks away.

She smiles back at him before he leaves and it melts my heart how sweetly he talked to her, the big softy. I walk to the bathroom and grab and wet some paper towels and take them back to her and hold them out and silently asking her if it's okay if I wipe her face and arms off. She nods and I sit next to her on the Victorian fainting couch I use for props. As I'm gently wiping off her cheeks, I ask, "Can you tell me your name? Where are you from?"

"My name is Lexie Parker. I'm from Campbell, Kentucky. How far am I from home?"

"I'm not sure, Lexie. I haven't lived here long but I can look it up on my phone," I tell her and grab it out of my purse. When the screen lights up, I see a bunch of missed calls from Benelli, Zen and even my mom knows back in Arizona, geez. I hold up my finger to tell Lexie just a minute and call Benelli. He comes first.

Before he can say a word, I start, "Hey hon, I can't talk right now, but I'm okay. It was a little girl and I'm taking care of her. You're going to want to have church. It's a big one. Justice has most of the details. Are you on your way?"

"Almost to the shop. I talked to Justice right after you sent him to the coffee shop and church is already scheduled for 6pm, but I wanted to see you first and get some more details. I love you," he tells me.

"I love you too. See you in a few," I tell him, and we end the call.

"Is your husband a preacher?" she asks, and I look at her, confused.

"Ohhhh, no honey, that's what he calls meetings with his motorcycle club," I explain. I don't correct her that we are engaged not married yet. "So, back to looking up Campbell, Kentucky," I say, and open the map app on my phone. "Hey, it's only forty-five minutes away, you'll be home in no time." The smile on her face brings me so much joy. I am so glad she got away and come to my shop, of all places. We'll make sure they pay if I have to do it myself.

Just then we hear the door unlock and the buzzer go off. "It's just me, babe," Benelli calls out before heading to the back where we are.

I see Lexie tense, but I smile and assure her she's safe and then raise and walk to hug my man. "Lexie, this is Benelli, the one who's having church," I say.

## Benelli

I walk in to see the sweetest young girl with honey blonde hair and big, blue, doe eyes. It breaks my heart that this sweet little girl was taken from her family.

"You're the one who's going to get the bad men?" she asks me.

"Yes, sweetheart, I'm going to make sure that we save all those girls and make sure they take no one ever again," I assure her, kneeling down beside her and hold out my hand. She slowly puts her hand in mine, but then jumps into my arms and hugs me. I look up at Elle and see the emotion in her eyes. And she clasps her hands and holds them to her chest. I'll be honest, a tear escaped when that little girl hugged me and was happy about me wanting to save her and the others, but I had to be strong and pull myself together. I pull her back and set her back on the couch and ask, "I heard your name is Lexie. Lexie, do you know your parent's phone numbers?"

"Noooo," she says and puts her head down sadly, "but I know where they work, and I know the school has known them because they've called before. My daddy used to work for the Army, but now he's a mechanic at a place called Dino's Parts and Repair. It has a funny dinosaur on the sign."

"I actually know where that's at," I tell Lexie.

"You do?" she asks excitedly.

"I do. I've gotten some parts there. What's your dad's name?" I ask, wondering if I might know her father.

"My daddy's name is Scott and my mommy's name is Chelsea," she tells me wiggling in her seat, "do you know my daddy?"

"I do, sweetheart. Let me call him and we will get your mommy and daddy right here," I tell her. Man, I know this guy. Granted, I haven't seen him in a few months, but he's a good guy and I can't even imagine what he must be going through. I step into the other room and dial the number for Dino's.

"Hey, this is Benelli Neroni. Is Scott around?" I ask. The other man on the phone tells me yes and puts me on hold to get him.

"Scott, what can I do for ya, Benelli?" he answers, but I can tell by his voice he's not the same happy-go-lucky guy I knew.

"Scott, we found Lexie. She's here with us," I say, and here the phone drop and her father sobbing uncontrollably in the background.

"You found my little girl? Is she okay? Let me talk to her," he pleads, and my heart is breaking apart hearing him.

"Lexie, your daddy wants to talk to you," I tell her and hold out the phone. and she makes a mad dash for the phone.

"Daddy! It's me!" she tells him, and she gets choked up. Hell, we are all choked up at this point. Me, Justice, Elle, we're all a mess of emotion. She's silently listening to her dad on the other end. "I'm okay daddy, I ran away and hid in this shop. They're going to keep the bad men from getting me, and they're going to save the other girls," she tells him, then waits for his reply, "Okay daddy, get mommy and come get me, I love you too."

She hands the phone back to me and tells me that her dad wants to talk to me again. "Yeah, no problem," I tell him when he tells me to watch his little girl, and he thanks me. I give him the address to the club and tell him we're going to take her there and get her fed.

"Lexie, Elle is going to take you back to the clubhouse and get you something to eat. Your mom and dad are going to meet us there, okay?" I ask.

"Yes sir, daddy said you were a good man and to stay with you until he gets there," she says, and we get her into Elle's car and we all head back to the clubhouse. She fell asleep in the car on the way back and I pick her up and carry her in and lay her down on one of the couches before I head into church. My blood is boiling at the fury inside of me, knowing there are more girls out there somewhere needing to be saved. I need to talk to the little girl more, but I want to wait until her parents are there with her, but church can't wait.

"Men, we are taking on a rescue mission. The Vengeful pieces of shit have kidnapped some girls. One of them escaped and found Elle, man, she's only like ten years old," I say, raking my fingers through my hair. At that, the men are angry and ready to do whatever it takes to save the others and take them down once and for all. Justice and I fill them in on all the details we have at the moment, and we stop when we hear a knock at the door. It's Fireball letting us know Lexie's parents have just come through the gate. I put Justice in charge of the meeting, telling them I'll be back after I've talked with the family. I don't know how long the girls have been or will be at the silo, and we need to find it ASAP.

Scott and Chelsea burst through the door, looking frantically for their little girl and spot her eating like she

155

hadn't eaten in weeks on the couch. They both burst out crying and calling for Lexie, and she runs and jumps into their arms. After many hugs and kisses and I love you's, Scott whispers to Lexie, kisses her on top of her head and walks towards me and grabs me in a tight hug, "Man, you just don't even know, to not be able to find your little girl and to keep the family from falling apart, I just, I, thank you," he says.

"I can't even imagine what you've been through. I know you just want to take her home and hold her tight. I know I would, but man, they've got other girls, we have to find them. I wanted to wait till you were here to ask her more questions. We don't know what kind of time we have to save them. I know it's probably going to be hard to hear what she might say, but we've got to find them. How long was she gone?" I tell him and ask.

"Thirty-seven days, thirty-seven long and miserable days. I took off work at first and did everything I could to try to find her. The police couldn't do it, she just... disappeared. We don't have any savings and the bills were piling up. We've got two other kids at home and the money from missing work, man I had to go back, and it killed me," he tries to explain.

"I get it bro, you had to take care of your family, but she's back now, she's back," I say, patting him on the shoulder.

We get the family settled on the couch and I sit in the chair catty corner to them, take a deep breath and begin asking Lexie anything and everything that might help us find the others. She does really good considering her age and what she's been through, and we don't ask her about anything they have physically done to her. We don't need that information for our mission, and I will let her family handle that part of it, though I did have Zen with all of us, just in case. Lexie tells us how she overheard two of them fighting outside the silo and how they planned on moving the girls on to somewhere she couldn't remember on the eleventh at 9pm, that only gives us 49 hours to find the girls and take the VD out. I try to get any and all clues as to the location of the silo. It's farm country here, so finding the right one is not going to be that easy. We know it has to be reasonably close because she escaped when they opened it up that morning around sunrise to give them little to nothing to eat and drink and she made it to the shop around... I check the time on Elle's call; it was at 10:16am. Sunrise in October is around seven a.m., so let's say she was walking around five hours. Little girl, also hiding from people, resting. We can probably cut that window down to half at least. She said she didn't come to a town the whole way until Elle's shop that leaves us with only one direction she could have come from which helps but unfortunately; she said the dirt road from the silo to a regular road was very long and she couldn't see the main road from it.

I step away and pull Virus out of church to get us a grid to work with. I give him all the details she gave us and the time frames. He pulls up all sorts of maps and applications, working away in a fury, and within about ten minutes he has it narrowed down to a five-mile area. That right there is why Virus is our IT Specialist.

Scott comes over and stands next to me while I'm going over the findings. "I want in," he says stoically.

"You need to focus on that little angel over there man, we'll handle it," I tell him.

157

"Listen, they took my girl, but there are more out there, and I want in on taking them down," he says, frustrated.

"Scott, I get it, I do, but this is a club matter now. We will handle it. I'm sorry but no," I try to explain.

"If it's a club matter, then patch me in. I want in and I'm not taking no for an answer!" he demands.

At this point Virus looks up from the computer and lowers his glasses down his nose, wondering how I'm going to react to a demand. Granted, I would probably deck anyone else, but I know the feel for revenge, and I respect him for wanting to not only be a good father but a stand-up man. I nod to Virus, and he picks up his laptop and the printouts he just made and takes them into church to share with the club.

When he closes the door I begin, "You want to be patched in? You think it's that easy? What then? You run out guns blazing and take them down, save the day and then what? You think you go back to your normal little life forty-five minutes away. NO, being a member of the Unfortunate Souls is a life decision. It doesn't affect you, but your entire family. We decide to give you a trial. Then you're a prospect, the lowest rung on the totem pole slightly above club whores. You do anything we say when we say it and without question. You NEVER talk to a patched member, especially the president, in the way you just talked to me. Just like when you were in the army, we are your superiors and you show respect at all times, no exceptions. Your loyalty for the rest of your life belongs to us, and it's not pretty to get out. You don't just make this decision on a whim. You discuss it with your wife, you uproot your entire family to come here, your kids are raised here, your family becomes our family. You willing to do that, soldier? You willing to give up your life and your family's life and start a new one? Do you even own a bike?"

"I'm sorry sir," well at least he learned the old army way fast, "I've wanted to reach out to you about becoming a member for a long time now and yes, Chelsea and I have discussed it at length about what that would mean for our family. I want this Benelli, not just because of what happened, but partially for that exact reason. There's a need to be a part of something important. I want to be part of a group of men that all have military backgrounds, that know the life and discipline I've lived. You know what it's like. I want the bond you and your brothers have, and I want to belong to something bigger, the men who don't sit back and let bad things happen, but they make them right, they stand up for those who can't stand on their own. I really want this Benelli, my family needs this, and I won't let you down. Oh, and yes on the bike, it's a Harley Breakout in Barracuda Silver," he ends with a small smirk but quickly becomes serious again.

I look at him and then back at his family and watch how Elle and Zen are interacting, I look down and shake my head before looking back up to him, "let me talk to the others but I'm serious, this is a lifelong commitment and you will have to relocate here and the men will give you hell being a prospect, it won't be easy. You sure?"

"Yes sir, I'm sure," and he looks over to his wife and Lexie and smiles. They look up and smile back and I can tell by his wife's face that what he said is true. They have already discussed this and they're as ready as they can be for not knowing our life.

# CHAPTER FOURTEEN
## Benelli

I step into church and sit down at the head of the table, placing my calloused hands flat against the resin wood, smooth against my palms. I stare into the carved symbol of our club, soldiers, everyone in unique positions and roles, all together working for the good of the country. I look out to my comrades in arms and the pride I have for this group of men engulfs me to my core. Not one man in this room questions whether we should take out the evil in this world, their only question is when. I took on this leadership role at the death of one of our own. The man who started this club with just a handful of soldiers wanting to do good in this world and enjoy the brotherhood that it brings. To band together on our steel machines and to fight the good fight as one solitary unit. We are and will always be members of the Unfortunate Souls.

"Brothers, we've seen bad in this world, and we've all fought against it. We have given our souls to this country and to this club. We've fought for injustice, and we've fought for peace. I see how you have all come together in solidarity to take on this mission of saving these girls at any cost. To take down those that are vial and try to hurt others. Those that hurt innocent young girls, to turn a profit and feed their demented, perverted minds and bodies. We WILL put it to an end. I know that I haven't been this serious as a leader, but this changes now. I've now seen up close how cruel this world can be when we let these demons live in it among us, and I want it to end now. We won't be doing this one mission, saving one group of girls, and taking out one group of pathetic scum. I want us to make it a continued effort to save those that need saving, to help those that cannot help themselves. When the world thinks of Unfortunate Souls, I want them to know that there is someone out there to help them. When they think all hope is lost and for those that are causing harm and fear to this world. They will know that they will eventually deal with us and they're going to meet their end. All in favor of this..."

Instead of yay's or fists pounded on the table, it's completely silent. My father, Ruger, pushes back in his chair and stands and gives me a salute. Immediately next, my uncle Winchester, my brother Remington, my cousin Colt all stand and salute. Following them is Justice, Lucky, Phoenix, Virus, Mac, Toxey, Brick, Nato, Red Bull, Cuda, Fireball, Grinder, Rooster, Rivet, every single member of our club joined this meeting and packed into church tonight and everyone stood and saluted in agreement of our club's new direction. At that I saluted back with such enormous pride at the men in my life.

After the emotions of the moment eased, I brought up what Scott had asked about joining the club. The points that he had made to convince me to sponsor him as a prospect. A few of the other members knew him from either the army or Dino's. Not one had anything negative to say and every member agreed to allow him to prospect. We go over anything else that needs discussed before we bring him into the meeting to discuss our plans.

I shoot Xena a text to send Scott in, and he quickly enters and stands before us quietly. "Scott, I've agreed to sponsor you and we have voted you in as a prospect. I will give you a rundown of what all that entails later. Along with a handbook we've made when we get this shit taken care of. But for now, time is of the essence so welcome to the Unfortunate Souls, don't let me down," I say. Scott thanks me and shakes my hand and the hands of those around him. He then backs and stands, leaning against the wall of the full room. Quietly listening to the plans and what specific orders we have for him. Normally, we would never allow a brand-new prospect into a meeting. In fact, it was rare one made it in any meeting in church, but due to the situation and the new direction of the club, I wanted all to hear, and be in agreement of this, so we allowed Fireball and Scott in.

"We have less than forty-seven hours now to find this silo and get the girls before they are moved to another location, possibly out of the country. Virus has amazingly nailed it down to a five-mile grid. We are looking for a dirt road off of this main one." I say pointing to the map spread across the table, "we're not going to be able to see it from the road, so we are going to have to trek down each one. We're not going to be able to take the bikes on this surveillance mission because it will be too obvious. We're not going to be able to wear our cuts on it either. We want to seem like we belong in that area, farmers, good 'ol boys, hunters, things like that. The hunting thing might actually work since it's bow season.

We'll go in groups of three down each road and field and if anyone questions us, we say we have permission to hunt and got off the property line by mistake, got it? Virus and I will drive out that way tonight and mark any dirt roads on the map so we will know exactly how many we need to check. Lexie said they bring them food a little after sunrise because there are some holes in the silo and the sun shines through. I'm going to guess that's when they switch out their watches so there will be double the men at that time. We need to hit it a few hours before then to give us time to search. Everyone go home, get your hunting gear together, get some rest and meet back here at 0330, we'll pull out at 0400. If anyone has extra camo or bows bring them for those that don't.

After church is adjourned, I walk out with Scott as he rejoins his wife and daughter. Xena and I set them up in one of the larger bedrooms at the clubhouse and get them settled in. I walk my beautiful and amazing fiancé to her car. I tell her that Virus and I will probably be busy all night narrowing down the possible locations. I assure her we won't be taking on anything on our own. I grab her in a tight embrace and kiss her goodbye. She tells me she's just going to run home and grab Luna, my hunting gear, and a change of clothes and come back here with the truck. I agree with her about that and thank her for being so thoughtful.

"Babe, you're it for me and I know I can't do much to help, but anything I can do to make this easier, I'm going to do. Anything I can do to help, please, let me know. I love you and I am so proud of you doing this, saving these girls, taking all this on. You take my breath away," she tells me.

"You don't get it do you? I am the lucky one in this relationship, I have you. I am the proud one. You have come so far, and you are so strong and so brave, my Xena. I'm just so damn lucky," I tell her and then give her one more kiss for the road. The quicker she leaves, the quicker she comes back.

By the time she gets back, Virus and I have all the maps printed out, our thermoses filled with coffee and ready to hop in the truck. I give Luna a few big scratches on the back and give my girl another kiss for luck and we head down the road. It's pretty dead considering the time with only a few vehicles passing every once in a while. Virus makes marks on the maps every time we see a field road. We go a little farther than we need to, not sure how much ground the little girl covered, but we want to be safe. He highlights the areas we think are definite possibilities to try first, and we turn around and head back toward the clubhouse. Once we have everything printed out and marked, the lists of who goes with who and what areas each group is going to check. We have only two hours to rest. Luckily, our military training taught us to sleep anywhere, in any position, whenever we got the chance. I set my alarm and curled up in bed with my girl and my dog; I was out in minutes.

When she is sweet and kind, she is my Elle and when she is a warrior and goddess; she is my Xena. When I awake to my alarm going off and she isn't in bed, my long, dark-haired beauty with the intoxicating eyes is a little of both. My minx had apparently snuck out of the bed at the clubhouse shortly after I was out because she had my camo laid out for me on the end of the bed. I go downstairs. She had organized the women to get together, and they had thermoses of coffee ready, lined up with homemade breakfast sandwiches wrapped up to go, along with some fresh muffins, bags of trail mix and water to take, coffee handed to each man the second they walked into the kitchen. The women also lined up all the bows, arrows, quivers. They'd even had Bowie knives each in strap-on leather cases aligned on another table along with several sets of binoculars and fully charged mini walkie-talkies with earpieces for each and every man. Hell, they

even have bottles of doe urine and anything else we need
to look like legit hunters.

"You've been busy," I say as I wrap my arms around her in
an enthusiastic embrace and plant a fiery kiss on her lips.
"I wish I had you helping me on all my missions," I growl
into her ear playfully.

"We wanted to do our part any way we could, this mission
is just as important to us," she replies. "Now, get the men
together and go out there and save those girls," she says
as she slaps my ass teasingly.

"Yes, ma'am," I say, standing up straight and giving her a
salute.

When the men have all arrived, we hand out the individual
maps and supplies. We go over who is in which unit and
what location they are assigned, and load up our trucks.
Virus has even made a list of some landowner names. That
way, if we get stopped by anyone, we can use it on the
neighboring land, and it sounds legit. We don't want to all
head out at the same time because it would be too obvious
if a truck heads out every ten minutes. That will give each
group time to get to their location and quickly hide their
truck before the next one comes through. My Uncle
Winchester is our tail gunner, so his truck and crew will be
the last to leave the clubhouse. They are all told to rally
back here by 8am.

I have Scott and Cuda with me. We decided to divide the
groups up with an officer around my age, a newer
member, and a seasoned member. There are 6 groups in
total with Virus staying behind to monitor the IT along with

Red Bull because of his broken leg. Neither one wanted to stay behind, but Virus knew he'd be more help to route everything. He'd track everyone's progress and Red Bull, well, we can't exactly have someone on crutches trying to maneuver around with a bow and gear in the woods. He's in charge of getting the Intel to Virus, relaying it back to us and making sure each group gets back and checked in.

My group gets to our appointed section. We hide the truck off the road where it can't be seen, but we can easily access it and hightail it out if needed. We load the bows to our backs and separate, but close enough to see each other. I motion with my fingers to keep our eyes open and then to move out. The morning is cool but not frigid as we walk along the edge of the woods and harvested corn fields, brown stalks, and ears beneath our boots. Cuda also carries a small, portable tree stand and finds the perfect tree to climb and scout the clearing ahead. Scott and I squat in our hidden locations, looking up to Cuda for his signal as to whether he spots anything. The sun isn't up yet but there is the lightness rising from the dark of the area knowing that the promise of the sun is upon us soon. Cuda spots something and motions to his earpiece for us to turn on our communication. We do and give a thumbs up we're good. He whispers, "There is something, about three clicks ahead, an old wore out barn, a silo and I only see three bikes, don't see any people though." I motion for him to climb down, and we meet him at the bottom of the tree.

"What's the plan?" Scott whispers.

"Let's see if we can get any closer to scope things out, it's almost sunrise so we need to be extra cautious.

## Elle

Slowly, group by group, they each return to the clubhouse to report they didn't find the silo. The women welcoming their men back and happy they are safe but disappointed that the girls have yet to be found. The only group that hasn't arrived is Benelli, Cuda and Scott. It's almost 8am, and no one has heard from them.

When Justice's group got back, he sent Rivet, Chelsea and Lexie to go get the other two kids and clothes. At 7:30am he sent the others to gather their families and come back for a temporary lock-down. At 8:05am, I looked over to Virus and Red Bull with pleading clasped hands and worry on my face. Begging them to give me something positive, but they shook their heads no.

Something has to have gone wrong. Time just keeps ticking, ticking, ticking and they aren't back yet. No one has heard from them. Family after family appears at the clubhouse for the lockdown. I am visibly shaken when the men have all arrived back with their women and children except for Rivet who wasn't expected back with Chelsea and the kids till 9:30am and that's if they packed fast. I'm still waiting on my man and it's pretty evident I am about to lose my shit. The women have got everyone organized as to where each family is going to stay. All the children are rounded up and playing in the main hall with Fireball in charge of the older kids.

I tried to distract myself with walking and bouncing a teething baby, but I just ended up crying right along with him. Remington pulled the baby from my arms and handed him over to his momma. He put his arm around my shoulder and led me over to the bar. Walking behind the counter he grabbed a bottle and two shot glasses and lined them up and filled them with the amber liquid, "drink it," he says.

"I don't, I mean, what is it?" I ask, stammering.

"Yukon Jack, it cures what ails ya," Benelli's brother tells me. He clanks the top of his shot glass with mine and downs it, so I join him. It burns all the way down and I nearly choke on its strength. "He's going to be okay," Remington assures me.

"How do you know?" I ask, hoping for some credible assurance.

"Because he's my brother and there is no other option," he says and pours another shot for each of us.

Benelli

We are approximately 100 yards away and clearly see the men at the entrance to the silo. We hear bikes revving their engines and duck back into the cover of the woods a little further. I look down at my watch and see that the time is 7:00am, Lexie had said around sunrise, and she was absolutely correct on that matter. I look towards Scott and Cuda and tap my watch. As those bikes pull up and start unloading items out of their side compartments, they converse with the other three about how the night went. "Same as it is every night, quiet as hell except for the coyotes. Those damn, crying kids, get worse at night. We just bang on the sides and that shuts them up. I'll be fucking glad when we get them out of our hair and onto the barge. I'm sick and tired of spending my nights without a woman and not allowed to touch any of these."

"Yeah, Krull keeps saying the price skyrockets for virgins," the replacement replies. "He better be fucking right, and give us our share when this is done tonight. See you at 7pm, the entire club has to be ready to go for the move." The three bikers that had been there all night jump on their bikes and leave, now the fresh three remaining. One is short and stocky and stands back with his shotgun drawn. The other two are at the door, one carrying two gallons of water and a couple loaves of bread, the other opening the metal door. We had managed to move closer while the six men were talking. Now with them busy, we take that opportunity to gain some more ground and find the perfect hiding spot in the dilapidated barn. What the fuck do you know? There's an old, short bus in there. I bet that's how they are planning to move the girls. We set down our bows and equipment, freeing up our movement and scope things out.

Being that close to the silo and smelling the rancid, rotting flesh Cuda is doing everything he can not to blow chunks. I shake my head no like that will stop it but it's too late. Cuda just lost his breakfast, and we hear the men alarmed outside and start heading this way. I cover the side door and Scott gets behind the main, Cuda who gets his wits back about him, ducks and covers behind a round bale drawing his weapon. As the main barn door slides open, Scott slams his gun barrel to the back of the man's head and knocks him out cold. I motion for Cuda to take my spot at the side door and cross over to the sliding door, abandoning my cover. When man number two enters with his gun drawn, I do a one-eighty spin and lift my right leg. As I do, managing to connect my steel toe boot upside his greasy head which in turn knocks the gun loose from his grasp. In that time, the third man had entered the side door watching the kick and downfall of his partner. Just as he is about to draw on me the man hears the click of the gun being readied by Cuda's steady hand and Cuda tells him to drop it. Goon number three does as he's told and drops the weapon and raises his hands to the sky. Scott picks the gun up off the strewn hay and I cold-cock the guy and he's out with one mighty punch thrown.


We decide to keep them alive and hog tie them, getting the keys from one of their pockets as we did. We then threw them in a stall full of dried horse shit, leaving behind Cuda to watch them. If he couldn't handle the stench from the barn, we are pretty certain he couldn't handle the inside of the silo.


We cover our noses with our hunting masks and open the door. The scent of unbathed bodies, the feces. Only masked by the dead bodies is a shock on its own. What we saw with our eyes was beyond anything I had ever come across in my life. They huddled together as close as they could get, filthy tears streaking down their faces. The youngest looking to be approximately five years old, with the oldest being in her early twenties. On the other side of the round metal building lay five dead bodies. Judging by their clothes, the females were either club girls or belonged in some way to that life. The two men were too decomposed to gather any information as to their identity. I recognized the hair of one female and her hallowing face, the ratted black hair, and blonde chunks it as clear to me it had been Chains' old lady Lilith.


"It's okay girls, we are here to rescue you." Scott says, as he squats down and brushes the tears away from the youngest of the group. "I'm Lexie's daddy, and she sent us here to save you." The young girl looked up at her savior and wiped her arm across her face to remove her tears, only smearing the dirt into sideways lines now. He bends down and picks her up and she wraps around him, holding on for dear life. As he heads towards the door with the littlest angel, shielding her eyes from the bright morning sun that she hasn't seen clearly in a very long time. The older girls helping the other, younger ones out of this above ground, pit of hell, each one unaccustomed to the daylight.

Not knowing what to do next but knowing we have to get out of here ASAP with these girls, thirteen in total. I walk to the open front of the red barn door and go towards the school bus, with any luck the keys we found on the men starts it and we can just haul everyone back easily. Finally, the last key I try the engine wakes up and revs after pumping the gas pedal, *"Yes!"* I think to myself. We then spend the next several minutes figuring out what to do with the three men we captured. Do we take them with us or end them here and now? We rearranged the ties and get them loaded on the bus, tying their ankles to the bars underneath, holding up each seat. Once we are completely sure there is no way they can free themselves, we load up our bows and things. We get the girls loaded and settled inside and head down the road, stopping by to have Cuda drive the truck back behind us.

We arrive to a huge welcome of everyone cheering at our return and with the trafficked girls to boot. I know we are going to have to make a quick plan to take them out when seven pm comes. When their entire club shows up to find the girls gone.

## CHAPTER FIFTEEN

# Elle

When I saw that school bus pull up, I immediately knew that my hero was back. I pushed and shoved my way through the crowd of club members and took off in a dead run, jumping up into the muscular arms of my future husband. Benelli spun me round and round as I peppered him with kisses. Once he stood me back down onto my two feet, my boots crunching in the rock, my emotions started getting the better of me and I slapped him in the chest telling him to never do that to me gain. What he said next was the sweetest, most heart melting thing about always coming home to me. I love that man so very much.

While we were reveling in our reunion, Sheila got the girls inside the clubhouse, and that's where the shock of the situation really registered with everyone. There was this little girl, and I mean little. I thought Lexie was too young to be kidnapped for trafficking, but there were girls younger than her, one only being five years old. Why would anyone think of someone so young in that way? Were any of them already raped like I had been?

I can't even put that thought in my mind right now. I picked up that sweet little angel and just held her, not even wanting to imagine. Her gangly arms and legs wrapped tightly around me. I can tell she hasn't eaten, and she is covered in filth. "What's your name, sweetheart? Do you want to take a bath?" I ask the small sprite.

"Brenna," then she lowers her head meekly, "Can I have a bubble bath?"

"Of course, Brenna, there must be bubbles!" I exclaim and spin her in circles, still clenched in my arms, and she giggles.

In the tub Brenna is loving her bath, I've put so much bubble bath in there you can only see her little, angelic face. I style her hair in a shampoo mohawk, and I can tell it's blonde now that it's properly washed. I rinse her hair, tipping her head back and making sure to hold my hand on her forehead so no soap runs into her little blue eyes. Her hair is so pretty, like strands of spun gold with the natural highlights that little children have, and we adults pay a small fortune to get. I heard a light tapping on the door and I open it a crack and peek my head out. It's Lyric. "Hey, some of the women brought in clothes their kids have outgrown. I think this might work for now," she says handing me a folded stack of clothes. I thank her and get back to Brenna before shutting the door.

I get her out of the tub and help her get dressed and brush out her locks. "Now, are you ready to go fill that belly?" I ask, giving her a Pillsbury dough boy poke.

"I'm so hungry I could eat food bigger than this whole bathroom," she says, stretching out her hands wide to show how big.

That much food! That's a lot," I say, trying to look shocked. We head out to the banquet hall and get in line. The others had been rotating, getting cleaned up in some of the other bathrooms and eating. I fix her and my plates along the buffet and we go to a table to sit with Lexie and her family. Benelli comes and places a kiss on the top of my head and sits on the other side of me.

"Lyric has been getting all the girls an outfit to change in to and after that, her and Remington will walk around trying to gather the addresses and phone numbers for the girls. There's a big stockpile of clothes the women brought in to donate. Look at that pile over there!" he says and points to boxes and boxes of clothes. "We're going to have to set up an entire bedroom as a closet for all this stuff. With the direction we want to go with this club, I'm sure it will come in good use."

I see Lyric walk up with a clipboard, "Brenna, this is Lyric, she's going to ask you some questions."

"You're so bootifull!" Brenna tells Lyric, and she blushes.

Lyric sits down beside the girl, "thank you, I think you are very beautiful too."

As she asks the little cutie patootie questions, I look around the room at all the girls; I notice how the older ones, closer to my age, have taken on mothering roles with the younger ones. Some of them look so frail and malnourished, you can tell who's been locked up longer than the others. I think how that could have easily been me in that silo, had they had not rescued me so quickly. They could have sold me to someone, God knows where and who knows what kind of life I would have had to lead. I turn and lean over to Benelli and give him a kiss on the cheek, I didn't have to say a word for him to know what I was thinking, "I know babe, it's okay, we got you and these girls before it was too late."

After the girls are all cleaned up and stomachs filled, we gather up all the sheets Lyric and Remington have filled out. Zen and Dr. Karen Lipe have each set up rooms where they will talk to the girls and give them checkups. That way they were treated both physically and psychologically, at least temporarily. Virus has set up his laptop and input all the info into a file. It turns out that these girls were all from around the Tri-state area of Illinois, Kentucky, and Indiana. After finishing, he closes his laptop and heads into church with the rest of the men.

## Benelli

This was going to be a tricky situation. We need to get these girls home to their families, but we can't have people coming in and out at the clubhouse with all the shit that's about to go down. We need to maintain the lockdown until we have led the Vengeful Demons to their demise. The Indiana charter, led by Mayhem, Lucky's brother, arrived just before we called church. Lerch is on his way with some of the St. Louis chapter to guard the clubhouse while we are gone. We don't know what's going to happen and need all the manpower we can get.

"I hate doing this, but the girls are going to have to wait before contacting their families to come get them or we take them home. We need to plan this out and get it done ASAP so they can see their families. We can't have a bunch of people coming here we don't know, and you know that the second these people know we have found their girls, this place will be crawling with strangers," I tell the men and they agree. "Any ideas how we kill these fuckers once and for all without the police coming down on us? You know they won't like the fact we did this on our own without getting them involved."

"I say we blow those mother fucker's up in that prison silo," Phoenix states angrily, his jaw clenched. There's a dangerous look on his face, his eyes the color of a moonless night, dark and void. I've only seen that look one other time, and that was just outside Bagram, twenty-five kilometers north of Kabul in Afghanistan, he had come across a man strapping a bomb to a young boy and before the man had it all the way on the child, Phoenix had snapped the man's neck. He got it off of the kid before it was detonated, took it to where the young boy had pointed, a small building holding several men, chucked it in, and he calmly and methodically walked away, clicking the detonator with his raised arm pointing towards the building and it exploding just as some men were exiting the building. Limbs and rock being flung into the air, and he just kept slowly walking away. I ran and grabbed him, pushing him with me behind a tank as the shooting began. His eyes were the same color that day.

I clear my throat and ask, "Okay, I like how you think, man. But anyone have any ideas how to pull that off without the cops coming back on us?"

"Make it look like a meth lab blew up," Justice states.

"I know where I can get a propane tank," Toxey chimes in ready for his first "real" heavy action in the club since being patched.

"We're down for that," Mayhem chuckles, linking his fingers and leaning his arms on the table, and his members nod in agreement.

"Momma didn't call you Mayhem for nothing," Lucky tells his brother and slaps him across the back.

"Okay, we've only got a small window before they find out the girls are gone. How quick can you get that tank?" I ask, grinning mischievously.

We get all the plans lined out of who goes where, what we do in possible scenarios, how to get the most VD members there at one time to trap them in the silo and we thought, what the hell, barn too, go big or go home, right? We are currently deciding on what to do with the three members we captured when we rescued the girls. Of course, my twisted enforcer brother wants to torture them as well as Phoenix and Apache. He is one of the more sadistic members of the Indiana chapter. He can skin a man like a big buck and not even phase him.

The plan is set. We have agreed to get as much info out of our hostages as we can before we take down the rest of their club at seven pm, after we have accomplished that and we are sure there is no more threat, we get the girls back with their families. Nothing like always having a miniscule amount of time to work miracles, but I know we've got this.

After we dismiss church Elle pulls me to the side, "Uhm, Lyric couldn't get any information on where Brenna is from or who her family is. She wouldn't tell her anything about her family.

"Nothing at all?" I ask her, "where is she now?"

"She's with Zen. I even tried asking her, and she gets terrified and quiets up. Brenna was a little talker before we started asking about her family. She loved her bubble bath. I just don't get it," Elle says.

Just then Zen walks over to us as we were heading over that way, "you are never going to believe this. Look at them." She motions over to Brenna sitting on Phoenix's lap and she's talking and laughing and smooshing his face with her hands.

I look over at them and my mouth drops open; I mean, I did see him keep an eye on that boy that he took the bomb off of, but I've never seen him like this in all the years I've known him since we got stationed together.

"All I know is I told him that she closed off when we asked about her family and he whispered something in her ear and now this," Zen says, pointing at him.

"What did he tell her?" I ask.

"Hell if I know, she hasn't left his side ever since he came over after church," was her reply.

"Well, I've got to get everything lined out. We are going to pull out of here at 5pm." I say to the two women before me.

"Do I need to grab him for you?" Zen asks.

178

"No, they're fine. I'm going to guess he needs this as much as she does," I tell her.

We go about our planning and getting things ready, and our woman are kicking ass making sure all the extra people from being on lockdown on top of the girls we rescued are all taken care of. We eat an early supper and kiss our families goodbye as we head out to take down the club.

As all the Unfortunate Souls, New Freedom and Indianapolis, Indiana chapter head to the site where we found the girls, loaded down with weapons and all the ingredients to make it look like a meth lab explosion. I pull Phoenix off to the side. "You good man?"

"I fucking hate people that do shit to kids. They can all fucking die. I'm glad we're doing this, taking this kind of shit on. We needed something like this, ya know? Like a direction, not just owning businesses and fun runs, I need this," Phoenix replies.

"So, you ever gonna tell me what happened to you?" I ask point blank.

"It's fucked up bro, my life was fucked up, I'd just rather keep it locked down for now," he states then adds, "C'mon, we got evil to destroy," and shoves his shoulder into mine with his hands in the pockets of his well-worn leather coat.

We get the propane tank and all the explosives set up and ready to go. We have all of our bikes and vehicles hidden but ready to ride and the entire place surrounded by two chapters of Unfortunate Souls. It's really important that we take the whole crew out this time. Not one single Vengeful

Demon is worth a pot to piss in, especially when they are all going along with the trafficking, but that ends today. We are all hidden in different areas of the farm, some in the old barn, some behind the silo, and the rest in the woods or hidden in the fields. There is no way they can escape. Now it's just a waiting game until they start arriving.

At exactly 18:57, we hear the rumble of motorcycles and my muscles tense in anticipation. I raise my fist in the air for the men to hold their position. Two by two bikes are pulling up to location and parking in a long row from the corner of the weather-beaten barn and ending by the remnants of the harvested cornfield. Behind them, two brand new Obsidian Black Mercedes-AMG G63 SUV's pull up and park. Someone has money, I think to myself, and look over to Phoenix. He is pissed and I know why. Someone with that kind of money has to have been trafficking for a while now.

I watch as I see men exiting the vehicles in custom-tailored suits, the obvious security guards with their unnecessary sunglasses standing in front of the shorter man that stands trying to look superior adjusting his gold cufflinks. The men walk only a few steps towards the Vengeful Demons and then take their stance; the guards stand erect but not stiff, their feet shoulder width apart and each having their one hand clasped over the wrist of the other arm in front of them, giving them an air of not only confidence but power. They might fool the Demons, but they don't fool me, I know that tactic.

I watch as Snake walks up to the men. His patched jean jacket with its rips, tears and years of filth built up on it do nothing to impress the rich man. "Where is your boss, Calibar?" one man asks.

My ears perk up at the name. "He is close and will be here once you've seen the girls and agreed to our terms," says Snake.

"I feel that you and your leader are mistaken. We already have a deal set in place. The price is non-negotiable. I was promised fourteen girls with at least ten of them being virgins. Those that are not must be high-quality beauties," says the well-dressed man speaking in Mandarin, and then translated by the first asking about Calibar.

"Well, we only have thirteen," Snake stammers, "but they are all high quality." He motions for the men to get the girls out of the silo, and they unlock it, realizing it's empty except for those dead bodies left behind and that's when I lower my fist. My men unload their weapons on the Vengeful Demons and the high-power men in the SUV's. The bodyguards surround the man that spoke Mandarin and have their weapons drawn. They shove him into the pricey SUV and shut the door.

The men have injured Snake and taken down most Demons. Remington takes out one guard, but not before he took his shot. I feel a burn in my left shoulder and the force of the bullet swings my body around and I am pushed back against the tractor tire. Lucky pulls me back and around behind it and I fall to a sitting position on the ground. It sounds like a war zone with all the guns going off around me. I roll to my stomach and pull out the rifle I had on my back; I prop my arms up the best that I can with my injury and take aim. It hits the center of the glass on the back passenger window of the SUV. Fuck, bullet proof, I should have known.

Just as the driver takes off with the vehicle I hear a combine start, it's mowing over anything and anyone in its way, which includes some bodies of the Demons we've taken out. Blood and ground body parts spew out from the back. It takes some effort, but the combine tractor is climbing up on the hood of the SUV and smashes the windshield and driver in its weight. As the hood is caving in, I see the door try to open but it's unable to with the roof smashed down, I then see the window go down and the Asian trafficker is going to escape that way, I have my gun aimed and take another shot and this one is right between his eyes and his body slumps half in and half out of the vehicle and is instantaneously shredded when the combine has successfully chewed it, taking the guards near the automobile with it. With all the blood and guts spewed everywhere, we are going to have to tweak the meth lab explosion idea and fast. We are out away from everyone, but there is no way at least someone hasn't heard all the gunfire.

As the shooting has wound down and we realize it's only us, we stop, and I see Remington, Phoenix and Justice surveying the area and making sure everyone is dead and the ones alive are secured. Right now, we've only found Snake and one other member still alive. We gather once the area is swept, and check our crew. Everyone is accounted for but one with me. A bullet in my shoulder. Rivet took a shot to his side, but the rest are good, except we can't find dad, where the fuck is my dad?

"Spread out, find Ruger, NOW!" I demand. This is not happening. I'm not losing him.

"Ben, Rem, get over here, man," I hear Lucky call out from the barn.

Remington and I dash to the barn and see our father laying in a pile of dirt and hay, a shot to his heart. He's not moving. Remington throws his head back, his fists clenched and yells out in a guttural angry roar, "Noooooo." I am standing there in complete shock and then fall to my knees next to his body. Rem storms away, dragging back one of the few Demons left alive to our dad's body. As he holds the man up by his greasy hair, he takes his knife and slices his throat and throws the man's body to the ground. He climbs on top of the man and rips open his shirt and cuts out his heart. He's holding it in his hands when we hear a cough come from our father.

Everyone turns towards Ruger, and I put my arms around him, setting him in an upright position. "Damn, that fucking smarted," he manages to rasp out and reaches inside his chest pocket and pulls out a blue tinted square, flat stone with a shattered bullet against it. "Stacks gave me this before she left back to Arizona. It's a synthetic sapphire with her name on it. She said it was as tough as me and to keep it close to my heart, I think that damn woman might be psychic."

I throw my arms around my father and hug him, then Remington pulls him to his feet and gives him a hug too. Dad looks down at the man with the slit throat and the heart laying next to him, "Damn, get a little violent there, Rem?"

"I thought you were dead," is all he says.

"We need to get this done and get you guys out of here. Cuda, get the truck and get Ruger, Rivet and Benelli out of here," says Justice. The pain finally hitting me, I let him take over. I know he's got this. We get loaded in the truck

183

and head back to the clubhouse, where the docs are waiting. When we get about twenty miles away, we hear the explosion and look back to see the sky where the silo was located turn black and red.

We get back to the clubhouse and they work on Rivet first since he's in the worst condition. By the time they are getting started on me, the men are all back. Justice, Remington, and Phoenix are working with Lyric and some others, arranging for the families to get the girls. Elle is by my side and refuses to leave me, as well as Aqua Net by Rivet's side.

By morning I awake to Elle and Brenna curled up tight against me. My movement wake Elle and she smiles up at me and gives me a kiss. "Good morning," I say.

"Good morning," but then her smile turns to a pout, and she whispers to not wake up Brenna, "I told you not to scare me again. How's your shoulder?"

"But I'm here now," I smile and try to plead my case. "I'm sore as hell, but I'll heal. Are the other girls still here?" I ask, kind of confused.

"No, they all have left with their families or Mayhem's club is giving some of them rides back to Indiana and meeting a few families there," she says and looks down at the little girl and kisses her on top of the head, "we still don't have all the answers on this little angel."

We manage to roll out of bed without waking her, and we head to the bathroom. I'm doing my business while Elle is brushing her teeth. "So, do we know anything?" I ask.

"Not much, she talked to Phoenix a little last night, I think her mom died or something, she said she was sick," she says, "we can talk to him when we're done in here and see if he found out anything." We switch spots and finish up, check back on the girl who is still out, and head to the kitchen, leaving the bedroom door open in case she wakes. Phoenix is sitting at the table stoically with Zen next to him, her hand on top of his. I walk over to the coffeepot and pour two cups as Elle gets the creamer out of the fridge for hers.

"Hey man, you okay?" I ask Phoenix.

Zen pats his hand lightly, and he shakes his head, stirring him out of wherever he was. "Yeah, I'm okay. That little girl, it's fucked up, man. She said her mom was sick all the time," he shakes his head again, "she told me her mom used needles to give herself "medicine" and then would sleep a lot. One day after her medicine, she never woke up. Still had the needle in her veins. She was shooting up in front of that little girl and didn't fucking give a shit. That five-year-old girl had to take care of herself because her mom was too out of it to do it. She said it got worse after her dad left and didn't come back earlier at the beginning of summer. Want to know some more fucked up shit?" he says, now staring blankly ahead, "he wore the same patch as those pieces of shit that had her locked up in that silo! He was a fucking Vengeful Demon!" he states and slams his fists down on the table and slams his chair back and it falls backwards to the ground. Zen and Elle jump at the action. He stands now with his fists clenched and gritted teeth, "if that's true, they took that little girl to sell after her worthless mom died in front of her. No loyalty to a club member's family, no honor, they were going to sell her to the highest bidder."

# CHAPTER SIXTEEN

## Elle

The words Phoenix said made me want to throw up. Just the thought of what Brenna has been through and what could have happened. It broke my heart, and it was more than I could take. I ran to the nearest trash can and started retching. When there was nothing left, I leaned back on my heals and realized Benelli was holding my hair back out of my face. Zen was ready with a wet dishrag. Two little, tiny feet tap, tap, tap up to me and her small fingers tug on my clothes. "Are you sick too? Are you sick like my mommy was?" a small, scared voice asks me.

"No baby, I'm not sick like your mommy was. I'm okay honey," I tell her and grab her into an enormous hug.

"Good, because I want you to be my new mommy. I want to stay here with you," she says and grabs me tighter.

Holding her, I look up at Benelli, and tears stream down my face. I can't let her go back to the world she was in before. I won't. Even if we find her father, he's from a club that did horrible, inconceivable things, and I won't put her back into it. "Okay, baby," is all I say, my voice cracking.

Brenna pulls back, looks at me and takes her tiny little hand and wipes the tears from my eyes. "Don't cry Elle, I'll be a good girl, I promise."

"Oh, sweetie, you are a good girl. I'm just sad you had to go through all the awful stuff," I tell her, quickly. Not wanting her to ever worry about anything else, I add, "Are you hungry? Let me go brush my teeth and I will cook you whatever you want. Do you want to go brush your teeth with me?"

She takes my hand, and we walk back to our room at the clubhouse. I'm so glad we stayed here last night instead of going home. "So, what do you like to eat for breakfast?"

Brenna shrugs her shoulders and says with a mouth full of toothpaste, "I grab a box of cereal if we have any."

"Do you like eggs, pancakes, bacon, anything you want?" I ask her after rinsing my mouth. She watches me and does the same, but she spits too hard, and water goes all over the sink and wall. Just then, Benelli comes through the open door and kisses me on the shoulder.

"I'm sorry, I'm sorry," she frantically says and grabs a bath towel, trying to wipe it up. She's in tears and looks frightened at Benelli. I can tell she's scared and must have gotten hit by her father for anything and everything. Benelli sees it too.

He pats her on the head and gently takes the towel from her. "It's okay sweetie, I'll clean it up." Her bottom lip quivers and that man of mine puts his finger under her chin and lifts it so she has to look at him. She closes her eyes. "Brenna, look at me honey," he says gently, "no one will ever hit you or hurt you again, ever, do you understand?" and she nods her head, but I can still see a little uncertainty in her eyes and actions. "Angel," he continues and squats down to her level, "I will promise you, just like I promised Elle, I will never, EVER, let anyone hurt you again and I always keep my promises, don't I Babe?" and they both look up to me.

"Cross my heart. When he makes a promise, he keeps it, and that's why I love him," I say, making the cross motions across my chest.

"So, you guys love each other a lot?" she asks.

"Yes, yes we do," Benelli and I say in unison.

"If Elle will be my mommy, does that mean you will be my new daddy?" she then asks.

"You don't want us to find your daddy?" he asks, but I can see that look in his eye. He's as hooked as I am and is praying, she'll say no. There is no way that he'll let her go back to that life than I will.

She takes his index finger and wraps her fingers around it. "I want you to be my mommy and daddy and I want to get to see Uncle Phoenix and Aunt Zen too."

He lifts her up with his good arm and gives her a hug and he takes her hand and holds it in his and gives it a sweet, quick kiss. I actually see the tiniest of tear drops in the corner of his eye and to lighten the mood I say, "Ahhh, look, dad, she's already got you wrapped around her finger."

"Yeah, yeah," he says, rolling his eyes and kisses me on the cheek. We walk back to the kitchen as he carries her all the way there and plops her down on the counter. "Okay, what are we having?"

"I asked her, and she said a box of cereal. She didn't answer when I mentioned all the other stuff," I say.

"I've never had any of that other stuff," she says, and we look at her blankly.

"You've never had eggs, bacon or pancakes or anything?" I ask, blown away. I mean, even if she was a drug addict mom, she cooked nothing for her?

She shakes her head no and we tell her she is going to have it all. We guess at about how many people stayed at the clubhouse last night and get to cooking. I line a giant baking sheet with bacon and put it in the oven. I know some people cringe at that, but I learned that in the oven it's straight, perfectly cooked and I don't get burned from grease splatters. It's a win, win. Phoenix took the eggs over while Benelli was on pancake duty. She gets a big kick out of him, making shapes and then flipping them in the air. I have gone all out for her first "real" breakfast, and I have Brenna help me make biscuits from scratch. She's having a blast squishing her fingers in the dough, then helping me roll it out and we use a couple coffee cups to cut out the biscuits, placing them on a cookie sheet. Zen is making juice, more coffee and cutting up any and every kind of fruit we have.

Lucky strolls into the kitchen. "What's all this?"

"Brenna has had nothing but cereal before," I tell him, and his mouth drops open.

"Well, I want in on the fun too," he says and pokes her belly, and she giggles.

"We got to make biscuits and squishy all the stuff together. It was fun!" Brenna tells him.

"I wanna squishy stuff too!" he says, and pretends to pout.

"Please mommy, can we let the guy with all the colors on him squish stuff too?" she looks at me and pleads with her hands clasped together.

I want to tear up at her calling me mommy, but I try to hold it back and laugh at her description of Lucky and his tattoos.

"This colorful guy is Lucky and yes, we can make something else you guys can squish," I say.

She pulls on the end of his long, red beard and tells him, "I like your name and your colors. My old daddy just had a black, scary skeleton head with red eyes and a snake coming out of its mouth." I freeze and drop the coffee cup I was holding.

"Elle?" Benelli asks.

I tense and all I get out of my mouth is, "Frodo."

Brenna being busy with Lucky and not noticing the fear on my face or even looking up from her playing with the extra biscuit dough, "Yep, that was my old daddy's name, he was a meanie, but my new daddy says he won't let him hurt me no more," she states and looks up and smiles at Benelli.

"That's right, Pumpkin, you are, for sure, going to stay with us forever now," and walks over and kisses the top of her head. "I'm going to go talk to Elle, I mean mommy, okay? You stay here with Lucky."

"Okay, daddy," and she says, oblivious to any tension in the air.

Benelli leads me to the other room and wraps me in his arms, "her dad is, was, Frodo," he states flatly.

"I remember that tat on his forearm when he, he," I stammer out.

"Shhhh, it's all over baby, he's never going to hurt either of you again," he says, comforting me. Trying to change the subject, "Sooooo, I guess we're mom and dad now. Are you ready for all that?"

"I feel like I was put here on earth and went through all of this so I could be here, at this moment, for that little girl, ya know?" I say rationalizing my trauma, "I mean, what if all that I went through, was so I could be here when she came to us, to know maybe, some of the things that she's been through, so I could understand and be here for her."

"To make you the perfect person for her, the perfect mommy for her? I think you were sent here for me, and I hate all that you've gone through, but it made you who you are. You are so strong babe, I feel you are here to be in both of our lives," he says and pauses and then shakes his head, "I'm a dad now, I mean, not officially, but that's our little girl."

"I know," I smile and look up and touch his cheek.

"I fell for you so fast Elle, faster than I ever thought I could for a woman, but that angel in the other room," he takes a breath and holds my hand and his to his heart, "I already love her, she's MY little girl now and I will spend the rest of my days to make sure she never has to go through anything like that again. Just like I promised you, I promised her, you two are my family and I know it's fast and crazy and we have to make it all legal and shit, but I'm not going to let either of you go."

I reach my lips up to his and kiss him. I kiss the man that saved me; I kiss the man that is willing to raise a stranger and give her a better life without a second thought. I taste him and I taste promise and future and a life full of happiness in his kiss and I could make an entire life with just the taste of that kiss.

Everyone is gathered together now in the dining area. We put a little bit of everything on Brenna's plate, well plates, it took three to fit everything. I set one down and her juice and Benelli sat the other two in front of her. Her eyes were like saucers. "Is that all for me?"

"Yes, sweetie, but you don't have to eat all of it," I laugh. "I just thought you could try a bite of each and see what your favorites are."

One of the plates was just different kinds of eggs, from sunny side up to scrambled with cheese to a ham and cheese omelet. Good grief, we went a little overboard. She stared at all the plates and contemplated what to try first. She reached out and picked up a strawberry and her eyes went wide as she chewed, and a smile erupted on her face. "This is so good!" she exclaimed and picked up a piece of banana. That one she said was okay, but not her favorite. Next, she started on the eggs and the creamy, scrambled ones were her favorite of that, but it needed ketchup. She tasted each and everything we gave her, including the biscuits we made, one with gravy and one with honey butter. "I've never eaten so much in all my life. Look how poochie my belly is," she said, pushing it out even more for effect.

Her belly was a little poochie, so I figured I'd better have her stop before she got a tummy ache. I hope I wasn't too late. When I started cleaning up and putting the leftovers away with the other women, she jumped in to help, too. I told her to go play with the other kids and her face lit up and jumped excitedly and took off in a run. Fireball and the club's newest prospect, Scott, who is Lexie's dad, are washing dishes and sweeping. I'm used to prospects doing the grunt work by now, but it's odd for me to see Scott doing it. Maybe because he's already a family man, but I know he has to earn it like all the others before him. Benelli and the other men met up to handle some business from yesterday that we women aren't supposed to know about, but I saw Remington and Justice dragging someone into the factory when I looked out the window last night. I hope they pour boiling tar down his body for kidnapping and harming those girls. I hope they torture him and make him suffer.

I'm distracted from my dark thoughts by Aqua Net. "So does that little girl really have no family and you're keeping her? I heard her call you mommy earlier."

"Looks that way. It's crazy to me that someone so small could already have had such a hard life that she immediately picks herself out, not only new people she can trust, but new parents," I say.

"Kids that young are funny that way," Nettie says. "That's kind of how we ended up with Rocky, ya know?" I shake my head no and she continues, "Rivet and I couldn't have kids, we tried and tried, went to all sorts of doctors but it wasn't meant to be." Every woman in the club was having babies except me. I took it in stride when Sheila had Colt and Barbie had Benelli and then Remington, but then years later when Sheila had little Pistol, I was a basket case. I went into a dark place for a long time. Rivet one day forced me out of bed and dressed and took me on a trip.

Now, I had no clue where we were going, but we hopped on a plane and went to the Ukraine. He took me to an orphanage. Apparently, that lug had already been in contact with them several times. I was sitting outside just watching all these children play and I put my hands to my face and cried. Someone touched my face and wiped away my tears and I look and it's this tiny little boy with crippled legs and braces on them. His arms were so skinny, but he reached them out for me to pick him up. He was only two and a half, and he chose me. He chose me to be his mommy." by this time we are both sniffling.

194

"I haven't met Rocky yet. Where is he at now?" I ask.

"Oh, he's grown now and away at college. He's going to school to be a lawyer at Yale. Me, a kid at Yale, can you believe it?" she replies proudly.

"That's really great. I bet you're one proud momma," I reply.

Later that morning, Zen and I decide to take Brenna to town to get her some clothes and toys. The guys are still busy, so we shoot them both text messages. Of course, Benelli makes us take Fireball with us and tells me to get his credit card out of his office and go nuts. We decide to make it a girls' day and do our hair too, but that I will pay for. I know we are going to be married, but I'm making my own money now and business has been great. Of course, thinking of that, I wonder how people manage full-time careers and parenting. I wonder how mom did it. I figure I better give her a call before we leave to shop till we drop. She's going to kill me for not letting her know about Ruger and everything that's happened sooner.

"Baby girl! How are you? I haven't heard from you in over a week," mom says.

"I'm good. There's just been a lot going on. The club has kind of taken over a new task," I say and fill her in on finding Lexie in the shop, rescuing the girls, then last but not least Benelli getting shot in the shoulder and then mention Ruger.

"Is he okay? I had this horrible dream before I came down last time, and I gave him a synthetic sapphire plate with my name on it. They were at a show and ordered them with the business logo on it, but something told me to make one more. I didn't know what drew me to them, but I later read on the informational sheet that came with the order that they were super strong, and they were literally bulletproof." She rambles out.

"Well, he can testify that they are very much bulletproof. If he didn't have it in his front pocket, he wouldn't be here right now. They shot him in the heart and other than an enormous bruise, he's completely fine," I say.

"Oh my God, are you sure? Do I need to come now? I mean, I was planning on coming the week of Thanksgiving, but I can come now," she asks.

"Mom, I swear to you, he's fine. He's in better shape than Benelli, and even he will be fine. Is there something you want to tell me about Ruger mom?" I question her.

"No, I mean maybe, no, we're just friends, we text and talk on the phone more than you and I do now, but no, damn it Elle, can I be real with you?" she stammers.

"Of course, mom," I reply with a little joy. I mean, mom's been single pretty much my entire life and I've always wanted her to find someone, and I saw how they hung around together and interacted on her last visit.

"I like him, like I think I like, like him," she says.

"Wow, four likes in one sentence. This must be serious," I joke.

196

"I haven't really liked a man since your father. I mean, I've dated some..." she says.

"But no one had that butterfly effect until now," I add.

"Exactly, it's been over 23 years since I've had butterflies Elle. I'm forty-two freaking years old. What am I doing?" she asks.

"Mom, it's your time and you are a young 42 and a smoking hot babe. If you want to be with Ruger, you have my blessing. All I ask is, you let us get married before you, so I'm not marrying my stepbrother," I joke.

"Oh God, I didn't even think about that!" she exclaims and then laughs, "now that's funny right there. I promise, I am in no rush to get married."

"Well, I might be. I haven't told you the big news yet," I say.

"Better than they both getting shot? Oh my God, are you pregnant? Are you making me a grandma?" she asks excitedly.

"Yes and no, or should I say no, and yes? I'm not pregnant, but we are making you a grandma," I tell her.

"I am so confused," mom tells me, and I tell her all about Brenna.

"That settles it. I've been thinking about selling the shop and moving there, but I was going to wait until next year, after I found a delightful spot for a new one. That moves the timeline up between all the new things in your life I'm missing out on, wanting to see what happens with Ruger, and now an instant granddaughter, I'm putting it on the market this month!" she tells me.

"Well, I know I would love to have you close. I miss you. There is a building that just went up for sale a few shops down from mine. It's the one on the corner and it would be perfect. I will check into it. I'm going to have to get off of the phone now, mom. I promised a little girl a shopping trip before I called you," I look down at Brenna who is pleading at my side now, "I love you mom, I'll call you tomorrow about that building."

"I love you too, baby girl," says mom before hanging up.

The rest of the day is spent first getting our hair done, then we eat lunch at the little mom and pop diner the club owns, then Walmart for the basics she'll need, the cutest kids' boutique where we really went nuts in and finally, the toy store. Brenna stepped in the door and her jaw dropped. She looked at me, then back to the toys, then back to me, all while her little mouth gaped open, finally asking, "Is this Santa's workshop?"

"It looks like it, doesn't it? Why don't we pick you out some toys since you've been such a good girl," I say. She grabs my hand and then Zen's, "come on Auntie Zen, help me pick out some stuff."

We end up with two baby dolls and some clothes for them, a few learning toys like a LeapStart, a marble run toy, puzzles I think she could do, a tea party set because Zen and I can't wait to see the guys do that with her and of all things a stuffed Armadillo, not a teddy bear, puppy or kitten, noooo an Armadillo, Fireball helped her pick that one out.

I text Benelli to tell him we are on our way home and he tells us to just come to the house. His dad, Phoenix and he are all there and they are grilling one last time before it gets too cold.

We get to the house, and Fireball is carrying in the majority of the items for us. Brenna runs in ahead of him and looks for Benelli. "Look at me, look how my dress swooshes out when I spin," and she spins for him.

"Oh, you look so pretty sweet, girl!" he tells her.

"Look, look, it even has pockets," she exclaims.

"I see. That is so cool," he says.

"Girls like pockets," I say, and laugh.

"I've got something to show you too," he says and takes her hand and leads her upstairs and I follow.

"Oh, honey! You did all this today?" I ask with my hand on my heart. He had fixed up the old room I used before we became a couple into the sweetest, lilac little girl's room with a canopy bed, toy chest, and cute little decorations on the walls.

"The guys all came and helped after we were done... handling things," he pauses between.

"This is for me? All for me? You're the bestest daddy in the entire world and I'm so glad I picked you!" Brenna says.

He leans down and kisses her on her cheek, "I'm so glad you picked me too, Pumpkin."

# CHAPTER SEVENTEEN

## Benelli

We are in the kitchen and Phoenix has just told us about what Brenna had told him. His words punch me in the gut. The life that little girl has had to lead. After seeing Elle and her snuggled up against me when I woke and hearing this, I know what I want to do. I will not let her go back to that life. I know my future wife will be on board, but will that little girl? Does she even want to be stuck with another biker family when the one she had was so horrible to her? I know she would have a good life here, but will what she went through with one club make her not want to be part of another?

Elle runs to the trash can and is throwing up and within seconds I am by her side holding her hair back for her. I know how she feels. The information Phoenix gave us made me sick to my stomach, too. I can't let that little girl leave now. I won't. Thoughts are running through my head like a speeding train. What do I do? How do I make this happen? What about all the other kids in the world that are going through this? I have all these ideas and plans whizzing back and forth in my brain, so many different directions. There is one thing that will help me clear my head and its justice. Just as I've decided, that's what I need to do. Stat, Brenna walks up to us and tugs on Elle's shirt and asks if she is sick like her mommy was. That rips me to the core. Elle assures her that she's fine and hugs her, and then she says it. She wants Elle to be her mommy and stay here, and that's all I need to make sure she does exactly that. I make plans in my head to fix the spare room Elle used for a short time at my house, correction, our house, into a room for Brenna.

While Elle and Brenna go to brush their teeth, I make a quick call to Brick to see if he's free and what I'm thinking about the bedroom. Luckily, he can push back his job for the day and gather some of the guys to help me out. I know I better get the approval of my old lady and walk to the bathroom; the door is open, so I stand there for a minute watching and listening before I enter. Just the sheer normal family vibe with them both at the sink makes me want this life so strong. I was single for so long, just going along thinking how great my life was with only the club and the pleasures that the club girls could satisfy me with, but this, this right here is what I truly desire, love, faithfulness, family. I hear that little angel tell Elle that she's never even had warm food and I enter just as she's rinsing and spitting into the sink. It went everywhere and I want to laugh.

I come in and kiss Elle on top of the head and then see the complete panic in Brenna while she's apologizing and trying to wipe up the mess. I pat her head and take the towel gently, telling her I will do it for her. Oh, that little lip, I just can't, my heart. I lift her little chin to look at me and assure her it's okay and that no one will ever hurt her again, just like I promised Elle. She asks if we love each other and if I thought I wanted to adopt that girl before, when she says she wants me to be her daddy, it seals the deal.

My heart shattered. Any wall that I've ever had up just came crashing down like a sledgehammer to crystal and she had me right there. I ask her to be safe if we should find her other daddy and that girl wrapped her hand around my finger and I know I'm done for. I lift her up with my arm not wrapped up and hold her. Yes boys, I'm a goner and Elle tells me as much. We go back into the kitchen and plop her on the counter, and we decide to make that girl a breakfast extravaganza she'll never forget. She giggles and claps at my expertise in pancake shapes and how high I flip them. Yes, this is what it's all about.

The next thing I heard was Elle say "Frodo" and a crash. I kiss Brenna on top of the head when she says he's not going to be her daddy anymore, that I am, and I lead Elle into the other room to talk. Well, that makes it official. Her father and mother are both dead and I'm going to do everything in my power to be her daddy. Wow, saying it out loud to Elle makes it real, so real.

As much as I hate either of my girls going through anything bad, Elle makes a good point. Maybe fate took us in all these fucked up directions so the three of us would be here, right at this point in time. We head back in and I watch that little angel fill up her belly. Probably more than she eats in a week, I think, but then tries to shake off that image of her life before. I can't get the picture out of my head, though, and I excuse myself to take care of this business once and for all.

I nod my head towards the warehouse, and the men get up to follow. We walk into the room where we have the four men shackled up, the three from the rescue and the one they call Snake that was at the last mission. "Now boys, which of you is going to tell us what we need to know?" I ask, rubbing my palms together.

"We're not telling you shit," Snake says and spits his useless venom at me, missing.

"Oh, I think you will," and nod towards my brother Remington, and he punches the viper in his face. His body is jerking back and swinging from the chains like a weight bag and the man spits out a couple of teeth.

I walk with casualty and purpose to the next man, "how about you? Anything you want to say?" he shakes his head quickly in a no and I nod for Remington to do something to this one. I'd do it myself, but he eats this shit up, so I let him. He picks up a sledgehammer and, like a professional ballplayer, slams it into the man's knee. "And that's a home run, fans," I call out.

The man screams in pain and says, "I don't know anything, all I know is we were supposed to watch the silo on our shift."

"Tsk, tsk, tsk," I sound out. "Now, I know better than that. You see, we were watching you when you were talking to the other three you were relieving." This time Phoenix jumps up to bat and shatters the other knee. "Don't lie to me boys, I know more than you think."

"Just, just wait till Calibar and the men get here. You're all goners!" the third man yells.

"Shut up, Goofy!" Snake spits.

"Goofy, you say? I think I'll keep this one alive. What do you think?" I tell my team and chuckle wickedly, and my men nod in agreement. At the nod of my head, Justice takes his piece and puts a bullet between Snakes' eyes. I methodically walk up to the fourth scum, "how about you? Do you want curtain number one to live like Goofy, curtain number two, we torture you like, what's his name?" I ask about number four.

"Balls, he's Balls," Goofy offers up, hoping upon hope that his cooperation really will keep him pain and death free. Foolish, foolish man, but I play the game.

"Do you want to feel our wrath like your friend Balls here? Or would you like curtain number three and we seal your fate like your second in command, Snake?" I ask easily, as if it were a dessert tray.

"You really gonna let Goofy go if he cooperates?" number four asks, contemplating on what to do. He's quickly analyzing that Goofy is gonna break, and he hasn't been struck yet, and the other two options aren't really appetizing. Fuck, if Goofy's gonna spill anyway, why not get in on it?

"I am a man of my word," I tell him plainly.

"You're a fucking idiot, Hash, if you think they're going to let you live. If they don't kill you, Calibar and the VD will," Balls screams at Hash.

"Oh, Snake didn't tell you, boys?" I acted shocked and continue, "We not only got the girls out of there, we took down your club. There's no one left. Let's just say it was a farming accident," I laugh.

"We spewed them through the harvester combine like they were stalks of corn," Lucky tells them, laughing darkly.

"Calibar..." Balls tells them, but is shot by Lucky before he can spill.

"Okay, okay, I'll tell you everything," Hash quickly spits out. "Chains started getting into trafficking before you guys got to him. The only reason I know you took out Chains, Frodo, and Luther is Calibar left and came back. He took over the club and the trafficking ring. He got some hoity, toity, Asian guy as a buyer and the guy gave us a list of what he wanted. Calibar would go from state to state doing recon and then send us in to get the girls and take them back to the silo. We were set to meet up with the guy so he could check out the product before shipment. I, I didn't want any part in it, but I was already in deep and they'd kill me if I didn't. When I joined the club, it was all about bikes, getting high and fucking hoes. I didn't want any part of this, but I had no choice."

"What about Frodo's kid? Why her?" I ask, daring him to give me a shitty answer.

"Calibar, Calibar did it, man, it was all him. After I found out about Frodo, I'd go and check on them every once in a while. Make sure they were okay, ya know? When I went over one morning, I found her dead with a needle still in her arm. What was I gonna do? I couldn't just leave the kid by herself, so I took her. I was going to give her to my sister to raise, but as soon as I got back to my place, he was there. He had me followed, man. He took the kid from me. I swear I was gonna do right by her," Goofy spills.

206

"Do you have anything else to add?" I motion to Hash, "Do you know where Calibar is now? Why he wasn't at the meetup?"

"No man, I figured he'd have been there," Hash stammers out and Phoenix walks over to him, we hear the click of the gun being cocked, "I thought you said you were a man of your word, you said if we talked, you'd let us go."

"I am a man of my word and I said I'd let Goofy go," and at that Phoenix put the final nail in his coffin.

At the third of the four men dead, Goofy speaks out, "Okay, they're dead. Can you get me down from this shit now?"

Justice walks over and releases Goofy from the chains and he falls to the ground but gets up quickly and rubs his wrists.

"What in the ever-loving fuck are you doing, Jus?" Phoenix asks, getting ready to put a bullet in Goofy, but Justice puts his arm across his chest to block him.

Goofy stretches out his hand to Phoenix. "Special Agent O'Neal, I went undercover to get the supreme leader of the trafficking ring, Zhang Xui Ying, but it seems like you've already taken him out for me. There's been rumors of Chains actions trafficking and I have been working on taking down Zhang for five years now, but I could never catch him and get the evidence. That's why I joined the VD to get Chains on the radar of Zhang. Then, when he kidnapped a club girl, you took him out. When Calibar took over, it was easy to get them linked up. My other connections leaked to Zhang there was a new, smarter leader that could get him the girls faster than Chains ever could."

"But how did 'we' know all this and why didn't anyone tell me?" Phoenix asks angrily, "and how the fuck could you do that job? Watching girls getting taken from their families like that and stand by?"

"So, you know when we brought them all back and put them in separate rooms? Ruger had balls, Justice had Hash, and I had him. He told me he was undercover. Of course, I didn't believe him, but he had his badge hidden in the heal of his boot. It was right there when I twisted the heal. I told Ruger and Justice because, well, we were all three together. We hung him back with the others, hoping we would get more info from them, and it worked. When he sang, we got more info from Hash. You and Benelli have been so busy with everything trying to find out about the little girl, I didn't get to tell either of you."

"I didn't get to tell Benelli until right before he came in," said Ruger.

"That's fucked up, guys. I know this mission has hit me pretty hard. Fucking with the lives of kids hits home, okay. But you," he points to O'Neal, "How in the fuck can you have let this go on and be a part of it, seriously dude, little kids!"

"I know it's fucked up, but it was for the greater good. Do you know how many girls Zhang got a hold of before I got involved? Seven hundred eighty-four girls before the ones you saved. Seven hundred and eighty-four girls got sent who knows where, and he got out of it every time. One was my sister, and I still haven't found her yet... but I swear to you, I will. If it's the last breath I take, I will find and save Liberty," he states.

"So, what's your plan now?" I ask.

"Hunt down Calibar. Thanks to you, we have the girls to testify against him," O'Neal says.

"Do you really think that's how we are going to let it go down? He raped my woman. He will pay for that, and it will not be a prison sentence where he gets released and can hurt another woman again." I tell him how it's going to be.

"Legally, I have to tell you that, but I've been in this world a while now. I've seen the damage it's doing to the girls. I don't need Calibar to find my sister. If I find him, I'll turn him over to you," O'Neal swears.

"And your report?" I ask O'Neal.

"It never mentions your club. You'll never be on FBI radar. Just make me a deal though?" he says.

"What's that?" I ask.

"When I find my sister and get out of this... you let me join your club and take out these scum the way it should be done. Deal?" he asks.

"We'd be proud to have you," and I shake his hand.

After we get anymore intel that O'Neal can give us on Calibar, we have church. After that, Dad, Phoenix and I stop and get some foo-foo girlie stuff and head back to my house to help Brick and the others with the room for Brenna. It's unseasonably warm today and us being men decided we better get the grill fired up before the girls get back.

Brenna swings, showing me her dress with pockets, and I show her the new princess room where she will be living at her new home. I've given Virus a heads up to figure out any way we can make this legal without a lot of time and paperwork. He tells me it would be a little smoother if Elle and I were already married. Looks like we are going to have to pin down a date, and soon.

We enjoy the evening with friends and family and some kick ass barbeque. Brenna falls asleep in my arms while we listen to Phoenix sing and play the guitar around the firepit. After everyone leaves, I carry her and put her into bed and tuck her in. I then spend the rest of the long day and into the wee hours of the night making love to my woman and, of course, setting a date.

# CHAPTER EIGHTEEN

## Elle

I enjoy having everyone over and especially not having to cook is a big bonus, but I am happy they all left because all I want to do is tuck our little girl in. Oh, my God. OUR little girl and after that I plan on getting it on with my man. We need to set a date though, and pretty soon, so we can get the paperwork in order to adopt Brenna. Virus and Benelli have been working on it, and I know Virus said it would be easier if we were already married, but he'd do his best.

I wanted to give her a bath before bed, but there is no way in hell I'm going to wake her up to take one. We can do it when she gets up in the morning. I follow him as he carries her up to her bedroom and pulls back the covers. He lays her down and kisses her on the cheek and covers her back up with her adorable purple comforter with butterflies all over it. They really did an outstanding job in this room today. I give her a kiss too, and he takes my hand and leads me to ours.

"You know, if anyone had asked me a year ago, hell, six months ago, I wouldn't believe it. That I would not only have a woman, but to be engaged to her. Plus, becoming an instant father to a five-year-old girl. I would have said they had lost their minds, but here I am." He places his palms on my cheeks and gives me a sweet kiss. "I am the happiest I have ever been in my life right now."

211

"I'm right there with you, babe, 100%. This has been a roller coaster of a ride and there are things I wish wouldn't have happened, but they did, and I've overcome them," I say.

"Yes, you have baby. I'm so proud of you," he tells me. "We need to lock down a date, though. I know you wanted to plan a big wedding, and we can still do that, but how much time can we really cut it down to?"

"I was hoping for spring, but is Valentine's Day too far out?" I ask.

"What about Christmas?" he asks, and I laugh.

"You're killing me smalls. That's less than two months. Can you give me a tiny bit more time here?" I laugh.

"New Year's Day, I know we won't get a place on New Year's Eve, but how about the day? Because I want nothing more than starting out the year with you as my wife," he says so convincingly.

"Well, geez, when you put it all romantic like," I joke and then kiss him.

It started out gently, but the more I thought about what that day would mean and picturing it, the more aroused I got. Our kiss became more intense, fierier. I reached my hand down and placed it on the outside of his jeans, and yep; he was feeling it too. His hand reaching down and unsnapping and unzipping my jeans. I shimmied and wiggled as he pulled them down and in an instant, picked me up and tossed me on the bed. I made quick work of getting his down and off too. The next thing you know, we were pulling and yanking our clothes off in a feverish frenzy. Kissing and touching and working our lips and hands all over each other. I pushed myself back onto the bed and he followed along with me.

"Get on all fours," he huskily says, and I eagerly do as directed. He teases my entrance with his cock, but I push back against it, not wanting to wait any longer to be filled. "You're ready, aren't you?" he asks in a low, sensual voice.

I turn my head, flipping my long hair over to the other side, and look at him hungrily. "Now, I need it now, Benelli."

He pushes into me and growls the name he calls me when I'm in power. "Xena." Throwing his head back as he thrusts into me harder and harder, faster, and faster. I work my body with his, pushing back, back, back against his steel body and he loves it. I keep my head turned, looking towards him, and it feeds his lust. His hands grip my hips and thrusts deep inside. I lower the top half of my body, angling down now so I can grab one of his hands with my own. His thrusts stop momentarily as he flips me in a swift motion, "ride me," and I do. I impale myself on to his cock and rise and lower my body in desperation.

He places his fingers strategically so that with every movement I make, his fingers hit my clit in exactly the right place. I'm about to go over the edge. He takes those fingers and places them in his mouth and moans at the taste. Then, he grabs my hips firmly and rapidly, forces my body up and down so quickly on his rock-hard shaft, and I throw my head back and lose all control. When I do that, the length of my hair falls and feathers against him and he too comes and growls Xena again. It's in such a carnal way that I feel like the most powerful woman in the world.

When the aftershocks finally cease for us both, we put our foreheads to each other, and we are so sweaty and breathless. I ease off of him and stand, holding out my hand, and he takes it and raises. We walk to the shower and enjoy another round before we decide we better get some well-deserved sleep.

It's been a few days, and I needed to get back to work. I have a boudoir session with the woman that I had to reschedule with when we found Lexie in the shop. I've honestly never done one before, but I've seen other people's work and they have a way of making women feel so empowered and beautiful.

"Hi, thank you so much for understanding about rescheduling, Mrs. VanZandt," I reach out and shake the woman's hand.

"Miss, and call me Marti," she says.

"Marti, what makes you want to do boudoir photos? A Christmas present for someone special?" I ask.

"Yes, someone very special... me. I lived with a man for way too long that abused me both physically and mentally. You're too fat, you're stupid, your hair isn't pretty, I'm the only man that would put up with you. Finally, I had enough, and I got away. I went back to school, I went to counseling, I found ME again. I want to celebrate that, and I guess I feel like this is the last piece to the new me, ya know. So, I can prove to myself that I am beautiful and sexy. So yes, someone very, very special," she says with a beaming pride that lights up the room.

"That is so inspirational. I wish more women could feel that way. Seriously, we all need to believe in ourselves like you do." Marti blushes. "Let's get started, why don't you get changed and meet me over in this room over here and I'm going to go lock the front."

Marti exits the dressing room, and she had her hair in an updo with a red bandana. She has a blue jean shirt that's tied just under her ample breasts and silky blue panties. The look is phenomenal. "I thought I would start with this. I have a couple other outfits too if that's okay?"

"Okay, are you kidding me? This is going to be a blast, and might I say, WOW, you are stunning. Rosie the Riveter would be proud," I say enthusiastically. I pull down the white backdrop and remember the guys left some tools in the back and go grab them. We do several poses, and we are both coming up with ideas and laughing. This is freaking awesome! She changes into a black lace bra and panty set and has her hair down this time. I do some shots of her posing, laying down with her legs up in some killer pumps.

These are coming out amazing. I remember I have some wicked black wings in the prop room and grab them. In one photo I have her standing with her back to me showing her black hair, wings, panties peeking out and those super toned calves in heals. Fuck me, I think I've found my calling. If this doesn't give women their empowerment back, I just don't know! We've talked throughout the shoot, and I find out that she's a counselor for rape and domestic violence victims at a woman's shelter about an hour and a half away. I show her some of the photos through the screen on the back of the camera, and she can't wait for the final editing and touches.

When I get home, I tell Benelli about Marti and how fun and amazing the shoot was. I tell him how I would like to get a special package together to support women getting back on their feet after feeling so defeated. I also really bonded with Marti and wished she wasn't so far away.

"Funny you should mention that. We had a meeting this morning and we want to go in a rescue mission direction with the club. There's talk about buying a home and opening it up for women and children. We get them out of critical situations, and they need somewhere to go. We're looking at a few possibilities later this week. I think Phoenix is talking to Zen about running it as we speak. We figured she would be perfect for this and sounds like Marti would too," he tells me.

"I love that idea!" I say.

Just then Brenna runs into the room and jumps up into my arms, "You're home! Man, I fucking missed you!"

"Fucking? Brenna, we don't use that word, okay," I say.

"Fireball says it. He said it a lot before Lexie's mom came and picked me up. He kept saying, I can't believe I'm in a motorcycle club and fucking babysitting," and I cringe and turn my squinted eyes towards Benelli, who is not too happy.

"Well, I'll make sure Fireball knows that it's a very bad word. Neither of you are going to say it ever again, right Miss Brenna?" Benelli says, trying to look menacing but not too much.

"Yes sir," she says lowering her head and crossing her feet and that's when the all-powerful president crumbles.

"I'm not mad at you baby girl." Aw, that's what my mom calls me, now I'm melting. "Now come and give me a hug," he says, and she smiles and does.

Just then, the front door opens, and its mom and Ruger. "Now, where is my new granddaughter? Aw, look at you, you are so pretty."

Brenna looks up at me, all confused. "Sweetie, this is my mommy, so that makes her your grandma."

"Noni, I want to be a Noni. Grandma makes me sound old," mom announces.

"What's a Noni?" she asks.

"Well, it's grandma," mom tells her.

"What's a grandma?" she asks. We all look at each other. Panic hits because none of us thought about seeing if she had any other family besides her mom and dad.

"Honey, did you not have a grandma and grandpa?" I ask worriedly.

"I don't know, what is that?"

Mom squats down beside her and pulls Brenna into her arms, "It's a person who loves you and spoils you even more than your mommy and daddy."

I have to roll my eyes on that one because, well, I just do. "No, I never had one of those, that's for sure," Brenna says.

"Well, you've got one now, baby girl," mom tells her.

"Hey, there, wait just a minute, what am I chopped liver? I'm your PaPa, and before you ask, it's like a grandpa but way cooler," Ruger says.

"Wait," and she holds up her hand in a stop motion and puts her other hand on her hip. "So, you're telling me that I've got a new mommy and daddy that are A-MA-ZING and love me. Now I get a Noni and PaPa that love me even more? You're kidding me, right?"

"I wouldn't say they love you more than me, but nope, not even kidding," Benelli tells her.

"I'm the luckiest girl in the whole wide world!" she yells loudly.

"And you know what Noni and PaPa are going to do? We are going to take you out to get a Halloween costume and some ice cream." Ruger goes right along with mom's talk like they had this all planned. I haven't seen my mom in forever, and they've snatched her up and are heading outside to the truck in a snap.

"Nice seeing you, mom. So glad you came to Illinois to see your only child. No really, love you too!" I call out trying to act deprived but honestly, that helps me out because I've got some serious wedding planning to do, stat.

## Brenna

I don't know all these people that have come into my life, but I'm so happy. It's probably not very nice, but if this is what real families are like, I'm glad mine are gone. I saw Elle get sick and puke and she still made me bunches of food. My other mommy was always sick and never made me anything, ever. My daddy never played with me, he never talked to me unless he was yelling at me and hitting me or mom. Benelli built me a whole princess butterfly room AND he played tea party with me and Uncle Phoenix. Now, I'm in a truck with people who are taking me to get a Halloween costume. I don't know what that is, but hey, it sounds like fun, especially the ice cream part.

We pull up to this store and walk across the parking lot. They each take my hand and when I jump up, they swing me, so guess what, I am going to keep doing it. I sometimes think of when that mean man took me and I was in that dark place with all those other girls, but I try not to. They were sad that they didn't get much to eat or drink but, shoot; it was more than I usually got at home, so that part didn't bother me so much and I liked not being alone all the time. They walk me into the enormous doors of the store and my mouth drops open.

"Are you kidding me?"


"What honey, what is it?" the one that wants me to call him Papa asks.


"This place is SOOOOO COOL!" I say and run up to this monster and it dances in front of me, so I dance too. The one called Noni has her phone out, recording me dancing. I ran to something else, and it started cackling, so I do the same. Then I go to a black cat, and it throws a hissy fit, so I hissy fit right back at it. I've never been to a store like this, but I love it!


"What costume do you want?" Noni asks me, and the three of us walk down the aisles. I wander off to another aisle and I see Lucky, and he hands me an arm full of costume stuff and shhh's me to keep him a secret. He then turns me and gently shoos me to go back to the other two. Lucky's so weird sometimes. He laughed and ran away. I don't know what that means, but I take the stuff to Noni and Papa.


"Here ya go," and I throw my haul into the cart.


They look at the cart, then at each other, then at the cart, then at me before stuttering, "Are you sure that's what you really want?"


"Yep, this is the one I want, it's perfect!" as I jump up and down in excitement, "Now, how about that ice cream?"


Papa laughs and picks me up in his big, old arms. "I think you will look great, honey bear. Now you just need a pumpkin," and he grabs one as we are heading towards the checkout.

"What's that for?"

"For you to put candy in when you go trick or treating," Noni says. "You know, when you knock on doors and say trick or treat and people give you candy."

"Shut the front door! People give you candy when you knock on doors with this pumpkin thingy?"

"They sure do, honey, but you have to say trick or treat," Papa says. I think he's fibbing, but I shrug my shoulders and go with it. Sounds too easy to me.

We get to the ice cream place, and I want to try this sucker out, but they made me leave it in the truck. What the hell! These grownups give me a thing to carry around and say trick or treat, but they won't let me use it. It worked out okay though because they gave me ice cream anyway and this stuff is the bomb.

We stop by the clubhouse after the ice cream, and I beg them to let me carry this orange thing; I want to try this magic candy thing out for myself. I knock on the door and this tall, skinny guy opens it, so I do my job, "trick or treat," and hold this thing out. The dude looks down at me and up at Papa, so I say it again, "I SAID, trick or treat," and I push the orange thing at the guy.

He leans over my head because I've got that sucker blocked and he whispers to Papa, "Um, boss, I don't have any candy, Halloween's not for another week."

"Fireball, I don't care what you have to do. Find something to put in her pumpkin now," Papa growls at the man. I guess he scared him because he started reaching into his pockets and putting stuff in it. Noni and I head to the kitchen while Papa goes to do something and I dump my stuff on the table and check out my haul. I've got a key, an open package of gum, and she counts the money for me, and I got $11.47, and a pocketknife! Hey, I like this trick or treating gig.

"Noni, I'm going to see what else I can get," I say and jump off my chair and take off towards doors.

"Okay, but stay in the clubhouse," she says and laughs, "I'm going to give Fireball back his key and pocketknife though."

I kick my foot at an imaginary rock, "Okay, fine, but I'm keeping the money and the gum."

I run to a door and knock and daddy answers, so I say "trick or treat" again and hold out this orange bucket with a face. He goes back to his desk and opens it and pulls out a Little Debbie snack cake and puts it in there. "Thank you," I tell him and run to the next door down the hall, but he hurries up and grabs me before the door opens. "What'd ya do that for?"

"Yeah, I think maybe we should wait for Halloween, sweetie. Not every door needs to be opened here," he tells me. I don't know what he means by that, but I tell him okay, anyway.

# CHAPTER NINETEEN
## Benelli

"Hey, Benelli, you got a sec?" Virus asks.

"Yeah, what's up?"

"I can't get very far on adoption without a birth certificate, any way we can go check her house for it?"

"I don't know if Brenna knows her address, or if it was a rental or what, but we can give it a shot."

I call and ask Brenna if she knows her old address. I'm going to guess she lives in Devil's Backbone since that's where the Vengeful Demons are located. She tells me it's a green trailer on what she thinks is Pencil Sharpener Avenue. I have to laugh and try to think like a five-year-old and it dawns on me, "Pennsylvania Avenue?"

"That's what I said, silly."

"Okay honey, can I talk to mommy again?"

When I hear Elle get on the phone, I tell her that Virus and I are going to go find her old house. We'll try to come up with a birth certificate. She wishes me luck.


Virus sets the GPS to the street we are looking for and we head that way. It was pretty easy to pick out the one that was hers. There was only one green trailer on that street. It was a beat-up old place that had to be from the early seventies; the grass was so bare we kicked up dust as we walked. When we knocked and no one answered, we tried the door and, to our surprise, it was unlocked. When we entered, the smell of rotted food and other items came from the sink and overflowing trash can. The livingroom and kitchen were all open together, threadbare olive carpeting covering the floor. We started at opposite ends of the trailer. In the back bedroom where I am, I spot a small file cabinet that's in the doorless closet. I kick away the dirty laundry that's in front of it and try the drawers. Of course, those are locked. I look around for key and remember spotting a key hook in the kitchen. I know it can't be that easy, but before I use my good knife on the thing, I'd try the keys for shits and giggles.


Virus hears me and comes out to the bedroom at his end of the trailer, saying he had no luck and I told him about the file cabinet. We decide to both check it out since there is probably no luck finding the document we need anywhere else. Grabbing the keys off the hook and heading back to the bedroom, he looks through drawers until I can get it popped open.


The first drawer he pulls is stuck on something, so he reaches his hand in there to move it around. Luckily, he did, because it was a loaded gun and with one more pull would have sent off directly towards him. "Brenna's parents were idiots," Virus tells me over his shoulder and shows me the gun. I shake my head in disgust as to the hand they dealt this little girl the first five years of her life. Right there, I vow to make all the rest amazing. This time when he pulled on the drawer, it easily came out, all the way out to the floor with the contents falling everywhere. "Bingo!" he calls out and I look over again after trying the last key I had, to no avail, and pulling out my pocketknife.

"What'd you find?"

"Here, try this," and tosses me a key he found in the hidden part of the dresser. He also found a small stack of papers. "Hey, don't worry about it, I found birth certificates."

I stop what I'm doing and step over to him, "Here's Brenna's," and he hands it over to me. Virus looks puzzled while looking at another birth certificate and then looks at me, "Um, Ben, what was your mom's name again?"

"Barbie, well Barbara Jean Neroni, her maiden name was Mifflington. Why?"

"You might want to take a look at this," he says. He hands me the second birth certificate.

It's birth certificate that I'm assuming belonged to Frodo. The age is about right, being about five years older than me, though I didn't know Frodo's real name. It says it was a male named David Carter; the mother being Barbara Jean Mifflington, and the father was, wait one fucking minute, I know that name, Curtis Carter, that's Chains' actual name. My mom had a kid with Chains?

Frodo was my brother? There is no fucking way that piece of shit was any relation to me. "This stay between you and me, okay? No telling anyone, not even Remington. I need to talk to dad," I say, and we get ready to leave. Something is pulling me back in there. I feel like even though I have what I came here for, my gut tells me to check the locked file cabinet, anyway. I hand the birth records over to Virus and tell him to hang out by the bikes for a minute. It's probably nothing, but I turn the key in the lock and slowly open the first of two drawers.

There are a bunch of file folders and I pull one out that has papers attached to girls' pictures. On the sheet it had information such as town, school, home address, things she did at certain times and on what days, like piano lessons on Wednesday 3:30-4:00. It also had a line that made little sense:

Picked up 9/11/02-Delivered 9/18/02 $2500

I started flipping through more of the sheets in the folder, each having a girl's picture attached. Some had different pick up dates but everything in these folder had delivered: 9/18/02 and a dollar amount. Some were higher, some were lower, but they all said delivered. I close that folder and open up another, same things but different delivery dates. They've been kidnapping and selling girls off for years! The whole top drawer of the file cabinet had separate folders like this, filed by delivery date. I know Frodo wasn't involved in all of these because he would be too young, but why have them? The only thing I can come up with is Chains kept them at his "sons" house for safety. Maybe he thought someone was on to him? I open my phone and call Virus, telling him to come back in here. I can't even pry myself away to go out and tell him, like they would evaporate if I took my eyes off of them.

I show him what I've found, and his reply is, "Man, this is too fucked up. We're going to have to get these to the cops. Also, before you protest, and I know you will say this is our new gig, it's not, not this part of it. We've got a lot on our plates right now and we can't do it all, hunting down these girls that are who knows where now, we can't do it all. Let's the cops handle this one Ben, if we show then that we are on their side, it will go a long way down the line when we need them."

I lower my head knowing he's right. I've got my wedding coming up, a new daughter we are trying to adopt, which is why we were here in the first place. We just bought the woman's home, Elle's mom just moved here and she's setting up her shop. As much as I want to be the hero, I need to pass that torch on to someone else.

"You're right, I know you're right. Do you know anyone on the force we can trust?" I ask. I mean, we aren't on the wrong side of the law, but we handle things our own way and not get them involved. They probably wouldn't be too keen on how we handle things. Case in point, taking out the Vengeful Demons that, according to the news, was blamed on a meth lab explosion.

"Yeah, I've got someone in mind," he says and scrolls down his phone. "Could I speak to detective Cagney?" I look at him puzzled but as soon as the other person answers it all comes clear. "Sara? Hey this is Virus, I mean, Dean." He takes a breath and pauses but I know what's coming and chuckle, "Winchester." He gives me a dirty look. "No, Sam isn't with me, smartass, and yes, I may have caught some demons, Vengeful Demons," he says with a snarl. Apparently, at the name of the outlaw biker club, whoever was on the other end took him seriously. "Yeah, you need to see this in person. Can you meet me at the old, green trailer on Pennsylvania? Yeah, the gangrene colored one," and he laughs, "Okay, I'll see you in ten." He ends the call. "Guess I should have given us time to come up with a reason we were here in the first place, my bad, any brilliant ideas?" He looks at me hopefully.

"Well, I can see your mind was on your dick, asshole. Since we are handing them pretty much everything anyway, I guess I tell them we found Brenna, but not at the silo. When she asks why we are here, let me handle that part," I say as I try to think fast. I know the entire process of adopting her would be easier with the authorities involved. I just hope they don't take her away from me, even if it's temporary.

Not long after, a dodge charger pulls up and out walks an extremely hot detective getting out of the car. I look at my friend and just shake my head and smile at him. She walks up to us and holds out her hand to shake mine, "Detective Cagney."

"Detective, I'm Matteo Neroni, and you know my friend." I shake her hand and I grin and motion towards Virus.

All the professionalism leaves her, and her face brightens, "Dean, if you wanted to see me, all you had to do was call," and winks at him.

"Excuse me, I need to make a call." I step away to one, give them some privacy and two, give Elle and dad a heads up about the possibility of someone coming to check on Brenna before I'm able to get back.

As much as we have grown fond of that little girl and would fight anyone that tries to take her away from us, Elle agrees that it's the right way to go about it. We brainstorm ideas as to how we came across the little girl whose parents are both dead. When I talk to dad, I mention mom's name on what I'm guessing is Frodo's birth certificate, and the phone goes silent. "Dad?" I ask.

"Your mom was right," he finally says on the other end.

"What are you talking about? Are you really telling me Brenna's dad, the man that raped Elle and that we killed, really my half-brother?" I ask, hoping and praying that it's not true.

"It's a really long story, but yes, it's true. I'll tell you what I know when you get home."

"Dad, don't tell Elle anything. I don't know how she would take it knowing I was related to him."

"You have my word, son," and I end the call.

"Excuse me, Mr. Neroni, can I have a word with you?" Sara Cagney asks from where she's still standing with Virus. Luckily, there is no way she heard any of my conversations.

"Yes, of course," I tell her and walk back to the pair.

"I was explaining to her how you had heard about your half-brother and his wife's death and came to check on your niece, Brenna, as soon as you found out. I also told her how you and your future wife took her in. How we came to look for her birth certificate." Virus gives me a quick, knowing look and I am grateful for the info.

"Yeah, that wasn't obvious AT ALL, dude," the detective says and elbows Virus in the gut, "you're lucky you're my friend or I would say you're interfering with the investigation."

"I know my step-brother," the taste of those words bitter on my tongue, "was not a good guy. He was in with a terrible group of men, and we didn't associate with one another. We only came to find the birth certificate when we found the other stuff and Virus, I mean, Dean, immediately called you. I just want to do right by my niece, ma'am. Whatever he was involved in doesn't concern me."

"I appreciate your cooperation. I will have to notify the authorities about the girl," she said, and I nod in understanding. "We will be in touch," she says, and we head towards our bikes and straddle them. Before we are about to start them up, she calls out, "By the way, I was wondering how you knew your brother..."

"Half-brother," I supply.

"Yes, half-brother, how do you know he's dead?"

FUCK! I screwed the pooch on that one. "I saw the news about the explosion and how the Vengeful Demons were there, I just assumed." Before she can ask anything else, I start my Harley and slowly take off back to my home and my girls with Virus right behind me.

When I get home, Elle throws her arms around me, completely frantic. "What are we going to do? They can't take her away from us, can they?"

"I will do everything in my power to make that not happen, baby. If they come, just go with whatever I say." Holding her, I look into her eyes and then bury my face into her hair and whisper, "I'll make this right, I swear."

"I know you will, I trust you," Elle says and releases a deep breath she'd been holding in. "Did you find the birth certificate?"

I run my fingers through my hair, pulling at the fist I had balled up in it, "yeah," and take a long, deep breath. "Yeah, I found the birth certificate."

"What's going on? What's wrong?" Elle questions, knowing me so well.

"Nothing baby, just thinking about how we're going to keep Brenna," I tell her and kiss her on the forehead.

"I know," she rubs her hand across my cheek, "I know it's going to all work out. It has to."

"Listen, I've gotta run and talk to dad and Remington for a bit. Where's my other girl?" I ask.

"She's upstairs playing with her toys in her room," she tells me, and I take the steps two at a time until I reach her open door.

"Hey, baby girl," I say before stepping in, the weight of the world on my shoulders.

"What's wrong, daddy?" she hops up and grabs my hand and looks up at me.

I pick her up and we sit on the edge of the bed. "There may be some people that come and talk to you," I let out and sigh.

"Oh," she says and looks down at the floor, "I've talked to them before. They come and check on me sometimes. Sometimes I have to go live with a stranger for a while. I don't want to leave you and mommy." Tears well up in those big, beautiful blue eyes, and I tear up too.

"I'm going to try my hardest not to let them, Pumpkin. Really, really hard. They may ask how I found you and took you, and that's going to start a whole lot of questions. They'll want to know who took you, how I knew you were there. I, I just don't know what to do or say," I tell her honestly.

"You shouldn't be in trouble for saving all of us. You are a hero for that. They can't take me away because you're a hero?" it's more of a question she asks than a statement.

"I'm not a hero baby, I just did what was right," I tell her and hug her like it's the last time I will get to. "Daddy has to go talk to Uncle Remi and Papa. I just wanted to see you before I left," I tell her.

I know it's not manly, but it's all I can do to keep the tears away on my way to dad's. I can't lose her. Her short little life has been nothing but a shit show, and I'm trying to figure out how to make it stop. I get to my dad's house and my brother is already there. I walk in and I can see through the sliding glass door they are out back on the deck. As I'm walking through the house towards the door, Michelle stops me and places her hand on my upper arm. "It's all going to work out." She lays her head against me, near her hand.

I place my hand on top of hers and let out a sorrowful breath, "I really hope so."

When I slide open the door, they both stand and look at me. "What the fuck is going on? Dad is acting like someone shot his dog and now, the look on your face, what is it?" Remington asks.

"Boys, have a seat," dad says and takes his spot on one of the wicker lawn chairs. Once we are seated, he pulls out a pint of Fireball from his cut and hands it to Remington. He then leans forward and clasps his hands together. "A long time ago, back before I met your mother, she was with Curtis Carter." I see Remington's fists clench. He then takes off the lid of the bottle, taking a healthy swig before passing it to me.

"Chains, OUR mom was with Chains? You're fucking kidding me, right?" Remington stands and starts yelling, which is understandable since he has no clue what has taken place today.

"Son, I know this is a lot to take in, but let me get this all out. Take a seat," dad says and motions to the chair and Remington, though steaming mad, sits back down.

"As I was saying, before your mother and I met, she was dating Chains. There wasn't a Vengeful Demons back then. They were in high school. Well, she was. Curtis had quit school and was working at a garage. Your mom got pregnant and had a son. She named him David and gave him his last name of Carter, assuming they would stay together. They were living together, and your mom started noticing Curtis... Chains, acting different. He was hiding things, drinking more, doing drugs, gambling. He got into some shady shit from what she told me. Some thugs came and beat the shit out of Chains, damn near killed him, and knocked your mom around. They took David and said if Chains didn't pay them, they'd kill the kid. He couldn't come up with the money and they told him that their child was dead. Your mom, believing her son was murdered, left Devil's Backbone and Curtis, as she knew him, and never looked back. Chains had started the VD right after your mom left him, but it was a bad club from the start."

He reached for the bottle, took a swig, and continued. "I met her a few years later when I got out of the military, and we all started the Unfortunate Souls. As soon as we were married, you kids came along, and I knew nothing about her previous life. It wasn't until we almost lost you, Remington, in that motorcycle accident. That's when she told me about David and losing him."

Remington and I both look at each other, trying to take in all the information we just received from our father. It's a lot to take in and I get mom thought her son, our brother, was dead. My question is, though, how did he end up in the Vengeful Demons and back with Chains? Did Chains raise him? Did he even know Chains was his dad? "Dad, you said on the phone mom was right when I told you about the birth certificate. What did that mean?"

"The night you mother died in that wreck, we fought. She had been acting sketchy for weeks. She was constantly on that damn phone texting someone. I assumed she was cheating on me. She had been drinking rum a lot more than usual. It was her favorite. That's how she got her club name Malibu Barbie," dad looks at his calloused hands, rubbing them together as if he was trying to get something off of them. "I confronted her, accused her of cheating. We were fighting. She was drunk, and I didn't want to hear her excuses, and I wasn't about to tolerate her going to see some other man.

She screamed at me and shoved me. I tried to grab her to keep her here, she pushed me away yelling, 'He's alive,' and got away, jumping in the car, and then left. That was it. She had a car wreck and never came back. I didn't know what she meant by it. It's not like I could fucking ask her about it," he takes another swig. "She was dead, and I had you boys to take care of. Hell, I thought I was better off all these years," he says, then throws the bottle. It shattering against the side of the garage.

"You didn't know, dad, none of us did," I say and grab him and pull him towards me. Remington came in a slapped us both firmly on our backs three times and then and puts his forehead into ours.

# CHAPTER TWENTY

## Benelli

Well, just like clockwork, DCFS showed up at the house for Brenna. "We understand that you have Brenna Mifflinton in your care?" states the caseworker.

"Yes, she's in the kitchen with Elle," and I extend my arm in the kitchen's direction for her to follow me. Elle, this is Brenna's caseworker."

Brenna, who is covered with flour from helping her make homemade dumplings, hops off of her stool and hides behind Elle.

"Brenna, I was wondering if we could talk," the woman with wiry hair in disarray asks.

"NO! I know who you are and I'm not leaving! They are nice and they love me, and I even get a Noni and a Papa here! Do you know what that means? Do you? That means they love me even more and I... AM... NOT... GOING!" Brenna screams with her hands on her hips and stomps her foot.

"Brenna, that's not very nice. What do you say?" I say to her.

"I'm supposed to say I'm sorry," she says softer, "but I'm not sorry. I love you and I don't want her to take me away."

The case worker touches my arm. "Can I have a word with you for a moment?"

"Yes, of course," I say, and we walk to the other room.

"I appreciate the fact that you took her from that situation, we had problems with her parents when they were alive, but that's not how the system works, she needs to be with approved guardians, I'm afraid..." she states but I stop her right there.

"I'm afraid that she is in a stable home, more stable than she has ever known her whole life, more love than she's ever had, and I'm afraid she's staying here, and we are going to work towards adopting her," I tell her as fact, because it is. They will have to kill me before she goes to another home that only has her for the paycheck. I know that not all homes are like that, but so far, that has been where she has been placed.

"Sir, I can see that she is in excellent hands, I understand, but she needs to be put with a foster family while we look to see if she has any relatives that will take her in," she says.

"Ma'am, did the officer not tell you? I am her family, her only family, and she's staying here," I tell her matter-of-factly.

238

"Do you have proof of that fact?" she says in a snobby attitude, as if I'm lying.

"Yes," and I walk over to my home office and produce not only her birth certificate, but mine and Frodo's and I hand them to her, "As you can see, her father and I have the same mother, my mother has passed and therefore, I am the closest relative to Brenna, and we are more than happy to adopt her and raise her."

She is busy writing notes down and after scribbling on her legal pad for a good three minutes, she looks up and asks, "You mentioned we, is the woman with her in the kitchen your wife? What is her name?" I tell her Elle's name and that we are engaged and getting married January 1st. The woman looks back down at her notes and continues to scribble. "I want to look around and I would like to supervise her for thirty minutes or so. Is that fine with you?"

"Brenna, would you come with me so we can show her your room and stuff?" I call out to her.

"Okay daddy," and I normally always love hearing it, but I cringe and tense my shoulders, not wanting to look at the woman following us.

Brenna takes my hand, and we walk upstairs to her room. "Look. See. I have my own room now, and toys. Look at this bed! And over here..." she opens her closet, "see, clean clothes, all new." The woman nods. She continues to write things down. "Do you see this guy? I want him to be my daddy. I picked him and I picked my new mommy too, and she's downstairs cooking us actual food, like REAL

food, and she lets me help. Do you know what they did
when they found out all I ate was cereal out of the box?
They cooked me EVERYTHING! Just so I could try it! I have
not been hungry one time since they found me, not one
time. I've never been dirty and stinky, well unless we
played in the mud, but then I got to have a bubble bath
and I smelled pretty after. They tuck me into bed at night
and read me stories. I don't have to worry. Someone isn't
going to come in and hurt me. You see lady, I've never had
this, not EVER! I love them and they are going to be my
new mommy and daddy. That's all I've got to say about
that."

I wipe the tears that were stinging my eyes only to see
that Elle had come in. Both she and the social worker were
crying. I walk over to Brenna and pick her up into my arms
and kiss her on the cheek, "You're not going anywhere,
angel, okay?" and I look over to the social worker and as
she's wiping her eyes with a Kleenex she dug out of her
purse she emphatically nods that Brenna will stay with us.

As the woman is heading out the door to leave, Brenna
hops down the stairs. I forgot to show her my Halloween
costume! "NOOOO! Brenna, I mean, sweetie, she's super
busy and maybe you can show her some other time," I
say, thinking to myself, if they see that five-year-old's
costume, she may reconsider her decision. I know my dad
and Elle's mom tried to talk her into something else, but it
is disgusting!

The day has finally come for her to go trick or treating. We
started with all the club member houses that are built here
at the club. I know it's gross, but apparently, it's too gross
for Elle because she's in the bathroom losing her cookies.
Elle stays behind at the house, hating to miss her first
Halloween, but apparently, she's caught a bug. Brenna and

I walk down the sidewalk, and I look back at the house. I know she was looking forward to going. She can't make it out of the bathroom long enough. As we walk along, we come across some preteen boys. "Oh man, that is the coolest costume ever, dude."

She didn't pick out your standard princess, bunny or any other five-year-old girl, ready-made costume. No, she got all the makeup and fake latex shit to go with it. She's dressed like a zombie, but one eye is closed and covered with latex and has a fake eye dangling from her head. She has a rope around her neck and make up "bruising" around it, That's just for starters! It's a good thing Zen was in drama back in the day. She knew how to apply all this stuff because I had no clue. Did I mention the gremlin looking thing attached to her looking like it's eating her intestines that are hanging out of her body? Yeah, that's why I'm out alone taking her trick-or-treating without Elle, but I have to say, she's raking in the candy. I, luckily, brought along a big bag that I stuffed in my pocket because she's had to empty the pumpkin out 4 times.

We are finishing up trick or treating when we spot Lucky, and he gives her a high five and some other secret handshakes they have created with each other. He walks with us and continues back to our house. She dumps all the candy all over the table. She's going to have candy from now until next Valentine's Day, if not longer. "Your idea was really cool, Uncle Lucky. I scared bunches of people!"

"What are you talking about, Brenna?" Elle asks her, cocking her head to the side.

"Well, I think it's time for me to go. I'll see you guys later," Lucky calls out, rushing to the door, his hand already on the knob turning it.

"I saw Lucky at the Halloween store and he just handed me all the makeup and eyeball and stuff and told me to give it to Noni and Papa," she says as she looks towards the door and just as I yell his name and look back to where he was the door is shut and he's gone. That fucker.

## Elle

The days have gotten shorter, and the nights are even colder. Our new little family has settled into a routine. We've enrolled Brenna into kindergarten. While she was behind at first, she is quickly catching up with the other kids. I pick up mom on the way each morning and we drop her off at school on my way to the studio and mom's gallery that only has the coffee shop between us. I love having her back in the same town. Even more so, our shops being so close. She sells some of my photographs alongside her sculptures and paintings, and we meet in the middle for coffee and a sandwich at lunch. Jamie and Jaclyn know our orders by heart.

Tank and Flo walk in, and I wave them over to our table. "You're back from your trip!" I say, "tell us all about it."

Mom looks up, jumps out of her seat, and slams her arms around Flo, "IZZY!!!" she shouts.

"Chelle Belle! I can't believe it. It's you! I did not know Elle was your kid! You should have called me! I've been trying to find you all these years!" Flo says excitedly.

"Your Aunt Izzy?" I question and give her a big hug, "I've heard so many stories about you and never knew you were the same person."

"So, you ended up with the club," mom says and pulls out chairs for them to sit.

"Yeah, I should have stuck with this one the first time he asked me out," Flo says, and gently pokes the lovable biker.

"Damn right, you should have," and he gets up and gives her a quick kiss, "I'm going to go get our coffee. You ladies need anything?"

"No, thanks Tank, we're good," I tell him, and he walks over to the counter next to another customer.

"Well shit, this must be reunion day. Craig? Craig Edwards, son of a bitch, how are ya?" Tank booms out and places his hand on the man's shoulders.

"Sam, what are you doing around here?" Craig asks, shaking Tank's hand.

"Me and the ol' lady just got back into town. What are you doing here?" Tank asks and picks up the freshly brewed coffee concoctions, motions over to our table, and leads the two men this way.

"In the area visiting my brother, he's going to meet me here and we're going to check out the art gallery next door," Craig says.

"Well, it's not open until I get back over there," mom says with a laugh and introduces herself.

I keep looking at this man and I can't help it. I'm staring. "I feel like I know you from somewhere," I say.

"Craig's been in the movie business, our hometown star," Tank says.

"Well, I don't know about that, but I've had some small parts," Craig says shyly, trying not to be boastful. I can tell that's how he is. He has kindness and a fun-loving look about him.

"Come on now, Craig, who else can say they've been in American Gothic, Matlock, and other stuff," Tank grabs Craig's shoulder, giving it a gentle shake.

"Oh my God, I know where I know you from!!! Empire Records, Rex Manning fan, I just watched that the other day!" I say, probably too enthusiastically.

"Guilty, as charged," Craig replies. "I also worked on the set of Dawson's Creek and enough TV movies to fill a cable channel," he says, chuckling.

"Shut up!" I say, "You know them? I seriously had the biggest crush on Pacey."

"I do," he says but the door chimes and in walks someone, "I'd fill you in but that's my brother. Do you know about how much longer before the gallery opens? I don't want to rush you."

"Oh, no problem. I'll head over there now. Izzy, we are catching up tonight!" mom says, pointing at Flo.

"I'll bring the Boonesfarm," Izzy says, laughing her ass off.

"If that doesn't bring back some memories!" mom laughs too and tells us all goodbye before heading next door.

"I just can't believe all this time you were Aunt Izzy," I say, shaking my head and give her and Tank hugs before heading to my shop.

I do a few photo shoots, and some editing before Zen shows up to do some wedding planning. There is little time to do it all. I've already got my dress and I have a fitting scheduled for after Thanksgiving. Pretty much everything is set. We're just at the Michael's picking out flowers now. Figuring silk would be easy enough and we can do them early, not worrying about the real ones wilting. We're crafty bitches, we've got this. After filling two carts full of flowers and decorations, bouquet stems, floral tape, wire cutters, we head back to my house.

"What in the hell?" Benelli takes in the giant piles all over the living room floor.

"It's probably best if you go have a boys' night." I look up at him from my position on the floor, "this might take a while."

Benelli is shaking his head and goes to answer the doorbell, "there's more of you?" he says as he lets in mom, Izzy, Sheila, and Kitty all holding either wine, pizza, or dessert.

Before he can shut the door, in walks Lyric with a glue gun and a bag of glue sticks. "I'm locked and loaded, ladies!"

"Okay, that's my cue. Do you want me to take Brenna with me?" Benelli asks, kissing me on top of the head.

"No, she'll be fine, we promise not to get too wild, she just got to sleep and if she wakes up, we will put her to work," I laugh, "go have fun," and I swat his butt as he passes after stealing a piece of pizza for the road.

The night is a blast. Mom and Izzy sharing crazy stories and catching up, planning Thanksgiving at the clubhouse. More wine. I think there is more laughter than flower arranging. I wouldn't trade it for the world. These are memories in the making. We're all getting slap happy when Benelli walks through the door. "You ladies are still at it?"

"What time is it?" I ask.

"It's one o'clock in the morning," he says, looking at the time on his cell.

"No freaking way!" Lyric says. "I've got to get out of here. I have finals coming up soon and I need to hit the books all day tomorrow, well, today."

"None of you are driving, I have Fireball, Remi and dad all out in the driveway waiting to escort you ladies home," Benelli states.

"Now I know I won't get any studying done," Lyric states, but none of us know what she means and before we can ask, she's out the door.

The door closes as the last of the wedding mafia leave and Benelli struts towards me all sexy, "and now that they're gone..." he says and whisks me up into his arms and carries me to our bedroom. I was getting drowsy right before the girls left. Somehow, I am recharged and ready to go. Funny how some great cock will do that to ya.

# CHAPTER TWENTY-ONE

# **Elle**

I wake up late the next morning after flower making and lovemaking, and I am utterly miserable. My head is stopped up and I'm congested. Benelli tells me good morning, and all I can do is groan.

"Long night of drinking there, princess?" he raises an eyebrow and asks.

"I feel like dog shit!" I say and sound as if I'm holding my nose while talking.

"Oh crap, babe, you sound like shit! I'm going to make you some hot tea and call doc Karen," he hurries out the bedroom door, pulling his phone out of his pocket as he goes. He doesn't even give me time to protest and say I'll be fine.

In no time at all, he's back upstairs with my tall coffee mug. It says, "Witch better have my coffee" on it with a picture of a witch on a broom. It's full to the brim with hot tea and a jar of honey with a spoon. I hold the steaming mug up to my face and the steam of the warm liquid feels good on my face. I take a drink and wonder how he made it so fast, but then it hits me. He microwaved the sweet tea out of the fridge. He gets a big heaping tablespoon of honey and I look at him like he's lost his mind. The tea is already sweet. "Open up," he says, and I do, but it's more like my mouth dropping open wondering what he's doing and he does it. He shoves that spoon right in my mouth.

I make a face and swallow it down with a chaser of the hot tea, "what was that for?"

"Doesn't honey help when you're sick?" he asks, now worried he's done something wrong. He runs to the bathroom and wets a washcloth and brings it back, putting it on my forehead, "Doc Karen is on her way."

I adjust the cloth so it's not covering my eyes and stop him. "Slow your roll cowboy, I'm not dying. Well yet, I'm allergic to honey." The horrified look on his face. Man, I felt so bad for doing that. "I'm just joking, Benelli, you need to calm down, here take a seat," and I pat the bed.

"Woman! I'm gonna kill you! Don't do that shit to me!" With his one hand over his heart and the other covering my entire face. Then he gets serious. "You are hotter than a firecracker! Where's the thermometer?"

"Middle shelf of the medicine cabinet," there is no use fighting him on this.

He comes back and turns it on and shoves the dang thing in my mouth. I'm trying to talk and he's hushing me, holding it in place. "102.1! That's bad, right?"

"Really? It's that high?" I mean, I knew I felt bad, but geez, that's pretty high. When he looks at me like I'm a dead man walking, I ask, "Have you never been around anyone sick before?"

"No, not really. Remington and I haven't been sick since we were kids," he says.

"Lucky you," I grumble, all moody now. Even living in Arizona, I think I've gotten sick almost every winter. Freaking sinuses! Come to think of it, it usually hits when I go up north to visit my Uncle Josh for the holidays.

A few minutes later, the doorbell rings, and Benelli has led Karen up the stairs. As soon as she walks in the room, she takes one look at me, "Yep, you're sick." Benelli looks at her aggravated, but I accidentally snort a laugh which sounds horrendous with a stuffed-up nose, and then I start the coughing fit.

She checks me out and sure enough, it's a sinus infection moving swiftly towards bronchitis. Apparently, all the puking I've been doing has been mucous attractive, I know. She gives Benelli a list of the OTC meds I need and a script for antibiotics. "But I don't have time to be sick!!! Next week is Thanksgiving and I have Christmas shopping, a dress fitting, photo shoots, the list goes on for MILES!"

"Well, now you don't," Benelli says flatly. "I'll cover Thanksgiving dinner," I snort again and start coughing, "Okay, so your mom does the dinner. I'll get your new assistant to reschedule the shoots. Zen can reschedule the dress appointment, I will do the Christmas shopping, and don't give me that look Missy. I can shop and do lots of things, I run a motorcycle club and a lot of businesses."

"Okay, okay, I will just lie here in bed and do nothing but sleep," I say, throwing my hands up.

"Resting and recovering," Karen says, and when she sees my glare is at her this time, she clasps her bag closed and turns, "and with that, I'm off. I mean it though, rest girlie!"

I realize Benelli is definitely a keeper. He's taken care of me, his work, cooking and cleaning, taking care of a worried Brenna. Who once she realized that her mom's sick and my sick will NEVER be the same, was fine. I am feeling better and trying to get up and do things, but I get shooed back into bed. "But babe, it's a woman cold, not a man cold," I try to protest, but I guess since the ass never gets sick, he's not buying it. I mean, I milked it for a couple days but come on!

By Thanksgiving morning, I'm feeling like a million bucks and ready to cook. I shower, dress and head downstairs and walk straight to Grandma Neroni's apron that Ruger was sweet enough to gift me along with a shoebox of her handwritten recipes. I guess Sheila and Pistol didn't want it, but Ruger said I was the first woman in the family worthy of the honor. As I'm sliding it over my head, Benelli starts to protest, but I point my finger at him, give him a death glare and then wiggle my finger no. He throws his hands up in surrender and grumbles something about acting just like his grandma, grabs Brenna and hustles out of the kitchen.

I click open my phone to Pandora and put on hits from the 50s and 60s. Nothing like a little do-wop to get you moving in the kitchen. Brenna has sneaked back in and I'm twirling her around the kitchen. Once her little hands are clean, I have her help me make sage dressing and let her mush the bread, eggs, and other ingredients all up together. Mom gave me a list of who's making what and how many we are expecting yesterday when she stopped by. I made the dressing. I'll do the mashed potatoes there. The turkey and pies are covered along with all the other essential Thanksgiving stuff, so I also make a "better than sex cake." Yeah right, I think and luckily, I stop myself before calling it that in front of the girl child.

Telling her it's a "better than playing in mud cake" so she is expecting it to be the best thing she's ever ate. I flip through some recipes in the box and decide what the hell and make Grandma Neroni's lasagna, even down to the homemade lasagna noodles. When I say that Benelli kicked butt at doing all the chores, I wasn't kidding. He bought enough groceries to last a good month and a half. As soon as the oven door opened for me to take it out, Benelli comes into the kitchen with Remington, their noses leading the way.

"That smells just like Grandma's lasagna. Please tell me that's Grandma's lasagna!" Remington walks behind me, planting his head on my shoulder.

"Hey bro, get off my woman. Go find your own," Benelli tells him. He takes the enormously heavy pan from me and sits it on the giant island with the other goodies.

"If she cooks as well as Granny, I'm stealing her away," he says and gives me a peck on the cheek and winks.

"Wow, Rem, I've never seen you this happy," I tell him.

"It's my favorite holiday and now with my favorite food, what's not to be happy about?"

"It's one of my favorites too," I admit.

"Okay, quit sucking up to my wife and let's get this stuff loaded," Benelli tells him and shoves some potholders into his chest.

"She's not your wife yet there brother, there's still time," Remington says and winks again at me and Benelli pushes his booted foot into his brother's butt.

While Remington is outside loading the SUV, I grab my man from behind and squeeze, "You're still my favorite Neroni, baby."

"I better be," and he whips me to the front of him and dips me and plants a big kiss on me.

"Oh Benelli, you make me swoon," I laugh and put the back of my hand to my forehead and pretend to faint. He lifts me back to a standing position and I add, "But seriously, what's up with your brother? I have never seen him so, so, I don't know, happy and social."

Benelli laughs, "He's social," I raise my eyebrow at him, "Okay, he's sort of social. What can I say? He's a different person from Thanksgiving to Christmas."

"Well, I like it. Now we know what kind of time frame we have to find him a woman that's going to knock his socks off."

"I wouldn't go that far. He hasn't even been visiting Goldie, Breezy or Jinx lately," and he realizes his mistake as soon as it came out of his mouth. "Now baby, do not look at me like that, you know I haven't either. In fact, they haven't been seeing much action from anyone lately except for maybe Lucky."

"I get it. Single, desirable men and club girls, but damn, the part I just don't get is why a girl would just decide to be that. Don't they want, I don't know, more?"

"Yeah, I mean, some girls do, but some don't. Some just like the thrill. To be devoted to a small group of men and not out getting it from random strangers. They know who they are with and stay faithful to the club."

"I never really thought of it like that."

"I thought we were loading the car, not having a deep discussion about the life of club girls," Remington says. "Come on you guys, I'm ready to get my grub on and I've already got Brenna buckled in."

"I thought it was a little too quiet in here," Benelli says and picks up the now covered lasagna, careful not to smash the foil onto the gooey cheese."

When we get to the clubhouse, Fireball, Scott, MacGyver and Toxey all shuffle out and have everything unloaded before we are out of the car. Now this is service.

As soon as we walk in, we're greeted by my Uncle Josh, my Aunt Cathy, and their families. Josh and Cathy are my mom's older brother and sister. "Oh, my God! I didn't know you guys were coming to us this year!" I exclaim, giving enormous hugs to one and all.

"We had to come see for ourselves what made both the Burrow women pack up and leave Arizona," Aunt Cathy says.

We spend the entire rest of the day stuffing our faces with the giant smorgasbord, catching up with family and friends. Aunt Cathy sees me with Benelli and Brenna. Yes, she kept catching mom and Ruger constantly looking at each other. She leans over to me, "now I can see why," and just smiles from ear to ear. "It's about time... for both of you. You've both made a glorious life here and these people are amazing."

I look at her, a little puzzled. How does she already know they are amazing? I mean they are, but? "I've been here visiting since Tuesday," she says, like she's reading my mind.

"And why am I just hearing about this?" I ask.

"Because I didn't want your funk," she cackles. Yep, that's my Aunt Cathy.

The guys, mostly, are all spread out in front of the enormous television, getting ready to watch the game. I bring over a bottle of beer for Benelli just as a news segment comes on:

Several missing females from the Tri-state area are giving thanks today due to local detective Sara Cagney. Detective Cagney discovered files from a home of a deceased man who we now know to be in the Vengeful Demons Motorcycle gang. You will probably remember our story of the meth lab explosion on an abandoned farm containing the remains of many, if not all, of the illegal group. Also, found at the scene was crime boss, Zhang Xui Ying. We now believe had connections to the club involving trafficking, not drugs, as originally thought. Detective Cagney refused an interview and states that she was glad to see the females were home. The investigation is ongoing. We leave you back to your regularly scheduled pre-game programming.

Everyone was silent during the whole broadcast. Many had filtered into the room to hear it. Everyone looked at one another. Some of the men letting out a deep breath that as far as the media and police were concerned, they still thought the Unfortunate Souls are not involved. The women began exiting the room (except for the die-hard females) and as I am about to leave, Benelli pulls me down to his lap and kisses me. He whispers in my ear all the wicked things he's going to do to me tonight and my cheeks flame.

I look around to see if anyone heard. Luckily, everyone is too engrossed in the game to notice us. That is except Lucky, who puts the lip of his beer to his mouth, licks his tongue around the edge and then flicks it across the top before sticking it inside. I lean over to slap his chest and fall off of Benelli's lap into the floor when I pull Benelli down with me. Lucky, who was about to die laughing but can't because he got his tongue stuck in the bottle.

I laugh, Benelli laughs. We are gaining the attention of everyone when Lucky is struggling to release his tongue. He jumps up and is running around trying to pull it off but can't because he's too freaked out and won't calm down. Mom and Aunt Cathy come to the rescue and lead poor Lucky to the kitchen and away from the laughter. I decide to follow behind; I have to see how they are going to fix this.

They have him settled in a chair, away from prying eyes, except mine, of course. I'm hiding off to the side. Mom gets in front of him and stares into his eyes. "Okay Lucky, calm down. It's going to be okay, I promise," she almost coos in the calmest of motherly voices. Lucky takes a slow, deep breath and lets it out. "Good, you're doing good," another slow breath and she nods to Aunt Cathy.

Lucky turns his eyes to her. She picks up a bottle of olive oil and drizzles it down her fingers. Slowly, it drips from her fingertips down to the top of his tongue, using her fingers to coat it. She puts her hand on his neck and pushes his head downward so that the oil runs down his tongue and into the edge of the bottle. Lucky gulps, because let's be honest, if it wasn't for it being my aunt, this would seem sexier than a rescue effort. My aunt is 51, but she owns it and rocks it. My aunt leans over and whispers something into Lucky's ear. His eyes go wide, and he chokes. Mom yanks the bottle and there is a loud pop from its release.

Lucky is now free and hugs my mother and kisses Cathy straight on the mouth. No tongue, of course, and heads out of the kitchen. I have to know; I just have to. I catch up to Lucky and bump his body with mine, "Soooo, what did my aunt say to you?"

He looks over his shoulder where they still are, then back to me and leans down towards me, "she said, what else does that thing do?"

My hand flies up to my open mouth and I turn to look back at the kitchen, where my aunt is standing in the doorway. And winks at me and shrugs her shoulders. "It worked, didn't it?"

Brenna stays the night with her Noni, so we are pretty stoked about a kid free night. We decide to take his bike that he had at the clubhouse and go for a ride. I wrap my arms tightly around him and slide up close. It's been a weird season. Most days, we don't even need a jacket, which Benelli tells me isn't normal this time of year. Being from Arizona, I didn't know what to expect here. "Let's ride down by the river," Benelli says over his shoulder.

"Good thinking," I say, and place my palm on the now growing bulge in his jeans. We barely made it to the deserted boat dock. He pulled over and parked, far enough off that no one can see us. We took the blanket he kept wrapped and tied to the bike and spread it out on the wooden dock over the water. It moving as we did. We feasted on each other and relished this alone time. We stayed there making love and then staring up at the bright moon and stars. You could even see Mars from where we lay. Once the chill of the night started filling the air, we packed up and continue this night at home. He swung back by the clubhouse so I could follow him into the SUV, where

I had stashed the bottle of redi-whip and desserts. We continued to have fun half the night.

# CHAPTER TWENTY-TWO

## **Benelli**

That woman has me up at 4am in the damn morning, after I sexed her up good and proper too! We are out the door by 4:30am and standing in line at a store by 5am. What is this lunacy? She calls it Black Friday shopping and I call it my own personal hell. Now, I realize why Michelle volunteered so easily to keep Brenna all night. I know she's not and I'll regret thinking about it later, but right now, the only thing in my head is, "THAT BITCH!" I could have just had my little one at home. Both of us still asleep and the two of them out in this hysteria.

No, I'm here because it's some sort of tradition or rite of passage or some shit. I beg, I plead, while I push this damn cart as she whizzes all around chucking stuff into it. I try to tell her I will buy it all at full price if she gets me out of here. I pledge her all the tongue lashing she can handle. Hell, I guarantee her a new car AND a honeymoon in Europe if she lets me leave. Nope, not happening, ugh. We weave from store to store until I'm becoming a completely grumpy asshole and then it is magically lunchtime, and it's over. I survived. We can't fit one more thing in the SUV, and I plop down in the booth at the club's mom and pop restaurant like I've been wounded in a war. I lay my head on the table and groan. The waitress comes to the table and asks what we want to drink, and I don't even lift my head. I tilt it to the side and say, "Coffee, make it a double."

While my head is turned to the side, I notice the other men in there looking as pitiful as me. Elle pats my head and tells me, laughing, "But Baby, you were such a good sport today."

"Grrrrrr," is all that comes out of me. The waitress is back and sets down my coffee and Elle's sweet tea and I sit up to guzzle it. By the time the girl comes back to take our order, I'm ready for a refill. Sip by delicious sip, I come back to life. "You know, I thought football players were tough. I have to hand it to you ladies, you can fake, spin and make a touchdown better than any running back in the NFL."

She blows on her fingers and brushes them across her. "Yeah, I'm a seasoned pro at this. But look at all the money we saved. By the way, other than your present, I'm done shopping for Christmas."

"Really? Like done, done?"

"Yeah, I think so. I mean, I will double check my list when we are wrapping them up, but yep, I think we are done."

"Please tell me when you say 'we', you mean you and your mom, right? The new car is still on the table, just throwing that out there."

"The car I have is fine. Say you throw New Orleans in for a honeymoon, and we move the date up a day to the 30th?

We are in New Orleans watching the fireworks on our honeymoon. You have a deal."

I shake that woman's hand faster than she can blink an eye, "Deal!"

"Awesome! Since the club owns the catering and the hall and we have all the decorations, it won't be a big deal to move it up a day. I don't have that many people coming from out of town and I'm certain it won't be a problem, right?"

Ah hell, I can see her second guessing herself. I better jump in quick, "We can get everything switched, and it actually works out better because we turned a business down that wanted it for New Year's Eve. I'm sure the caterers were scrambling, trying to do the wedding and all the parties going on. This works out great babe!"

She takes a deep breath and relaxes her shoulders, "You're right, this is going to work out even better. Can you make all the travel arrangements for the honeymoon?"

I pick up her hand in mine and give it a kiss. "I've got this, babe, don't worry. Our honeymoon is going to be unforgettable."

After lunch, we get home and unload all the presents down into the basement, hiding the stuff she got for her mom and Zen. She's going to get them over here to help wrap and work on the wedding stuff. I talk her into waiting until tomorrow to put up the tree. Thank God! I kind of lied and told her they had Black Friday deals on travel too, so I needed to spend the rest of the day planning that. Hell, I don't know if that's true, but it got me out of more manual labor.

There we have an extra tall ceiling in our log cabin home and French doors in the back. We picked an extra-large tree when we took Brenna to the Christmas tree farm. We decided to make Christmas extra special for Brenna and went all out. The tree farm had hot cocoa and even horse-drawn carriage rides. She had an absolute blast! We invited our family and close friends over for dinner and decorating after. I was going to need help to get that puppy in the house and stood up. I don't know who was more excited about it, Brenna, or Remington.

We always celebrated Christmas at the clubhouse, but we haven't made as much fuss about it since mom died. Uncle Winchester always dressed up as Santa for the kids and passed out presents. We spent Christmas day at their house with Pistol home from school, but as for our own homes, it was nothing as grand as this. We put the tree close to the stairs so it would be easier to decorate, well part of it at least. She could put the star on with a little help.

The girls spent an entire weekend baking up at least a dozen different cookies. Hundreds and hundreds of them, some sugar cookies in shapes and decorated, some of your standard chocolate chip, you name it; they had it. I swear I was going to have to get bigger clothes if they kept this up. I think Elle ate a few too many herself because she ended up in the bathroom, losing those cookies.

The club spent several days delivering gift boxes of the sweet treats all over town. While we were at it, we gave out the Christmas bonuses to all our employees. Luckily, it was unseasonably warm, so we were all on our bikes with the prospects following us with all the stuff. I've been riding every single chance I get, only taking the SUV when we are doing family things.

Elle has gotten sick a few more times over the last several days. I stop by Lipe Family Practice with the cookies, I pull Karen off to the side. "Hey, would you mind checking on Elle? I think she has that damn bug again."

"Sure, no problem, I'll swing by after we close up today."

"Thanks, I really appreciate it. I'm hoping maybe she's just overdoing it trying to make Brenna's first Christmas with us extra special. She's gotten sick a few times and she seems more run down the last couple days."

"That's probably all it is. I wouldn't worry."

"Thanks doc, have a Merry Christmas if I don't see you tonight. We'll see you at the wedding on the 30th though, right?"

"I wouldn't miss it for the world. You have a Merry Christmas too, Benelli."

I was still in my office getting ahead on paperwork, so I missed Doc Karen's house call. When I got home, I asked Elle how it went.

"Oh, it went fine. She gave me some vitamins since I've been so run down. I'm going to swing by the office tomorrow for blood work. Stop making that face Benelli, it's nothing, normal people that actually go to the doctor get blood work all the time."


Okay, maybe I was making a face and overreacting. I need to chill out. I pull a beer out of the fridge and ask if she wants one. She says she's good and I decide since it's a beautiful day, I'll grill our supper.


Christmas Eve went pretty spectacularly at the Neroni household tonight. Elle and Brenna set out cookies and milk for Santa. Brenna said that explained a lot when we told her what it was for. Sometimes I question that she's only five. I did, however, see her birth certificate and can vouch her birthday is April 16th and she is, in fact, five.


Remington, dad, and Michelle came over and spent the night, not wanting to miss the look on her face in the morning. That worked out great because we really needed the help of putting toys together before morning. Elle and I were tucking her into bed and trying to convince the excited girl to go to sleep. We convinced Remington to get on the roof and make sounds like a sleigh landing, and he even used his phone for "reindeer" sounds. That convinced her to shut her eyes and at least act asleep. Just to be safe, and good thing we did, we had Tank come over dressed as Santa and when she sneaked downstairs and was caught by Old St. Nick eating the cookies, she ran back to bed and didn't come back out till morning.


She ran to our room and jumped in the middle of the bed, luckily missing some important parts but still getting a knee really, really close. "Is it time? Is it time? Can we go downstairs now?"

"Ugh, it's like," I roll over and look at my phone on the nightstand, "Brenna, it's 6:00 in the morning. Can't you sleep just a little longer?"

Elle sits straight up in bed. I don't know which of my girls is the most excited this morning. "Come on baby, wakey, wakey." They both jump out of bed and are pushing me to get up.

"Okay, I'm coming." They both got more sleep than me last night. We may have gone a little overboard on the presents. We will probably regret that for every future Christmas, but we will deal with that next year.

We get downstairs and bless that future mother-in-law of mine. She has made coffee and I believe I smell cinnamon rolls. She is handing us cups as soon as we hit the bottom step. Dad and Remington have their phones ready and record her face as soon as she sees her jackpot. Brenna's mouth drops open and she's stopped in her tracks. Her smile is gigantic and there's a few tears leaking out of those baby blues. "Is this for me?" she asks, slowly walking to a giant doll house, reaching out her hand ever so slowly to touch it.

"That is for you sweetheart, Santa brought you that," Elle tells her.

"I saw him last night. I know I wasn't supposed to peak, but I saw him eating the cookies," Brenna says.

"What? You peaked? I don't know about letting you open the other stuff," I say teasingly.

"Pretty please, with sugar on top, I promise to never, ever peak again," she pleads with her little hands clasped.

"Well, if you promise," I say, handing her a couple of wrapped boxes. She opens each one so slowly that Remington plops down on the floor with her and takes it out of her hand and rips the paper off.

"Uncle Remi, you need to calm down," she says, and we all bust up laughing. She is so sweet and grateful. She thanks whoever got her what and gets excited about each and every item, including the socks.

Once she gets distracted by some of the dolls and furniture for the house. We pass out the presents for each other. I got Elle a new camera, some backgrounds and props I saw her heart on Amazon she forgot to log out of. Also, a Sapphire tennis bracelet since that's her birthstone. She's crying way more than I expected. I mean, I knew I did good, especially with the photography stuff since that was way easy, but that's a lot of happy tears. She puts on the bracelet and shows her mom, then grabs Brenna and they go upstairs. They come back down and Brenna and her have gotten dressed, but I really didn't pay attention to what they were wearing, to be honest. Brenna hands me a gift bag. I reach down in it, and I look at her, still not noticing the shirts. All of a sudden apparently everyone else has because there are gasps and hugs going towards Elle.

I see there is a key ring with a key on it, the key ring flashes #1 dad, "Oh, that's so sweet Brenna, thank you baby girl."

"Okay, you don't get to see what that key is to until you take out the last thing," she says getting a little frustrated and I am so lost.

I dig through the tissue paper to find a little square black-and-white picture with a little peanut in the middle. That's when I get a look at the shirts. Brenna's says big sister and Elle's says "future member of the Unfortunate Souls" with a little red heart on her belly. I look at her and I look at the picture, then back at her. "Really?"

"Really. Apparently, those antibiotics canceled out the birth control pills," she says, "Are you happy?"

I jump up and spin her around. "Are you freaking kidding me? I'm the happiest man on Earth!" I kiss her, and say with tears in my eyes.

"Spin me, spin me," Brenna jumps up and down. I pick her up and give her a big kiss and spin her too as she giggles.

"Now, let's go see what this key goes to," Remington says, adding, "Brenna, Uncle Remi got you something out there too."

We get outside, and Phoenix and Zen are standing beside our SUV. I walk around the other side and it's Reaper's bike, fully restored. "I remember that bike! That's Reapers." Michelle exclaims. Man, between finding out I'm going to be a dad and getting Elle's father's bike, I'm trying to be a strong man, but I'm an emotional mess.

"Here's yours, princess," Remington says, and carries over a battery-operated Harley motorcycle for her. She runs into the house and comes back out with her new leather coat and her sunglasses and hops on it.

"Look at me! I am a motorcycle princess!" she roars, while revving her bike and riding all over the blacktopped driveway.

I lean over, wrap my arms around my Elle and tell her, "this is the best day of my life."

"There's more best days to come," she says, kissing me back. "Now, give me a ride on that beautiful machine."

The two of us hop on and we take off down the hill. The ride is cold, but we don't seem to care; we are enjoying this moment. For her, it's a little piece of her father and for me, the founder of the club that I'm proud to be a president of.

## CHAPTER TWENTY-THREE

# Elle

Today is my wedding day, December 30th. I'm standing in front of a full-length mirror, my hair all curled and put in a half up/half down design with delicate baby's breath around an intricate veil with an attached tiara in it. My gown is fitted with delicate beads and sequins across the bust, fully decorated at the top, and less and less as it goes down my body. A fellow photographer that was in my classes back home came to do the pictures. Mom is trying not to cry as she comes up behind me and places her hands on my shoulders and we look at each other in the mirror. "You look so beautiful, baby girl," and I place a hand on top of hers.

"Stop that, I'm hormonal anyway, don't make me cry," I tell her.

Aunt Cathy peeks in the door, "It's time."

We exit the dressing room and line up in the foyer. The doors open and Brenna starts the procession with a basket of rose petals she is dropping really purposefully and REALLY slowly, one at a time. Benelli is trying to get her attention and get her to move just a little faster, but she's not seeing him motion to her. I can't see or hear what's going on, but it's all caught on video. Apparently, my dear man finally calls her name loud enough, so she'll hear and tries to loud whisper for her to come on. She then takes gigantic handfuls and runs down the aisle throwing them in big, wild bunches at the guests, looks up at her almost dad and screeches to a halt when she sees him shaking his head and face palming.

Next to go down the aisle are Lyric and Phoenix. Lyric is in a tea length red halter that accentuates all her beautiful curves while Phoenix is in motorcycle boots, blue jeans, and a tuxedo top half, including a red cummerbund. Hey, I compromised, they aren't wearing those horrible shoes and I let them wear jeans. Next Zen and Remington head down the aisle and then it will be time for me, mom, and Ruger. I love that he offered to walk me down the aisle. About halfway down the aisle the two couples stop, the guys nod at each other and they switch walking companions. Zen and Phoenix walk together, and Lyric and Remington. Most brides would probably go Bridezilla about now, but I just chuckle. There's no doubt in my mind that Phoenix and Zen will be next down the aisle.

Once they are all the way down, the music for me starts and they lead me down the aisle. That is when I see his face and he sees me. I'll be honest, I couldn't wait for this part. To see the emotional look on his face. Yeah, that's the stuff dreams are made of. I'm not saying I wouldn't have married him without "the look," but it's definitely something I was hoping for.

Preacher, that came from the St. Louis chapter to marry us, guided us through the rest of the ceremony. Since he gave in on the tuxedo top half, I promised him we could do the traditional wedding vows. The ceremony was relatively short and sweet and before I knew it Preacher was

announcing, "You may now kiss your bride," and he did.
Oh man, he did.

He grabbed me and dipped me, and I was breathless. Only
lifting me back up when the whole crowd went wild. He
looked down at me with a wink and a smirk and all I would
do was say, "Wow!"

Once we walked down the aisle, we stood in line as each
guest passed us, hugging, shaking our hands, patting
Benelli on the shoulder and once everyone was through,
we made our way through the bubbles and birdseed to our
waiting Cinderella, horse-drawn carriage. I wasn't
expecting that, and it took my breath away. I put my hand
to my heart and looked at this wonderful man of mine.

"Don't look at me," he said, "I'd like to take credit for that
look on your face, but it wasn't me."

Mom leans over to me, "when you were little you used to
dream of having a Cinderella carriage."

"Mom! It's amazing! Thank you!"

"I wanna go! I wanna go!" asked Brenna excitedly.

"Of course, I have to have my queen AND my princess with
me," Benelli says, and scoops her up into his arms.

Once we get to the reception, that's when the partying,
singing, and dancing begins. The only thing I'm missing out
on is the champaign, but I wouldn't trade the baby I'm

Benelli's Elle

carrying for the world. It's a small sacrifice for the little peanut growing inside of me.

Everyone did an amazing job decorating the clubhouse to the hilt. The food was phenomenal; the celebration was epic. When we cut the cake, we did smash just a little bit into each other's face, and I held out my icing covered finger and he took it into his mouth. Yeah, we were going to have to start this honeymoon, and soon. I thought for sure it was going to be Elle catching the bouquet, but it was my mom who wasn't even remotely trying for it. Benelli seductively took off my garter and I could tell Ruger was, in fact, trying for it. He elbowed and pushed his way through all the other single men like he was at the Superbowl trying to intercept the ball. And he did. Not that many of them were actually trying, unlike the girls were for the bouquet.

The celebration was winding down, and we didn't want to wait to get each other in bed any longer. We said our goodbye's, and we stopped at the first hotel we saw on the way to our honeymoon. While he slowly worked my dress and undergarments off, I shimmied in anticipation. As soon as I was free from my clothes, I practically tore him off and shoved him to the bed, climbing on top of him. Let's just say round one was fast and furious. Round two, we took it slow and worshiped each other's bodies like every taste, touch, lick, and suck we needed for our survival. It was the most erotic we have ever been together and continued for hours until we both fell asleep wrapped up together.

We got up the next morning, showered, and had another round before checking out and heading on our way to New Orleans. We get there in time to spend the evening out to dinner and I am devouring some true Cajun cuisine. My new husband had booked us at an amazing New Year's Eve celebration, and we celebrated the New Year with a midnight kiss underneath the firework brightened night. He had booked an entire condominium in the French Quarter with a beautiful, private garden area outside and a balcony overlooking the happenings below. It had way more bedrooms than we needed, but we christened every one. We spent the days visiting the Frenchman's Market, the City Park, shops, Jackson Square, you name it; we saw it all. The nights either making love or having wild monkey sex, depending on our mood.

The last day, I talked him into going to a tarot reader/medium. He didn't want to go, but he did for me. We enter the building and a woman wearing her hair in dreads with a colorful wrap around in leads us through a beaded entryway into another room where we are seated. She first takes his hands:

You're a nonbeliever. You're on your honeymoon. (eye roll), You have found the love of your life. You've had to do some dark things in the past year, very dark things. You did what was right.

She releases his hands and takes mine. You have been through a lot in the last year. You have a bright future ahead, mommy.

She lets go of my hands and looks over at the corner behind us. There is someone here with you. He showing me the grim reaper, but he's not. I don't understand.

My father went by Reaper.

Ah, now that makes sense. His name was Jon. He's telling you two to beware of a man from your past. This man is near, but he doesn't know that you are close. He is not a good man. I would say stay clear of him, but your father says you must take him down. Be very careful.

I am freaked the fuck out, and Benelli sees it. "Okay, we get it. How about some good news?"

She shakes her hands in the air like she's flinging something off of them and then takes my hands again. "I see a little girl and a baby boy. You will go to court in the very near future, but it will be a joyous outcome. I see..."

"Let's just stop while we are ahead, thank you," Benelli says, raising and shaking her hand.

When touching his hand again she keeps hold, whispers something to him I can't make out.

He jerks his hand from hers and grabs me to leave. "What did she say?" I ask.

"Nothing, it was nothing babe, just some mumbo, jumbo voodoo shit."

Benelli

That witchy woman just told me that evil will come to the one of peace, but a bird of darkness will rise up from the ashes and save her. I know exactly who she's talking about, but don't know what's going to happen or why. Part of me wants to go back without Elle and find out more, but another part of me knows that it's all going to be in riddles if she tells me anything. Plus, it's not like I'm going to be able to stop whatever it is from happening. Right now, I need to focus on Calibar if he really is in New Orleans. I'm hoping this witch is just rambling, but way too many things are accurate to not take heed of what she says. I am on high alert.

Hopefully, if we can catch Calibar, then whatever is going to happen to Zen won't happen. I try to seem relaxed as we walk around, taking in more of the sights, but also scanning the crowds. We stop to get a drink before we head back, and I relax. Elle is sitting on the stool next to me and turns me so that my back is to her. She massages my neck and shoulders and I feel the tension easing.

"Dang babe, you're really tight," she tells me and digs in a little harder.

"That feels amazing! Yeah, let's just say that woman got me a little tense. Creepy how she knew Reaper, Jon, and everything else, huh?" I ask.

"Yeah, that was intense. On the upside, the adoption is going to go through, and we are having a boy if she's right," she says.

More tension leaves me at the thought of a son. "What do you think of Oscar?" I ask with a smirk on my face.

"Yeah, Oscar the grouch, that's not happening. What about Liam?" she asks.

I scrunch my face. "Like the actor? Not feeling it. Michael?"

"I like Micah," she suggests.

"Micah Neroni, it has a ring to it. What's the middle name?" I ask.

"I'd like him to have my dad's name, but Micah Jonathon doesn't sound right," she says.

"How about Jonathon Micah and just call him Micah?" I suggest.

"I like that, but what if she's wrong, and it's a girl?" she says.

"Well, since your mom is Michelle, and you're Elle, something along those lines?" I suggest.

She laughs and says, "I think that trend should end with me."

"Okay," I chuckle. "Is momma ready to grab something to eat?"

"Always," she replies.

We stop a couple of blocks away and fill up on the local cuisine. After I pay the bill, we decide to head back to the condo.

# CHAPTER TWENTY-FOUR

## Elle

That evening, we are walking to our condo, and I freeze. I can't move. Benelli is distracted when his phone rings and he answers, "O'Neal? What have you got?" I hear the words leave his mouth, but it's like it is in a tunnel where everything is moving in slow motion. I see him hang up and turn back to me. "Elle, we need to go. Elle? Elle!" I feel him shake me and I look at him and slowly come out of the trance I'm in. "It's him," I say slowly.

"Yeah, O'Neal's contacts say he's here."

"I know," and I lift my arm to point. He doesn't see us and he's barely recognizable looking clean cut, but I'd know him anywhere. He's flirting with a girl around my age. Flipping her hair off her shoulder and leaning to whisper in her ear and she smiles.

Benelli flips open his phone and dials him back. We spotted him. He's on Bourbon Street in front of..." I don't hear the rest. I just start walking that way. I'm dazed and confused, but my mind is telling me to save that girl. I'm stopped by Benelli, grabbing me, and pulling me back. "What the fuck do you think you're doing?"

"I need to save her," and I try to pull away.

"He has men in the area. They'll be here any minute."

"There's no time, I have to save her."

"Elle, stop!" he grabs me by both my arms and stares into my eyes, "you are not the one to do it, think of the baby."

I look down and place protective hands on my stomach. My baby, yes, I must protect the baby. I look up, though, and see them walk away. "Benelli!"

"Okay, go in here and stay where it's well lit. Call an Uber or whatever, but go straight to the condo and lock the doors, do you hear me?"

"Yeah," I nod, "Okay. Benelli, be careful."

I head inside the building and request an Uber from the app as I lose Benelli from my sight. I get back to the condo and do as I am told, locking the doors, and I check the windows too. I go upstairs and crouch down beside the bed on the floor, grasping my phone. I remember the gun that's on the nightstand and grab it. Time is ticking so slowly. An hour goes by and there is no Benelli. Just me, my knees tucked up, griping the gun tightly in front of me.

My phone suddenly lights up Benelli. I lay down the gun to hit answer, "Where are you? Are you okay?"

"I'm okay, Babe. Are you in the condo? I'm coming in the front door now," he says and the tension in my body eases.

"I'm here, I'm in the bedroom," I say, still a little nervous to move.

"Okay, I'm coming up," and he ends the call.

The doorknob slowly turns, and swings open gently. As soon as I see his face, I jump from my huddled position and run to him, throwing myself in his arms. "I was so scared."

"I know, baby, it's okay. We have caught him," he tells me and the fear that I've lived with, the one that has been having control over me, is gone and my body sways. Benelli catches me in his arms and steadies me. He's always been my rock.

He leads me to the side of the bed so I can sit. I rest my elbows on my knees and cup my face with my hands, "It's over," I take a lung filling breath and release, "It's really, finally over?" I say, turning my head to look at him.

He cups my cheek. "It's finally over. O'Neal is having Calibar turned over to him. Don't panic at what I have to tell you..."

"What?" my guard rising again.

"The plan is to take him to us. We will deal with his punishment after O'Neal questions him. He will say he escaped or come up with a reason he's dead, but he's ours to do with what we want after," he says in a calm but scary tone.

"He's mine. After you are all done with him, he's mine," I say with rage, pacing the room, clenching, and unclenching my fists, a power surge coursing through me.

"Babe."

"Don't you dare, babe me; he took parts of me and the only way I will ever get them back is to hurt him like he hurt me," I stop and stand so close to Benelli's face and stare into his eyes, "I'm taking what I lost away from him, he... is... mine!"

Benelli, just as serious as me, nods in agreement. "You take his final breath from him, you have my word, Xena," and at that I grip his hair hard and pull him to my mouth. I kiss him so fiercely that something changes between us. A powerful force, him and I united. We are a force to be reckoned with, like a tsunami of emotions and need filling us both. We go hard and strong, in a way we've never done before. I take the force that he's giving me and revel in it. I give it back in return.

He pulls my hair and I moan with ecstasy. I bite his lip and sink my nails into his back. It's carnal the way we are, like wolves under the moon. He takes me off of him, flipping me over and bending me over and though I haven't let him do it before, due to the buried vulnerability I'd felt in the past, but I feed off of it now. I take each forceful thrust and lean back into it. Wanting the power, he's filling me with. My alter ego, Xena, is all in and that's who I am right now, no longer the resignation that I didn't know that was buried deep within, I am a warrior, a goddess and a queen and I come with the satisfaction of it, and he follows right behind, a guttural roar as he does and then lays his forehead against my spine.

Once we have caught our breath, we shower and pack, leaving New Orleans behind. The city that gave me back my life, gave me back my power, and I am eternally grateful.

We drive through the night and arrive home the next day. O'Neal is already there, and they have Calibar shackled, but he doesn't know the location and has seen no one but O'Neal. He's arrogant, seeing his captor as nothing but a traitor to his club.

We go straight to where they have him, not even stopping to talk to family or the club. Benelli has given everyone orders for it to be just us three. O'Neal meets us at the door and ushers us to the other room, "I have got nothing useful out of him, he's not talking."

"I'll change his tune," I say and walk in with Benelli following. Calibar's eyes bulge when he sees the two of us. "Didn't think you'd see me again, did you?" I look down at the table of devices and delicately brush my hand across each and look up at him. "What shall it be, hmmm?" He spits in my direction, but he's too far to reach. I click my tongue in a "tsk, tsk, tsk," and Benelli punches him, his body swinging.

"I understand you aren't being very helpful there, Cal. Now, what should we do to change that?" I say, my fingers touching my chin, pondering, walking over to a table, carefully examining every item for pain imaginable. My hand stops on a nail gun, "Oh, this looks like fun." There is a small amount of worry now on his face, but he remains silent. Standing directly in front of him, I take aim and grip the trigger. A round of nails embedding into various parts of his body, nothing deadly, just enough to get his attention.

His breath hitches as each one hits his body. "We're needing some info there, Cal. Are you ready to talk?"

"Fuck you, cunt. Oh wait, I did," is his reply.

"Ow, that hurts," I say sarcastically. There was a slight punch to my gut at his words, but there is no way I'm letting him know that. "You know, that might have hurt me 6 months ago, but I'm a new woman. It seems you have forgotten who's in power today. Let me introduce myself. I'm Xena, wife of the president of the Unfortunate Souls." His eyes bulge in the new knowledge.

The three of us step out of the room to talk. "O'Neal, don't you guys have some sort of truth serum or something, or is that just in the movies?"

"I'm afraid you're out of luck. The only truth serum we have around here is getting him drunk and hoping his tongue loosens up," he says. "Something that loosens his inhibitions or puts him in a state between wake and sleep."

"What about alcohol and a sleeping pill? People get chatty when they're drunk, right? Benelli, you've seen me on Ambien and awake doing things. What if we combine the two and keep him awake? If it doesn't work, we aren't any worse off than we are now," I say.

"I say we bring in Remington and the others and get this over with," Benelli states.

"Babe, let's try this. If it doesn't work, we will just end him," I plead.

"Fine, you go get the stuff. We will stay here with him," he says.

I leave and head to our room at the clubhouse, grab the bottle of sleeping pills and head towards the bar. Going behind the counter, I grab the strongest bottle I can find. Remington grabs my arm as I'm about to leave. "I want in on this," he says.

"It's my fight, Rem, doing it my way," I reply. "I can think of 100 ways to do this gruesome, and who knows, I may end him that way, but that won't get us the info to save the other girls."

"Alright, but at least let me watch," he says, and I agree to it. We walk back to the place that we have him held. He's slightly worse off than when I last saw him, but he's still conscious.

"Let the party begin boys, I'm here," Remington states loudly and Calibar is noticeably freaking out.

I am in on him using fear, trying to get him to talk, and we have a plan. "No, we are going to do this my way, or I'm gone," I say, winking at Benelli, where Calibar can't see.

"Get him down and chain him to the table and chair in the other room, him and I are going to have a private chat," I demand.

The men do as I say, and they secure him in a chair, and I walk in, shutting the door. I set down two solo cups and the bottle. "You want a drink?"

He nods and looks at me quizzically. I pour the drinks and slide him one cup; he shoots it down. I get a bottle out of my pocket and pretend to take the pill. "Anxiety." I shrug and slightly laugh.

"Well, I could use one of those," he states, and I push one across the table and refill his cup.

"You know, I'm the only chance you have of getting out of here alive," I say.

"Like that's going to happen. I'm a dead man. You and I both know it," he says.

I talk to him slowly, carefully, calmly, all while making sure he's taking shot after shot of the alcohol. I think that I'm gaining his trust. I excuse myself, telling him I'm tired of all the death and ensuring that if he talks, he walks.

"I'm going to give him a bit for the alcohol and pill to take effect," I say, and we stand and watch him for about fifteen minutes. He's getting groggy, so I go back in.

He's slurring his words, and he is definitely in that state between waking and sleep where your guard is down. I use a seductive voice when I question him, and the answers flow out of him like a fountain. "You're the leader now that Chains is gone. I bet you know where all the other girls are, right? You're so much smarter than he was. I bet you know where all the records are?" I ask.

"I do. That old fool, he tried to keep that all between him and Frodo. Did you know he was Frodo's dad? Your men did me a favor. Frodo was next in line to take over after Chains, but I was the smart one. I should have been next to take over. Your club made it easy after killing them two. I came in and took over and took charge. I had respect."

"You should have been in charge all along. I bet Chains kept horrible records," I say.

"That fool had them all on paper. Files all over the place. I put them on a flash drive. I've got them all. Well, except for the missing files. I heard the news where they found them. That's why they were stupid. It's harder to hide a bunch of paper folders. That's where I'm smart."

"Yeah, I bet you even hid the flash drive in a safe place. I bet it's in a place no one would ever think to check," I say, seeming to be enamored and impressed. "You can tell me." I lean over the table and whisper.

He looks left and right and leans over the table, too. He can't reach me but honestly, he's so loopy now, he couldn't hurt me if he wanted to, "it's in the collar of my coat."

I don't know if the guys could hear that, so I repeat but louder, "The flash drive is in the collar of your coat! That is so smart! You just lay your head down and rest sweetie, I'll be right back." He does as he's told, and I rush to the other room.

O'Neal goes and grabs the sack of items they took from Calibar, brings it back to us and his coat is in there. He takes a knife and carefully cuts the collar and finds the flash drive. Benelli leads us to another room full of computers and other electronics. The files immediately start uploading and O'Neal stops on the file that includes his sister, Liberty. He now knows who she was sold to and where she is located and puts the info into his phone. He takes out the drive and palms it in his fist. "I know you're not going to let me take him in," he says.

"You're right. Go find your sister. The less you know about the rest, the better," Benelli states. "Remember, once this is all over, you're welcome to join the club. No probation," he tells him with a hand placed on O'Neal's shoulder. He nods and puts his other hand on Benelli's and gives him a look of appreciation for not just the offer but that he finally found his sister, with the club's help. Remington, Benelli and I went back into the room where Calibar was passed out. Remington handed me a knife and lifted the head of the man who caused me so much pain. I looked at Benelli and then back down at the man, "this is for all the girls whose lives you ruined, and this is for me," I say as I sliced the throat of my rapist.

I don't know what the club had ultimately done with Calibar's body, didn't ask. I washed the blood off me, and I took the hand of my husband; we left to pick up Brenna. Is it fucked up what I did? Pretending to be into the man that raped me just for information, then ending his life. Yeah, but sometimes vengeance is soothing to the soul. We got to Ruger's, where mom and our little girl was, mom just looked into my eyes and I simply said, "It's over," and she knew what that meant and nodded approval.

The next morning, we got a call saying that they approved the adoption. She was officially going to be ours.

When the day finally arrived for us to go before the judge, we were ecstatic. We filled the room with friends and family that have grown to love Brenna and became a part of her life. When he announced that she was officially adopted, and now Brenna Neroni, everyone yelled and cheered. The judge overlooked the raucous, happy to see how much better he knew her life would be. He'd had her parents in front of him on way too many occasions.

We left the courthouse and went back to the club for a celebration where she was the star. Now she can officially say we are her mommy and daddy, and my cup runneth over.

# Elle

## 8 months later

We are at the hospital, and they have induced me. Turns out this little man wants to bake longer, and I am more than ready to hold him in my arms. Benelli is a nervous wreck now that the contractions have started and getting stronger. As soon as I'm at a four, they are going to give me an epidural. Hell to the yeah, I may be a strong woman, but I am going to take all the comfort I can.

The nurse comes in and checks me and YES! I'm at a four. She informs the doctor, and they call the anesthetist. I don't want to see the needle; I don't want any part of it, but let's get this done. He takes one look at it and is looking at me all wide eyed, "Are you sure about this, Babe?" A contraction starts and I squeeze his hand so hard and that's his answer. By the next contraction, it's all in and I am feeling great. I'm social and laughing and wanting everyone to come in and visit.

I'm just having a grand old time. I've been sitting up super straight and telling jokes. This thing is AWESOME! I've just been pushing the button on it like it's a hit on a vape pen. The nurse comes in again to check me, and I've went from a five to a ten in an hour. She rushes out to call the doctor and have her get her butt here. They scramble and start setting everything up for the delivery.

The doctor comes in and I'm boisterous and laughing, "Heyyyy, Doc Karen, come on here, we are just in here telling stories."

"How about we get ready to push instead?" she says.

"It ain't time to push," I say, waving my hand at her and laugh.

"Are you sure they didn't give her something else along with the epidural? She's been chatty and cracking up ever since," Benelli states.

"I'm all for this. I had back labor with Elle. If she can do without all that pain, I'm all for it," mom says.

"You have to push, NOW!" Doc Karen tells me.

I bear down and focus as Benelli stands on one side, a hand on my back and one under a knee, my mom on the other side doing the same. "Zen, you help her from the back," she's told. Another contraction hits, but I'm feeling no pain. "Okay, push Elle, tuck your chin and push." After a bit she says, "Okay, last push, give it all you've got." I actually laugh and push and push and out he comes. Legitimately laughing the kid out. I look up, holding my breath until I hear the cry. It comes and we all let out the breath we were holding. It's strong, loud, and they do some quick checks before setting him on my chest. He has thick dark hair just like his daddy, explains the massive amount of heartburn I had during the pregnancy. We all have tears running down our faces. "Daddy, do you want to hold him while we finish up with Elle? She has a little more work to do."

"Yes," he says cautiously. The nurse takes him and swaddles him into a blue blanket and hands him to Benelli, making sure he holds the head and neck.

"So, what's his name?" one nurse asks.

"Micah, Jonathon Micah Neroni," Benelli tells her. Mom puts a hand on her chest because he's named after Elle's father.

# Benelli

## 10 years later

"Brenna, slow down! BRAKES GIRL! BRAKES!" I yell at my daughter.

"I am dad! Stop, you're making me nervous!" she replies.

"I'm making YOU nervous! I'm wondering if I paid my life insurance up," I tell her.

She pulls over and parks between two cars. "Dad, seriously! I've got this! See, I parked just fine."

"Okay, I'll give you that. You have mastered parallel parking," I admit.

"C'mon, I need to go take my test," she says, hopping out of the car, running around, and dragging me out.

I am so not ready for this! Forty-five minutes later, they are snapping her photo and she's cheesing it up. When she gets outside, she snaps a selfie with it and sends it to her mom and her Noni and Papa, who got married on

Michelle's birthday, May 25th, five months after we did. She said it gave him one less date to remember if she did it then.

We get back to the house for Brenna's sweet sixteen party and I think half the school is here. She is way too pretty for her own good, too many young bucks sniffing around. Her 10-year-old brother Micah has my back, though. He is patrolling the party like his way older than his years. Elle calls him her old soul. Someday he's going to take over the Unfortunate Souls and continue the legacy.

Their little sister, Delaney, is as sweet as they come, our easiest child by far. She turns seven this October fifteenth. She has my skin and hair color but her momma's beautiful looks, and those eyes, she got those from Elle, too.

## Brenna

I am having a great time at the party they threw for me. All my family and friends are here, and someone I haven't seen before. He walks over to my dad, and I notice he has on a prospect patch. Oh, he is hot! Like damn! Tall, dark, and yummy. Just my dang luck, I'm finally allowed to date, and my dad will never let me date this one, not a prospect for his princess, ugh.

There is just something about him, though. Do you ever just see someone and just know? Know in your heart that person, that person, is THE ONE. He doesn't know it yet, but I'm going to marry him.

# Benelli

## 25 years later

On the morning that I turn over my Presidency of the Unfortunate Souls, Elle rolls over and says, "Mr. President, I need help with something..."

"And what would that be?" I ask with a smirk.

Elle rolls me over and starts kissing me. Working her mouth down my body, nipping at my ear, my throat, my nipples. She slowly moves down between my thighs and grasps my cock. I still want this woman as much now as I did before, probably more so. She licked her lips and smiled up at me before taking me into her mouth. She licks and sucks my balls, but I need to be in this woman. I lift her up so that she is on top of me. Elle Baby, ride me. She is so wet from just sucking me that it turns me on even more. She sets the pace and then I don't know what got in her, but it's like she is riding for gold. So damn good, every single time. If I were to die now, I would die a thrilled man.

As we both come off our post sex hang-over, Elle asks me if I am sure that I am ready to retire. "Hell yes, let the young ones have it. Micah is more than ready for the presidency at his age." He's now twenty-four, but as Elle always said, he's an old soul. Elle and I want to travel and see our grandkids. We want to roam the states on the back of my bike and relax, enjoy the time we have left to the fullest.

Brenna is married to an MC guy and now has four kids, but that's their story to tell. Delaney is twenty-one and is here for the celebration and me handing over the reins to my middle child.

Everyone is in the clubhouse, and I give my son, Micah, the new job of being the president. The club was all in agreement. Though they didn't want me to step down, they agreed with who we chose. I had many incredible years running this club, and we helped a lot of lives over the years.

Wow, it seems like just yesterday that I met Elle and how our lives have changed over the years. I remember when the kids were all little. As I look around and see all the young bucks and the not so young ones, I notice my daughter Delaney standing to the side with her new friend. I'm not sure who she is, but I look over at Micah and see a shocked look on his face as he stares at Delaney's friend. It's almost like he knows her. Hmmm, I wonder what is up with that? I look to see if Elle is seeing what I am, and she just looks at me and smiles. That woman knows something.

I can't wait to see what Micah does with this club. Knowing my son, he will do great things, there is no doubt. I pull my wife to my side and wrap my arm around her waist. I don't know who has the biggest look of pride, her or me. The one thing I know for sure is she will forever be my Elle.

Check out the rest of the Unfortunate Souls MC series:
Stack'd Against Ruger
Phoenix's Zen
Feeling Lucky
Lyric's Enforcer

More from Debbie Mitchell:
The Biker's Baby
And coming soon, The Devil's Handmaidens MC
(Mystic Bayou Chapter is Debbie's)

If you are looking for something sweeter, try:
Hot Cocoa & Shenanigans or
Last Train

Also, find us on:
https://www.facebook.com/RomAuthorDebbieMitchell

Facebook
https://www.facebook.com/groups/unfortunatesoulsmc

Bookbub
Bit.ly//BBDebbieMitchell

https://www.goodreads.com/author/show/20925082.Debbie_Mitchell

https://www.bookbub.com/authors/leslie-staffey

Website
https://authordmitchell.com

PS... WE LOVE REVIEWS!!!!

Made in the USA
Middletown, DE
23 December 2022

20267500R00166